When Kim woke, she woke to deathly silence

She could smell damp earth, and mustiness and . . . cigar smoke.

She was trapped in a "House of the Dead." A crypt. A crypt inside the Alexander family cemetery. Horror drove her to her knees. She rocked back and forth, her arms wrapped tightly around her body. This was no nightmare. It was real!

She mustn't lose control. If she did, she might lose it permanently.

Reality intruded into one tiny corner of her mind. She had to get out and warn Shane! Without thought for herself or her own fears, she located the door latch, took off her thin shoe and began to pound away at it. Then she remembered the unloaded gun. She could use the gun butt to force the lock. Reaching into her purse, she found it and fancifully pointed the gun at the metal door, pulling the trigger.

A deafening roar filled the crypt, she was flung back and her hands were scorched. . . .

ABOUT THE AUTHOR

Lynn Leslie is actually the pseudonym for a very talented writing team, Sherrill Bodine and Elaine Sima, who live with their families outside Chicago, Illinois. Authors of Regencies and mainstream novels, both admit that romantic suspense is among their favorite genres. Profound believers in research, the team recently vacationed in New Orleans, to cull background for this novel. They're strongly leaning toward Florida as the setting for their next romantic suspense....

Street of Dreams

Lynn Leslie

Harlequin Books

TORONTO • NEW YORK • LONDON
AMSTERDAM • PARIS • SYDNEY • HAMBURG
STOCKHOLM • ATHENS • TOKYO • MILAN

To Mom-o and Pop-o,
whose love story is better than any book!

Harlequin Intrigue edition published January 1990

ISBN 0-373-22129-0

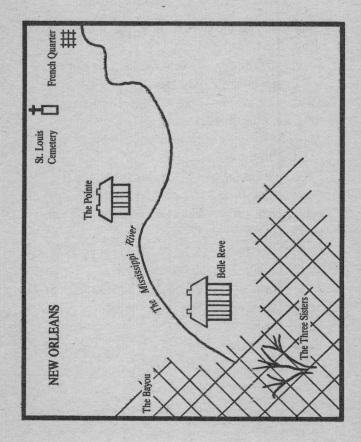

CAST OF CHARACTERS

Kimberly Campbell—Wandering into a voodoo shop, she found evil and love.

Shane Alexander—A playwright, his darkest writings wouldn't rival this.

Madame Loulou—Her voodoo shop attracted tourists, and murder.

Jeanne Carter—She was a policewoman with one too many beats.

Detective DeSable—Friend or foe?

Claude LaCroix—The perfect Southern gentleman, he was intent on resurrecting the glorious past.

Evangeline Paris—A tarot card reader, her readings were always on target.

Judge Rudolph—Full of Southern bluster and brawn, he seemed the eye in the storm.

Chapter One

Kimberly Campbell was lost. She couldn't remember the last time she hadn't known exactly where she was going. If her colleagues had been with her, they would have teased her unmercifully about not having the situation under control. But for now it didn't seem to matter. She hadn't the slightest idea which way to turn and yet she didn't care. Everything was so exciting. New Orleans did that to people, she'd heard. The old houses in the Vieux Carré with their dreamy courtyards and lacy balconies were too romantic to just rush by. There was so much to see, so much to do she hardly knew where to begin. This was her holiday. A treat to herself for surviving the first year as chairman of the Fine Arts Department. With three whole weeks to explore, she wasn't going to waste a single minute. She would start by finding the voodoo shop Dr. Van Meter had told her about.

Kim roamed slowly through the little streets of the French Quarter trying to decipher Dr. Van Meter's hand-drawn map. He had told her to begin on Canal Street—the Street of Dreams he had called it because its shops provided all manner of wonderful sights, from open-air vegetable and seafood markets to frivolous feathered Mardi Gras masks to the finest antique furniture.

The Quarter was exactly as he described and more. She dawdled under balconies, wandered through flowery patios. She explored the ins and outs of shops housed in old mansions: antique stores with crystal chandeliers and shining treasures, specialty restaurants, avant-garde art galleries and dusty bookstores. On Bourbon Street jazz floated through the swinging doors of cafés and bars, bathing Kim in its contagious energy.

Turning a corner onto a narrow side street, where bougainvillea climbed centuries-old brick walls, she finally found what she had been looking for: Madame Loulou's Voodoo Shop.

The shop door was open. Inside was dim and cool, a welcome respite from the blazing Louisiana July sun. Closing her eyes for a moment to adjust to the gloom, Kim sighed in relief and pushed away her hair from her neck. No one had noticed her entrance even though the shop was small. A tiny woman with skin like old parchment stood behind the counter gesturing toward a tall heavy woman wearing a long-sleeved shirtwaist dress.

"I promise you it is true. This recipe has been handed down through generations of beautiful voodoo queens." Madame Loulou's thin fingers quickly tore the clear plastic from a red bottle shaped like a female torso. "This is a true voodoo love perfume."

The tall woman shook her head, laughing nervously. "No, really. I don't think it's for me."

"Here. The fragrance is quiet pleasing." Twisting off the top, Madame Loulou thrust the bottle forward. "All you do is place a drop behind your right ear and then a line of scent in the shape of an *X* over your heart. The man you want will be yours forever."

"Thank you, but I'll just take these herbs I've paid for." The woman clutched her bag tightly to her bosom and turned away, pushing past Kim, almost tripping out the door in her eagerness to leave.

Shrugging, Madame Loulou gestured Kim closer. "Yes, miss?" The old woman's narrow lined face widened when she smiled, her pale skin growing slightly pinker, the faded blue eyes brighter. "Have you come for a love potion?"

"No." Kim laughed, not quite believing she was really here in this strange little shop. "I came for a voodoo doll. Is that what these are?" She gestured to the twine dolls that tumbled out of a large straw basket on the counter.

"Yes, dear. These are real voodoo dolls," the woman said, as Kim picked one up, turning it over in her hands. Its head was painted with black dots for eyes and a black slash for a mouth. Its body was made with loosely looped natural twine. A piece of rope was tied around the neck, a set of instructions hanging from its throat. "See, if you want to cast a bad spell, you take the black-headed pin and stick it into the doll. If you want a good spell, you use the white-headed pin."

The idea of Dr. Van Meter casting any kind of spell tickled Kim so much that she chuckled. She remembered the last few hectic weeks of school. A doll might get the attention of his anthropology students. "How much does it cost?"

"What is this doll for?" Madame Loulou asked abruptly, studying Kim intently.

Surprised, Kim looked carefully at Madame Loulou. Was it her imagination or had the woman's voice changed, become firmer, more cultured? Now Kim's holiday spirit seemed slightly frivolous in the presence of Madame Loulou's seriousness.

"I teach drama at a high school in Illinois. The anthropology teacher asked me to bring back a voodoo doll for his course on religion and voodoo's effect on Christianity in the nineteenth century."

"Then this is not what you want." Madame Loulou's lips curved in a dismissive smile as she removed the doll from Kim's hands. "These are for the tourists to take home and show their friends. Not for a serious student of voodoo."

She gestured toward the far wall. A tall case sat there. "The dolls there are the true voodoo dolls."

From the neck of her dress Madame Loulou drew a long gold chain on which a small key dangled. Unlocking the glass case, she carefully lifted out a wax doll shaped like a female. With perfectly proportioned arms and legs, its body was covered with a bright green cotton dress and ruffled neckline. But the beautifully formed head had no features.

"This doll is made of wax and is the kind used for hundreds of years to cast spells. Of course, believing the spells have power is the secret to why voodoo works in our culture today."

"Works? In our culture today?" Kim questioned gently, not wanting to hurt the fragile-looking older woman's feelings. If she chose to believe all this nonsense, Kim wouldn't judge. It just wasn't for her.

Smiling, Madame Loulou nodded. "It would surprise your anthropology teacher to discover the effect of voodoo has not dissipated so very much since the nineteenth century."

Kim tried not to look totally incredulous, but she must have failed, for Madame Loulou laughed, a soft warm musical sound.

"I know it is difficult for a modern young woman like you to believe there are people today who use these very same dolls to destroy their enemies or bring happiness and good health to their friends. The dolls are given power by adding a lock of hair, or a nail clipping, or a favorite piece of jewelry from the person you wish to cast a spell upon. I will make this doll look like you."

Shock made Kim step back. "Me!"

Again Madame Loulou's blue eyes grew brighter. "No need for concern, my dear. I promise to place a *good* spell on this doll."

Kim felt almost like a child beneath the old woman's wise gaze.

"Remember, it has power only if you believe it does. And since you do not believe, it will just be for your amusement."

Lifting scissors she gestured toward Kim's hair. "If you will permit me?"

"I don't know about this." Stepping back another pace, Kim shook her head, laughter again lacing her words.

"Let me snip one lock from beneath." Madame Loulou frowned in concentration, the network of lines in her face deepening. "Just one piece that has not been changed by the sun."

Kim hesitated, torn between embarrassment that she was having anything to do with this voodoo nonsense, and an absurd urge to go along with it just to prove it wrong. Suddenly Madame Loulou, in spite of the tall purple turban and huge gold hoops hanging from her ears, looked so sweetly earnest Kim made her decision.

"Oh, why not?" She threw up her hands, smiling. "You're right. All the kids will love the fact that Dr. Van Meter has a voodoo doll that looks like me. But if you don't mind, I'll cut a lock myself." Taking the scissors, Kim snipped from the back, near her nape, then thrust the hair forward, the small honey blond coil curling around Madame Loulou's outstretched fingers.

"Thank you. I know you will be pleased. Now browse a bit, dear. I should have—" She stopped abruptly. Her face altered, seeming to grow even narrower and paler, the high cheekbones and long nose sharpening.

Kim turned to follow Madame Loulou's stare. A man blocked the doorway, his lean body silhouetted by bright sunlight.

"You must come back tomorrow, miss."

Twirling around, Kim frowned. "But I thought—"

"Tomorrow. High noon. It will be ready. I must close the shop now." The words were urgent.

All the gaiety Kim had felt since she stepped off the plane in New Orleans drained away, replaced by a sudden intuition: something was wrong. Madame Loulou's voice had changed again and Kim could swear she heard fear in it. And the woman's hands were shaking.

Kim glanced back toward the door. The man was still there, lurking in silence.

Common sense told her it was none of her business. But this was an old and fragile woman alone in a tiny shop on an out-of-the-way street in a sometimes dangerous part of town. Suddenly Kim's sense of protectiveness and responsibility took hold.

"Are you all right?" Kim asked quietly, leaning across the counter. If Madame Loulou was afraid, Kim wouldn't desert her. There must be a policeman around here somewhere.

A reassuring smile curved Madame Loulou's thin lips and color stained her cheeks. "You are very kind, dear."

then moved to stand in front of a doorway hung with
ropes of tinkling beads that led to a back room. "Madame Loulou?"

Silence.

Sighing, Kim wandered along the counter, browsing
through the books on voodoo, macumba and voodoo
queens, fingering white beans in a porcelain bowl
marked MAGIC. How could fat white lima beans have
anything magical about them? she wondered.

Then she noticed the voodoo love perfume. Madame
Loulou had forgotten to replace the stopper. It would
evaporate if Kim didn't put the top back on. She lifted
it to her nose, surprised by how appealing the fragrance
was. It reminded her of gardenias, jasmine and roses, the
scent of New Orleans and dreamy moonlit patios.

She put the stopper back into the bottle. Some scent
was on her fingers so she spread it on her skin at the vee
of her blouse. Then for the first time she noticed a pamphlet on the counter. She opened it and saw the contents, which she read aloud in hushed tones.

"Bone to flesh
Flesh to bleed
Blood to tears
Spirit heed.
Tears to blood
Heart to purge
Eyes to weep
Spirit merge."

The words settled into the room, rustling echoes hovering in corners as if waiting....

Suddenly she wished Madame Loulou would come
out to the front. Placing her purse and the recapped

bottle of perfume on the counter, she rang the bell again.
It cut through the oppressive silence with a shrill no~~t~~
Her alarm returning, Kim moved carefully around the
counter. "Madame Loulou!" she called again through
the purple beads into the back room.

Something *was* wrong. Kim had sensed it yesterday,
and her instincts were rarely wrong. Swallowing her fear,
she crossed to the doorway separating the shop from
what she assumed were the living quarters and parted the
clacking beads.

The room was a treasure box and wonderfully normal looking. With no sign of anything amiss, Kim
walked in and noticed how perfectly neat and tidy Madame Loulou kept it. A huge settee with plump pillows
covered in dusky rose and blue-and-cream chintz sat
before a small brick fireplace. Next to it was a bureau
encrusted with patterns of gilt enamel set in tortoise-
shell. Knickknacks, carefully placed, lay about in profusion. Music boxes, dress swords, inlaid pistols, all were
lovingly displayed on beautiful, highly polished antique
dressers and tables. Through open folded doors, a lofty
four-poster bed elaborately carved and made of solid
mahogany took up an entire wall.

The voodoo shop was a tourist's delight, but this room
was a collector's dream, where Madame Loulou lived in
comfort surrounded by her treasures. Relief made Kim
smile. There was nothing wrong here.

Stirred by a sudden draft from the open door, the
beads clacked and Kim swung around. For the first time
she noticed the Chinese screen in an alcove to her left.
Jutting from behind it, barely visible, was the sole of a
thin bare foot. Fear rushed up, hot and sickening, to her
throat.

"Madame Loulou!" Kim cried out, her heart pounding in her chest. She felt weighted down by a stone, yet in reality she reached Madame Loulou in an instant.

The storekeeper lay crumpled on her side with one hand extended as if she were reaching out.

"Oh my God, she's had a heart attack," Kim breathed, sinking on her knees to touch Madame Loulou's neck. She checked for a pulse. A gurgle of sound brought hope.

"Madame, I'm here!" she cried, gently reaching her arms around to turn the old woman onto her back. A shock of pain throbbed through Kim's hand. There was a knife lying on the floor, and somehow the blade had sliced Kim's palm. Instinctively she picked it up, staring at the fresh blood staining its sharp edges. Shuddering, she flung it out of the way so it couldn't cut Madame Loulou.

Gently, Kim turned her, and she felt her fear turn to horror.

There was blood on the white skin of Madame Loulou's face and a wound in her chest was still bleeding. In seconds Kim went into action. Yanking the cotton scarf from her neck she pressed it to the woman's chest. Her lips trembling and a tear sliding down her cheek, Kim stilled the nausea in her abdomen, chiding herself that she must stay calm. She was Madame Loulou's only hope.

Madame Loulou slowly opened her eyes and Kim bent her head. "You're going to be all right. I'll go for a doctor," she soothed, brushing short white hair back from the ashen face. "I'll have to leave you to go to a phone, but I'll—"

"Promise me!" Madame Loulou whispered, her blue eyes staring into Kim's face. "Promise me!"

"Yes, anything. Anything," Kim stammered, laying her warm hand over the icy one Madame Loulou reached out to her. "Anything."

"Tell Shane...tell only Shane...no one else. You must promise me," her voice weakened and Kim gripped the cold hand tighter trying to warm it.

"I promise." She was desperate. There was too much blood and she couldn't stop the flow. "I must get help now."

Suddenly the icy fingers grew stronger, pulling Kim closer, the thin colorless lips next to her ear. "No, too late."

"It's not too late, Madame," Kim argued frantically. "Let me get help. I need to—"

A strong grip interrupted her. "Tell Shane—" the words came jerkily, interspersed with rasping breaths "—Maria is alive."

"Maria...alive." Kim repeated. "Did she do this to you? We'll find her. Make her pay."

"No, child...tell Shane...her power is strong. Warn him...Maria...Laveau...."

"I promise, Madame. I'll tell Shane."

The grip relaxed. Kim sensed the instant Madame Loulou ceased breathing, the blue-veined lids closing for the last time, but she couldn't accept her life ceasing to be. She rocked the old lady gently in her arms. Someone had done this to Madame Loulou. Someone—Maria Laveau?—had used brutal force against this helpless old woman. It wasn't right. Kim would make sure this Shane person got the message. She'd make sure the police hunted down Maria Laveau and made her pay for this brutal crime. Angry tears burned Kim's eyes.

Yesterday's image of Madame Loulou standing in the shop wearing the absurd turban and dangling earrings was at odds with the woman who had lived surrounded by priceless antiques in genteel comfort. Kim sobbed softly, shock holding her still.

"Louise! Louise! Are you back there!" The clear deep voice of a man called from the front of the shop.

Drawing a sharp breath, her eyes blurred with tears, Kim flung back her head and looked up as the beads parted. She knew immediately who he was. His hair was thick, with black waves brushed back from a high forehead, and his brown eyes were wide in a lean face. He was the man from yesterday, the one who had brought fear into Madame Loulou's voice.

Cradling the dead woman protectively in her arms Kim challenged him. "Who are you? What do you want?"

Swiftly he moved to kneel beside her, placing his fingers on Madame Loulou's neck. "Oh, please, God, no!" he whispered, the look of anguish on his face making Kim's heart skip a beat.

Perhaps she should feel fear now, but she didn't. Only numbness, and the certainty that the murderer would not have called for Louise nor appear so stricken by her death.

"I'm sorry," Kim said tonelessly, still not relinquishing her protective hold.

The man closed his lids tightly for a long minute before he reopened them to look into Kim's wet swollen face. He took a deep ragged breath. "Don't be afraid," he said quietly. "I'll call the police. The Vieux Carré headquarters are nearby, so someone will be here quickly. Then I'll be back to help you."

She watched him first drape a quilt over Madame's body then leave the room to phone the police. Strangely enough his words and reaction comforted

Kim. This stranger who had seemed to frighten Madame Loulou didn't frighten her at all. She sensed in him a deep pain. She also sensed that he was an ally.

"Here, let me help you," the man said from above her. She hadn't heard him return. "You've cut your hand."

He lifted her slowly to her feet and led her to a chair. "You'd better sit down while I get you some water and a towel."

She tried ineffectively to wipe away the bloodstains covering her clothes, but fresh blood oozed from the wound on her hand, smearing everything she touched.

"How did you do this?" he demanded suspiciously when he suddenly reappeared and began to staunch the flow from her wound with his own handkerchief. It was slightly damp and stung her palm. She could see his eyes were red...was the dampness his tears? Before she could answer a commotion broke out in the shop.

"Mr. Alexander!" boomed a husky male voice from the other room. "I'm Lieutenant DeSable. Homicide."

Startled, Kim twisted around and saw she was immediately surrounded by people. Two policemen stood inside the bead-curtained doorway. Three ambulance attendants crowded around the screen, while Lieutenant DeSable and a policewoman knelt beside the quilt. They flung it back and Kim closed her eyes, wanting to blot out the image of Madame Loulou's sad face. She felt strong hands grip her shoulders and was glad of them. Opening her eyes again, she saw that someone had put back the covers and Lieutenant DeSable was nodding to the policewoman.

"Carter, this is one for the coroner. Do what's necessary." While the policewoman named Carter began drawing a chalk outline of the body, Lieutenant De-

Sable grunted and rose to his feet, turning back to where Kim and the man he had called Mr. Alexander stood.

"You called the station at twelve forty-seven, Mr. Alexander. When did you discover the body?"

"He didn't find the body. I did," Kim said clearly, her eyes swollen with tears. Why did she suddenly feel so alone after moving away from those warm supportive hands?

Lieutenant DeSable brushed back a few imaginary hairs on his balding head. "What's your name, miss? And what's your relationship with Louise Le-Carpentiers, the deceased?"

"Kimberly Campbell." Then she gasped in surprise, blinking, as a flashbulb went off. They were taking pictures. Pictures of Madame Loulou's apartment, the scene. Forcing her gaze back to the lieutenant, she calmed her voice. "I . . . I didn't really know her. I was a customer."

Suddenly from behind them, in the shop, a woman screamed and began hysterically calling out for Louise and then lapsing into French.

"For God's sake, what the hell is going on?" shouted Lieutenant DeSable.

A young officer stuck his head through the beads, but before he could say anything a woman with bright orange hair rushed in. Crying out in French, her eyes searched the room and fell on the quilt. "Louise . . . *chérie* . . . *mon Dieu! Mon amie, morte . . . morte!*"

Carter took the woman in hand. "Who are you?"

"Evangeline Paris," the woman said between sobs. "I practice the tarot on Royal Street. Loulou was my best friend, and I cannot bear . . ." She sobbed even harder.

Lieutenant DeSable was rapidly losing patience. "Quiet her down, Officer Carter, and keep the crowd away. We've got some processing to do." Without missing a beat Lieutenant DeSable's small gray eyes turned back on Kim. "How did you cut your hand, Miss Campbell?"

Dazed, Kim looked down at the handkerchief. A line of drying blood marked her palm. "I don't really know. When I turned Louise over...I felt something."

One of the ambulance attendants appeared at DeSable's shoulder. "There's a knife over by the Chinese screen, Lieutenant."

"Bag it, Officer Carter. And anything else for the lab." The policewoman turned away from the tarot-card reader and once again the dark-haired Mr. Alexander moved close to Kim. He leaned down.

"Kimberly, the knife. Is that how you cut your hand?"

Before she could answer Lieutenant DeSable continued, "Did you touch anything else, Miss Campbell?"

"No, just Madame Loulou. Just her, in this room. But I touched a lot of stuff out in the shop."

Officer Carter handed her superior a clear plastic bag containing a thick-bladed knife red with blood.

"Oh, wait!" Kim interjected. "I think I picked up the knife...."

The lieutenant paused thoughtfully, studying the knife and Kim's reaction to it. "Perhaps we should go over this point again, Miss Campbell. You didn't touch anything in this room, but you picked up the knife?"

"It was under her." Kim tried to weigh her words carefully and keep her voice steady. "I cut my hand and without thinking picked the knife up to get it out of the way so it wouldn't hurt her. I must've thrown it farther than I thought.''

A new suspicion began in the lieutenant's eyes and Kim began to talk faster to counteract it. "I'm sorry, Lieutenant, I'm not thinking very clearly.''

"We also found this." Carter held out a plastic bag holding Kim's blood-soaked scarf.

"That belongs to me. I used it trying to stop the bleeding. But my hand was cut, so my blood will be on it, too," Kim said quietly, realizing how damning this must look.

"*Ma chère,* you helped my dear Louise!" Instantly the woman with the fiery orange hair sprang toward Kim to clutch her arm. "The spirits will bless you, *ma fille.*"

"Almighty Jesus, get her out of here!" DeSable bellowed.

"You must leave now, Miss Paris," said Carter.

Evangeline Paris released Kim's arm and cast a disgruntled look at the policewoman. "I'm going!" The brightly painted lips in her red-blotched face smiled at Kim and the man at her side. "You both are surrounded by spirits. Especially you, child. Your blood is mixed with my dear Louise's. You have a bond now.'' Tears filled the tarot-card reader's eyes again and she buried her face in her hands as the policewoman showed her the way out.

Kim stared at her. Evangeline Paris was spooky, that was for sure. But what mattered now was that she had a promise to Madame she planned to keep. She had to find a man called Shane and give him Madame Loulou's dying message.

Kim looked up to find Lieutenant DeSable glaring at his officers. "Do you think one of you could keep the gapers away so we can remove this body?" DeSable's

voice had lowered and his steely stare sent two policemen rushing to the front of the shop. Again his eyes fell
on Kim. "Officer Carter will get your full name and
where you're staying in New Orleans."

A wave of disbelief made Kim feel light-headed.
Could these policemen possibly think she was responsible? She hadn't given very clear answers at first, but
she'd been in a state of shock. At least the dark-haired
man hadn't accused her of anything. His quiet presence
was oddly reassuring, although he had been strangely
quiet since the police arrived.

She turned to study his stony profile, but a low whistle from one of the other officers distracted her.

"Take a look at this, Lieutenant." He was pointing to
the smashed pieces of bone Mr. Alexander had found so
interesting.

"Holy Jesus," the lieutenant breathed. "Get that
stuff in a bag quick. And not one word about it goes
outside this door. Understand?"

His gaze encompassed not only the policeman in the
room, but Kim and the man beside her.

Kim's confusion grew when the lieutenant shuddered
visibly. He pulled himself together just as Officer Carter reentered the room. "Escort them both to headquarters for further questioning," he ordered brusquely.

"Don't you think Miss Campbell's been through
enough for one day? Can't this wait?" the stranger
asked, threading his fingers through his thick wavy hair
as he stared into DeSable's set face. "While you're
wasting time, Louise's murderer is getting away."

The lieutenant blinked once before looking away to
motion to the paramedics near the screen. "Mr. Alexander, I said I'd see you both at the station." Again the

two men locked gazes. "That's the way we conduct criminal investigations in New Orleans."

The man was close enough to Kim that she felt if she needed to she could lean back on him for support. Bewildered that she should even think of doing so and a little frightened by everything that was happening, Kim turned to face him. She was in the middle of a murder; maybe she was even a suspect. Somehow this man, who had shown her kindness, seemed to be the only solid thing to cling to. But Kim never clung to anyone.

A small frown tightened his firm mouth and speculation deepened his brown eyes. "Don't worry. It'll be all right."

Kim took a deep steadying breath to show him that she had herself under control now. There was a flurry of movement as Lieutenant DeSable held back the ropes of purple beads for the attendants as they carried out the white-sheeted stretcher.

"Where are you staying, Miss Campbell?" the policewoman asked loudly.

Dragging her eyes away from the doorway Kim tried to answer but found her throat was dry.

Flipping open her notebook, Officer Carter glanced over the rim of her glasses. "Miss Campbell?" she asked again.

"The St. Charles Guest House on Louis Street," she finally managed. "Room four."

"And you, Mr. Alexander?"

"The Orleans Club," came his soft deep voice from directly behind Kim. "Suite 200."

"Your full name, Mr. Alexander?"

"Shane. Shane Alexander."

Chapter Two

Kim felt as if she'd been hit by a two-ton truck. She could hardly breathe, let alone think straight.

Stepping back, she blinked and again looked up into the man's face—Shane Alexander's. He was Madame Loulou's Shane. This striking-looking man with his thick wavy jet-black hair and piercing dark eyes, which had glowed amber when he'd first glimpsed Madame Loulou's body. Now, however, his eyes were hard, a brown so deep they were almost black. They narrowed in speculation as he studied her.

She sensed when his speculation turned to suspicion. His body grew rigid with distrust, his face hardening, the planes and angles of it sharpening with unspoken tension. Could she have somehow betrayed herself? Could he know, somehow, that she had been entrusted with a secret? A secret for him alone.

The words of the message shouted in her mind—demanding to be told. They had to be a clue to Madame Loulou's murderer. Kim wanted to blurt them out. But she couldn't in front of the police.

She wanted to erase the suspicion from Shane Alexander's face and give him the knowledge that might help solve this terrible crime. Perhaps, then, justice would be done. Perhaps, then, she'd be able to let go of this inexplicable sense of personal loss she'd experienced when Madame Loulou died. And guilt that she hadn't been able to save the old woman. What if Kim hadn't waited so long in the shop? What if she had immediately come into this room? Would Madame Loulou still be alive?

"Miss Campbell, are you all right?" Carter asked, breaking into Kim's thoughts. A thread of irritation had entered the officer's voice. "We're ready to go to the station now."

Kim nodded and forced herself to turn back for a last look at the room that had held Madame Loulou's treasures. If only its walls could offer an answer. Then her gaze fell on the chalk outline and dark stain on the Oriental carpet. A great wave of hot nausea washed over her. Not now! Later she would give in to these feelings, but not now.

Without a word she followed the policewoman out into the scorching afternoon sunlight. The summer air was still rich with the perfume of roses, but the little street was no longer still and peaceful. Just outside the courtyard knots of people whispered to one another while two policemen set up barricades, closing off the entrance to the voodoo shop. Across the street, huddled in a doorway by herself, Kim saw Evangeline Paris, her bright orange hair falling over her face as she wept into her hands.

The police car was stifling. The vinyl seats were sticky, and even with all the windows open the lingering scent of tobacco was overpowering. She glanced out of the corner of her eye at Shane Alexander. He was running his fingers through his hair, staring at her. Kim sat utterly still, looking straight ahead now, using all her resources to pull her thoughts into an ordered fashion. She had made a promise. How could she keep it and tell the police everything she knew about Madame Loulou's death?

The trip to the Vieux Carré police headquarters took only moments—they could have walked the half block as quickly. With great ceremony Officer Carter ushered them up shallow front steps to a towering white-pillared porch and then through a set of double doors. All show for the onlookers, Kim thought, and then caught herself. She wasn't usually so cynical.

At any other time Kim would have admired the large reception area with its lofty ceiling and walls covered in black-and-white murals of New Orleans history, but not today. She must be in shock. That had to be why she felt so odd, so unlike herself.

Taking a deep calming breath, she glanced around, trying to get her bearings. In the middle of the large room was a command post, surrounded by white wooden counters. Off to one side were stacks of travel brochures. Again it appeared this was all show for the tourists and not a real working police station. A stiff-backed officer approached and led them to an anteroom. Kim desperately tried to control her overactive imagination. She felt detached, as if all this was happening to someone else. Or maybe it was a horrible dream and she would wake up to find Madame Loulou still alive, wearing the absurd purple turban, her face widening in a welcoming smile as she stood behind the counter of her shop.

The slam of the glass-paneled door made Kim jump. They were in a small room lined with dark wooden benches. The two officers spoke in whispers before Officer Carter abruptly left the room. The other policeman politely offered coffee. Kim shook her head, but Shane accepted eagerly; the officer then left the two of them alone. She watched him drink the dark scalding brew in a gulp. She sank onto one of the benches—almost like a pew, she thought absently. This was no nightmare. It was real. Madame Loulou wasn't alive. There would be no miracle to bring her back.

Madame Loulou had died in Kim's arms entrusting her with a last message to be given to this man. She should tell him now, this very minute. Or should she tell the police and let them handle everything? But what did she really know? She concentrated on recalling the morning. The shop with its grisly and spooky contents. The serene and treasure-filled living quarters—and Madame Loulou. She must have been lying there for quite some time. Why hadn't Kim gone into that room earlier? Her presence had brought Madame Loulou to consciousness and she had been desperate to give the message. But, Kim remembered, not so desperate that she hadn't extracted the promise of secrecy first.

But why demand secrecy? Maria Laveau. The woman had been in the shop. Kim was certain of that. But who was she? And what had Madame Loulou meant by "Her power is strong"? The message would mean something to Shane. And it didn't necessarily make this Maria Laveau a murderer.

Still it was a clue, and should be given to the police. They were trained. They could take the few words Madame Loulou had said to her and piece together the truth. Kim was uncertain for the first time in years, a mixture of emotions coloring her usual good judgment. She needed to do the right thing.

Shane was prowling around the room as if the caffeine had loosened a caged animal.

"Did you hear what Carter said? We're to wait here until DeSable is ready to question us. Damn it! They're wasting time!" He picked up his cup, found it empty, crumpled it and threw it toward the wastebasket. The abused cup ricocheted off the wall and lay about a foot away from the metal can. "I've got to find out who did this!"

Her heart pounding, Kim stared at his taut face searching for answers. An inner voice warned her she must behave as normally as possible, but her first attempt at speech failed. She swallowed twice before the words "Who are you?" came out in a whisper.

He stopped and stared at her in sudden confusion as if his mind had been miles away. "My name's Shane Alexander. You know that...." A moment's silence, a frown still twisting his mouth. Then the tension seemed to ebb slowly from his body. He ran impatient long fingers through his hair, tangling the waves into disorder.

"Louise was my aunt." His voice was gentler now— the tone he had used in the shop when he had helped her with Madame Loulou. He stopped directly in front of her. "I'm in New Orleans for the summer at my Uncle Jerome's estate. I live in New York, working as a playwright."

He recited the words like an automaton. This is who I am—don't ask for anything more. Don't try to get too close or expect anything from me. Then he surprised her.

A ghost of a smile changed his mouth, softening it. "I know you thought Louise was frightened of me yesterday. She wasn't. I . . . cared for her. A great deal."

Kim knew that. She had seen it in his eyes. And she recognized him. She was surprised that his name hadn't registered earlier. Shane Alexander was the author of two of the one-act plays her advanced drama students had chosen to perform last spring. They were brilliantly written, but Kim hadn't liked them.

Suddenly her indecision seemed ridiculous. She had her answer. She could keep her promise to Madame Loulou and also tell the police what she knew. But she would give Shane his aunt's message first. If she didn't agree with his writing, if she couldn't accept his dark view of humankind, at least she could respect the honesty of the plays. The man who wrote them must be honorable; he would know what to make of the message. Then, when she was questioned she could tell the police and do all in her power to find this Maria Laveau; to get at the truth. Because whoever had committed this horrible crime should be put behind bars forever.

Taking a deep breath, she stepped closer to him. "Shane, there's something I—"

The glass rattled in the pane as the door was thrust open. Officer Carter stood on the threshold, beckoning her. "Lieutenant DeSable is ready for you now, Miss Campbell."

There was no time. Kim had left it too late.

Shane stepped away, his eyes flickering over her again as they had in the shop. "You're as pale as a ghost. Don't worry. Just tell them what you know."

All the way down the hall she told herself Shane was absolutely right. In a way his words influenced her. She had to tell the police everything, even if it meant breaking her promise.

The instant her mind was made up, the vision of Madame Loulou came back to her. She could again see the bright gleam in the other woman's eyes and feel her cold fingers gripping her hand as she had insisted only Shane must know the message. After exacting the promise that Kim would do this, Madame Loulou had died.

There was a strange kind of shaky relief in finally knowing what she must do. A part of her rebelled against it. Kim slipped into the chair in front of Lieutenant DeSable's heavily scarred mahogany desk.

As THE DOOR SHUT behind Officer Carter and Kim Campbell, a familiar emptiness gnawed inside Shane. Thank goodness this Kimberly had been with Louise at the end. His beloved aunt hadn't died alone like— His mind shut off automatically. He couldn't allow himself to follow where that path led.

Each time he lost someone the hollowness expanded; now there was room for little else except rage. If he had to scour every hellhole in New Orleans he would find the scum who had done this to Louise, and he would kill the person with his bare hands. He'd seen that act of revenge done twice before—once in the jungles of Brazil, the result of a rivalry between witch doctors; and once in the Serengeti when warriors killed their foes.

For the first time he understood the kind of emotion that caused a human being to take another's life. He supposed his veneer of civilization today was thin indeed. Louise had told him that he needed more beauty in his life so that his plays wouldn't be so unhappy, wouldn't reflect man's darker side. She was right as always. But now he felt consumed by the darkness.

Closing his eyes, he willed his pulse to quiet. He had been taught at a very young age that he must stay uninvolved. He'd learned from bitter experience that his capacity for emotion was overpowering, and that this power affected not only himself but everyone around him. Now he never allowed himself to feel too deeply.

He opened his eyes and found Officer Carter staring at him from the doorway. He hadn't heard it open and was momentarily shocked. Had she seen something on his face that should have been kept secret? Her expression was sufficiently hidden behind her horn-rimmed glasses, but her voice was completely neutral.

"Mr. Alexander, Lieutenant DeSable would like you to join them."

Straightening, he followed her to the lieutenant's door. As he entered DeSable's office Shane was surprised by the harassed look the lieutenant flashed him. Glancing curiously at Kim, Shane experienced another jolt of surprise. Her green eyes were no longer wide and vulnerable as they had been ever since he found her cradling Louise in her arms. Instead they sparkled with the determination he'd noticed the first time he'd seen her in the shop when she'd thought she was protecting his aunt. Her softly rounded chin had jutted out then with fierce protectiveness. Later he had been amused by the fact that this very attractive, seemingly fragile woman appeared to have a will of iron. Now he sensed that her iron will didn't come naturally, but perhaps had been nurtured and cultivated until it was an integral part of her.

"I think we can continue now." DeSable settled back into his leather swivel chair as Carter went to stand at his back and gaze speculatively at them. "I want you both to tell me exactly what happened in Louise Le-Carpentiers's shop this afternoon."

A low sob made Shane turn around to stare again at Kim's delicate profile. She was gripping the arms of her chair so tightly her fingertips were white.

"Lieutenant, I . . . I don't think I can talk about it now."

DeSable, exasperated, tilted his chair back, glancing up at the policewoman. She only lifted her brows, shrugging. With a deep long-suffering sigh the lieutenant shook his head. "Miss Campbell, we realize this is not easy. However—"

"Please!" Kim leaned forward, greatly agitated. "Don't you understand? I've never seen anyone die before."

Shane's life, professional and personal, was the theater, and he knew acting when he saw it. This young woman was giving one hell of a performance. Just the right amount of hesitation in her voice, her fingers nervously gripping together; but the soft trembling lower lip was pure genius. What could this be all about? She was a mass of calculated quivering womanhood.

But when she turned to look at him, Shane saw that the tears gathering on her lashes were real. And there was something else in her gaze, a silent appeal, that made him rise to his feet.

"Lieutenant, obviously Miss Campbell is experiencing delayed shock reaction. You'll get more coherent answers out of both of us in the morning."

Kim fell back in her chair, fumbling in her purse for a tissue. "He's right. I'm so confused right now I don't even know what I'm saying." With that she covered her nose and blew softly.

"All right then. Tomorrow morning at ten sharp," DeSable said, giving in none too charitably. He looked disgusted at the whole proceeding. "I don't suppose I need to tell both of you not to leave New Orleans. Everyone's a suspect until all the facts are in. I'll have a car take Miss Campbell home."

"That won't be necessary," Kim said blinking her tear-darkened lashes, a sudden determination paling her cheeks. "Earlier, Mr. Alexander offered to see me home." She smiled up at Shane. "Can we go now?"

"Not just yet." Officer Carter moved to block the doorway. "Both of you will have to follow me downstairs to give us a set of fingerprints."

The green eyes were vulnerable again. "But I . . ."

"It's just routine." DeSable stood. "We'll have to match them with all the others from the shop and on the knife."

"It's okay," Shane said quietly, not fully understanding what Kim was up to, but willing to go along for now. "I'm being fingerprinted, too. Don't worry."

"Don't worry!" she whispered urgently as they followed the policewoman down the steps to the basement. "They don't suspect you! Madame Loulou was your aunt, they would hardly think you'd murder her. But I'm a stranger to her, to you, to New Orleans. Why should anyone believe me?"

Kim was no longer playing a part. She was genuinely angered and frightened. He didn't blame her. Being in the middle of a murder investigation was intimidating, even if you were innocent. And his gut told him she was.

"Just stay calm. This will be over quickly and we can talk then. You have some explaining to do," he said curtly.

The searing look she bestowed upon him was reassuring; she wouldn't fall apart now.

By the time they were through processing Kim had gotten herself under control. He took her arm and led her down the front steps, but as soon as they reached the sidewalk she shook off his hand. Her eyes were still red from her earlier tears, but her lower lip wasn't trembling; it was as firm as her voice. "I need to talk to you alone, Shane."

"That was quite a performance in there, Miss Kimberly Campbell. Want to tell me what it was about?"

"Yes, well, it wasn't all a performance." She thrust up her chin. "But I'm glad for your support. You at least don't act like I'm a criminal. Everyone at the police station seems to suspect me."

"I keep telling you not to worry. That's just their way. Just keep telling the truth and you'll be fine. Now why was it so important to get us out of there without answering any questions?"

She stopped in the middle of the street to peer into his face. "I do have something to tell you. Only you. That's why I had to get us out of there. Your aunt gave me a message for you before she died."

She had surprised him before, but now he was stunned. And angry. If Louise had left a last message for him then why hadn't she told him right away?

This time the grip on Kim's arm was so firm she couldn't shake it off. "We can't talk here in the middle of the sidewalk. I know a place close by." His hold on her arm was just short of bruising, so she had no choice but to follow him none too gracefully the few blocks to Café du Monde.

He found a table for them against a high stone wall covered with brightly climbing flowers. He didn't know what they were but their scent was rich and sweet, almost overpowering. He was seething; how could Kim have left something so important this long?

Without asking, he gave the waiter their order of two hot chocolates and a plate of *beignets*—heavily powdered puffed doughnuts. The short walk had been made in complete silence. Now she sat, still without speaking, next to him at the small round table. He wasn't a patient man nor a particularly kind one, but he had tried to be both to this young woman because of Louise, because she had been with his aunt at the end. Now he found that she'd been keeping some message from him. His patience was used up.

"Well? You have something to tell me?"

The green of her eyes became almost opaque in the sunlight as she leaned closer, her fingers gripping the edge of the table. "I promised your aunt I would give you a message. She was most insistent. But I want you to know up front that after I tell you I'm going straight to the police with this information."

He was about to protest, but stopped to let this woman tell what she knew.

"I think I know who killed Madame Loulou," she said after a deep intake of breath.

"Tell me!" He didn't realize his hand shot across the table to grip her wrist. "Tell me exactly what my aunt said."

Her gaze met his steadily. This was the strength he remembered. Her words came out slowly at first. "She told me to tell you that Maria Laveau is alive. Her message to you was that Maria's power is strong." Rushing a bit she finished, "Do you know what that means? Do you know who this Maria is? Where we can find her?"

Shane released her wrist, leaning back in his chair, shock enveloping him. "Is that all? Nothing else?"

Shaking her head, Kim flung out her hands as if astonished. "All! What's the matter with you? Don't you see that this Maria Laveau is the prime suspect? Maybe even the person responsible for your aunt's death!"

"You're mistaken, Kim," he said softly, disappointment cutting through him like a knife. "Maria Laveau couldn't have murdered my aunt. She's been dead for a hundred years."

SOMEWHERE ELSE in the city, a woman, hideously dressed, reached into a bag she had set before her and drew out a doll. It was a beautifully shaped female in a green dress, with a delicate wax face. A lock of honey-blond hair curled down around the doll's features, making them seem to come to life.

"Whatever she knows won't matter," the woman intoned. "She'll soon be in our power."

Chapter Three

"She's been dead for a hundred years."

Shane's words settled around Kim, hovering at the corners of her mind, rustling echoes of the fear she had sensed earlier in the shop while reading the strange poem in the brochure. Now, like then, she shook free of her feelings and sat up straighter, glaring across the small table at him.

"What are you talking about? She was in the shop this afternoon with your aunt."

"No, Kim. Maria Laveau couldn't possibly have been there," he murmured, sitting even further back in his chair before a smile came over his face. "Unless..." His dark eyes grew even more intense as he stared into space, withdrawing completely from her.

"Unless what?" she demanded, her voice, to her disgust, cracking.

He returned from his private thoughts, almost surprised to find her there at the table with him.

"Unless it was someone made up to look like Maria Laveau," he speculated, his expressive eyes studying her face.

Kim couldn't even begin to guess what was simmering beneath the surface of Shane's gaze. But she needed to know. She'd been drawn into something beyond her scope of experience, and wouldn't let it defeat her. She needed more information. She needed to know what part she played in all of this.

"Of course you realize I don't understand what you're talking about." The bland smile he sent her across the table infuriated her, and her voice rose slightly as she demanded, "But I want to know what's going on. I think I have a right."

His face, wiped clean of that curious smile, was the final straw of a day that had seen her carefully controlled world tilt crazily on its axis. For an instant Kim lost her tenuous hold on her emotions.

"I lied to the police so I could keep my promise to your aunt," she spat. "I think I deserve some kind of explanation."

"Yes," he answered at last, his voice the one he had used twice before—low and beguiling in its gentleness. "I do owe you something for helping Aunt Louise. An explanation at least—"

The waiter chose that moment to appear before them, setting their cups of hot chocolate and a plate full of *beignets* on the table.

When Shane had ordered food she'd been appalled. How could he even think of eating? Because she had skipped breakfast, planning to lunch at an out-of-the-way Creole café a friend had recommended, and it was now late in the day, she was slightly light-headed from hunger. But the idea of putting anything into her churning stomach was abhorrent. Yet, the aroma from the plate drew her. Perhaps, to cover her agitation, she would try just one. She picked up a *beignet* and bit into it. It was delicious! Deep-fried, sweet, empty calories, which comforted her and made the horrible feeling inside her subside just a little.

She covertly studied Shane's profile as he turned away to pay the bill. His nose was saved from being aristocratic by a slight crook, while his mouth was sculpted like that of a dreamer, or a poet. There was no poetry in his writing, she knew, but certainly there were dreams—dark ones. She knew what kind of plays he wrote. What she didn't know was what kind of man he was and whether or not she could trust him.

She'd finished the treat and was licking powdery sugar from her fingertips before Shane turned his attention back to her. Cupping the mug of chocolate between his palms, he looked steadily into her face.

"I'll start by telling you that Maria Laveau was the most powerful voodoo queen ever to reign in New Orleans. Between 1820 and 1870 hundreds of people came from as far away as Europe and Africa to seek an audience with her. Even members of royalty visited her. She had fifteen children. One daughter called herself Maria II and took over the title of voodoo queen after her mother's death. Unlike her mother, though, this Maria used her powers for evil and for personal gain. She was sometimes very controlling, urging her followers on with fear and the threat of death."

"Maybe I'm dense, but what do those two women have to do with the Maria Laveau who was in your aunt's shop today?"

"Whoever was in the shop was a member of the voodoo cult keeping the legend alive," he said quietly.

"Oh, please!" Irritation warred with plain exhaustion in her voice. "This is the twentieth century. No one believes in that stuff anymore."

Shaking his head sadly at her naïveté, he leaned closer. "Voodoo may have gone underground in New Orleans, but it's still here, and it's very important to some people. That's what my aunt was concerned about, why she seemed so nervous yesterday. She had heard of a new voodoo queen, claiming extraordinary powers, who could be involved in rather questionable activities. Not just gris-gris bags, love potions, or juju."

"Gree-gree bags? Juju? What are they?"

"Amulets, and don't leave out the love potion. They were all very real to my Aunt Louise. She was a descendant of Maria Laveau, not through Maria II fortunately, but she did wield considerable power. That's one reason I was surprised to see her personal protective juju broken on the floor."

The sip of hot chocolate Kim had just taken burned its way into her stomach. She took a deep breath of air. "Shane, I'm not following this."

"In her apartment," he exclaimed impatiently. "The broken bits of bone you saw, which the lieutenant scooped up so quickly. That was a sacrificial juju, made especially for her own protection. DeSable recognized it. That's why he put it away so quickly. No need to start rumors in the Quarter." He brushed his hand over his eyes. "I'm afraid it's too late."

"The police believe in this, too?" she exclaimed.

"Maybe, maybe not. But DeSable knew my aunt's reputation. And he also knew that if word got out to the voodoo cultists that her personal juju had been broken, it would cause a lot of confusion and concern. On top of the other rumors . . ."

Kim's hand moved in frustration as she sought the right words. "You really believe in all this stuff?"

"This stuff, as you call it, is a very powerful ancient religion. Probably a derivation of the oldest religion known to man and it's still being practiced in cultures all around the world. They call it *Santa Rae* in Spanish-speaking countries and *macumba* in Brazil—but it's all the same."

She studied the intensity of his face, trying to understand. She knew he was an educated, intelligent, articulate man. How could he have such crazy ideas? "You can honestly sit there and tell me that by sticking pins in a doll or whatever the mumbo jumbo, someone can actually manipulate another person?"

"Let's just say I believe in the possibility."

She could see a strong pulse beat in his jaw. Almost in wonder at her instinctive perception of this man, she recognized that pulse as a signal of stress. How could she so quickly after meeting him feel this singular affinity with him?

Before she could voice an opinion he surprised her by leaning even nearer and saying, "I've seen it. Even experienced it myself—in Africa. In the Amazon basin of Brazil. In New Guinea. There are things happening in cultures all over the world that you wouldn't believe possible. But they do exist."

"How do you know these things?"

"I grew up knowing them. My parents were anthropologists. I spent my formative years abroad, experiencing those cultures." His eyes were too dark and narrowed now for her to read. He withdrew into himself, his face utterly without expression just as she had seen it before, as if he had told her more than he had intended and suddenly realized it.

She experienced again that sense of understanding him. Even so, she wasn't going to allow him to shut her out now. "This new...voodoo queen. Could she have something to do with your aunt's death?" she asked boldly.

His eyes flashed black pinpoints as he looked beyond her, unwilling to meet her gaze. For a moment Kim thought he wasn't going to answer.

"Yes. I think voodoo was behind it. I'm going to find out who was responsible and deal with them myself." His anger was so tightly coiled; the strong bones of his face and his tight mouth sent shivers down her back. He frightened her. There was no point in denying it.

"We have to go to the police." She forced firmness into her voice as she stood. "I am going to the police."

The look he gave her stopped her. "The police may well be part of it," he warned.

She slid carefully back into the chair. "You know something else."

"Only what Louise told me. People came to her, told her things." He shrugged. "They may all be rumors, but I'm not taking the chance." He eased back, away from her, his voice low. "I don't think you should, either."

"You're trying to frighten me away."

"Kim, this has nothing to do with you. Get out of it while you can." His eyes lightened ever so slightly. "Tomorrow morning tell DeSable everything. Everything that might help him in his investigation. Everything, except Louise's message for me. And then get on a plane and go home."

"I can't! DeSable had me fingerprinted. You heard what he said. I'm a suspect. He won't let me leave now."

Shane paused, sighing as he studied his hands. Then he looked up, his brow creased with concern. "You're probably right. But you should stay as far away from this as you can."

"I'm involved whether I want to be or not." She shook her head in defiance. "I have to stick it out. I want to help find who did this as much for myself as for anything else." She met his unblinking gaze steadily. "I want to do whatever I can to help find who did this to your aunt."

"Why?" Lifting heavy lids, he frowned at her. "She meant nothing to you."

Kim recoiled in shock. His face was still so hard and closed that she finally blurted, "Your aunt died in my arms! I can't just let that go. Don't you understand?"

Tears welled in her eyes and angrily she brushed them away. She had two and a half weeks of vacation left in New Orleans and could do whatever she wanted with that time. If she spent it trying to see justice done, Shane Alexander had nothing to say about it. And if he thought he could talk her out of it he was sadly mistaken. In a way she really had no choice—she'd been at the wrong place at the wrong time. Like it or not she was involved.

This time when she looked up, his eyes were distant and assessing.

"I don't understand you, Kim."

"Obviously." She stood. "I'll see you at police headquarters tomorrow." This time he didn't stop her. She slid gratefully into a cab at the curb and gave the driver her address. When she peered out the back window as they pulled away she found Shane still sitting at their table staring after her.

KIM HAD ONE of her nightmares that night. The almost forgotten evil enveloped her and the blackness pressed against her. She was powerless. Unable to move, locked in so small a space—almost a coffin—she felt the air grow stale, thinning itself of oxygen...thin-ner...thinner....

Her own whimpers woke her. She got up and re-moved her gown, which was soaked with perspiration. Mechanically she ran a bath and slid in.

She had built a bulwark of confidence slowly, bit by bit over the years, until she believed in it herself. There was nothing she couldn't deal with, nothing that couldn't be handled as long as she faced it squarely. Ex-cept for the dark, she had to admit ruefully. That was her only nemesis—her abiding terror of darkness. But she was getting better even with that as each year passed.

The warmth of the water eventually soothed her clenched muscles, and her breathing slowed to normal. Carefully she considered why the old feelings had come to haunt her, couched in a dream. Why was she again the child hiding in the closet? Why had the terror and un-certainty of being found and locked into the darkness against her father's bouts of drunkenness resurfaced to-night? He'd come home in those days, late at night, ready to battle. As a defense, Kim had hidden in her bedroom closet, knowing that since her mother's death, no one could aid her. Sometimes hours would pass until the sound of his snoring signaled all was clear and safe. For years, even after the child welfare center had put her into a foster home, she'd had nightmares.

Since those days no one had ever made her cower. When she'd grown old enough to understand the child-hood fears, she'd vowed no one or nothing ever would again. Certainly not some imaginary evil—voodoo queen, or whatever else Shane might rave on about. And he wouldn't frighten her away either. She looked down at her hand, the cut on her palm still angry-looking. She had removed Shane's handkerchief before going to bed.

She owed him a new one; her efforts to rinse out the bloodstains had been futile. She should put some more ointment on the cut and a new bandage.

She rose from the now tepid water and briskly toweled herself dry before finding a bandage for her palm. It was still too early to be up, but her adrenaline was surging. The way to regain control of her carefully organized life was to understand what had happened in that shop today... yesterday.

After dressing in a khaki cotton pantsuit with a red T-shirt, Kim studied her tourist brochures again, before deciding on a course of action. Shane believed the murder wasn't her concern, but he was wrong. She couldn't just sit around and wait for the police to decide whether or not she was a suspect. She would help herself, just as she always had. And she'd help Louise.

If no one else—Shane especially—would help her, maybe Louise's friends would. Evangeline Paris, the tarot-card reader, might be a place to start. But first she had a few things to discover for herself.

She accosted Mr. Charles, the manager of her guest house, just as he opened the doors to the tiny breakfast room.

"Miss Campbell, you're up bright and early this morning." His whiskers fairly bristled with pleasure. "I've just brewed some delicious chicory coffee."

"I'm sorry, Mr. Charles. I don't have the time now. But you could help me with something. I wonder if you could point out the location of the Voodoo Museum on this map of the French Quarter."

Frowning, he slowly took the pamphlet from her. "I know where it is, but it's not a big tourist attraction, you know."

"Yes, well, I'm curious. So I thought I'd stop by there." Sensing his hesitation, she smiled encouragingly.

"Doubt they're open this early, but there it is. On Dumaine Street." He marked the block with an *X* before handing the map back to her. "That's a tribute to a part of culture most of us in this city would rather forget, Miss Campbell."

"Thank you, Mr. Charles. I'll keep that in mind," Kim said with a big smile designed to douse any worries the older man might have had.

THE SIGN IN THE WINDOW read Closed, but the door was slightly ajar. Kim peeked in. A man, sitting at a long table, was spooning piles of what appeared to be crushed herbs into small red cloth bags.

"Excuse me, are you open?"

Startled, he looked up. "Sorry, no. Come back later."

Kim refused to be put off. Taking another step forward she asked in her best tourist voice, "Oh, please! I'm leaving on the ten o'clock plane this morning. My friends will just kill me if I don't bring them back some voodoo stuff from New Orleans." She giggled and pointed to the bags on the table. "What are these?"

"Gris-gris, miss," he answered automatically. "No. Don't touch. I'm in the midst of preparing them—a special order."

"Tell me about them. Could I buy some for my friends?" Kim asked, taking the opportunity to scan the tiny room. She recognized several things that had been in Madame Loulou's shop, but here most of the walls were covered with shelves of books.

"I'm only doing these bags because the regular tourist shop is closed," the man said, slowly starting to unbend. "I suppose I could do some for you if you could wait awhile."

It took a moment for Kim to realize he was talking about Madame Loulou's shop. Perhaps this man would be a good source of information if she was careful not to let him see through her playacting, the same skill she'd put to use at the police station yesterday.

"I'll be happy to wait." She settled into a chair in the corner and took a book on Maria Laveau off a nearby shelf. The phone on the desk rang and when the proprietor turned to answer it Kim noticed for the first time a sign off to her right that read Entrance to Museum.

The man mumbled into the phone and hung up. He turned back to Kim and brusquely inquired, "What kind of gris-gris do you want?"

"Are there different kinds?" she asked ingenuously.

"I do mostly bags promoting health and wealth. I'll need a name and age because each bag is intensely personal."

Kim thought quickly. "Wealth for John Van Meter, fifty-two." As an afterthought she added, "And health for Shane Al—Shane, um, I think he's around thirty-three."

"All right, miss. Of course, you can't stay here while I make them up. Perhaps you'd like to tour the museum?"

Kim nodded enthusiastically.

"That'll be ten dollars for each bag and three-fifty for the museum. Twenty-three fifty." He looked up expectantly.

Kim counted out the exact change and dug a small notebook out of her purse. "This is so fascinating, I may have to write it all down."

The entryway was darkened. As she passed through it, Kim became aware of a soft drumbeat and voices chanting. She hesitated, then realized there was a tape playing, but it wasn't like any elevator music she'd ever heard. Gripping her notebook tightly, she forced herself into the next room. It was only a tiny bit brighter, and a spotlight was directed at an oil portrait of a woman. She was beautiful, a sly Mona Lisa smile playing on her face. Her personality jumped off the canvas, compelling Kim to take a closer look. Next to the portrait was a card with a biography written in a matter-of-fact style containing the same facts Shane had recited to her the day before. Today they seemed real. Looking at Maria Laveau, Kim found it easy to believe the woman had attracted an enormous cult.

Tearing herself from her study of the voodoo queen, Kim glanced around at the contents of the museum. An altar was set up to one side. She was surprised at all the Christian symbols intermixed with bones and snake skins. Feeling repelled, she nonetheless took careful notes. There might be some clue here to unlock the mystery of Madame Loulou's death.

Across the room was a large aquarium, holding what a placard described as the "ritual snake." She stayed as far away from it as she could while reading the typed sheet on the wall near it. "Dumballah," it said, "is the most powerful of spirits." She shuddered involuntarily. Snakes had always made her squeamish. Right next to the placard was a small painting of a woman holding a large coiled snake above her head. Its caption was: "Maria II invoking the spirits to appear before the true believers."

While she gazed at the picture the music increased in volume, its drumbeat sending throbbing pulses through her head. The chant filled the room around her. Kim backed away from the snake's cage one step at a time. It was getting so hot. She loosened her jacket, and was ready to bolt from the room when another paper tacked on the wall caught her eye. The bold heading read:

JUJU

That must be what Shane had been referring to—the broken bones. Curiosity overcame her growing fear. The paper explained that juju was a sacrificial object that had been buried and retrieved. It contained protective spirits, represented by lines drawn on a clean skull, and was to be hung from the ceiling or high on an outer wall, where its power could act as a shield for the life of the owner. The example was a cow's skull. A green cross and several other symbols had been drawn on it. Kim dutifully sketched them in her book. Vaguely she remembered lines on the larger pieces of broken bone that Lieutenant DeSable had so quickly concealed.

She couldn't remain in this stifling atmosphere for another moment. Breathless, she scurried down the corridor as if the walls were closing in. A bright light indicated she was nearing the museum shop—just around a corner. In seconds, relief flooded her as she emerged from the museum into the shop. The proprietor was just hanging up the phone.

"Very good, miss." He looked around, his eyes shifting, as if he was apprehensive. "Your gris-gris bags are here. Now, I'd like to close up."

"Oh, but I need some reference books. This one here—" she reached for the book on Maria Laveau "—and a good one on the history of voodoo. What would you recommend?" Kim blinked in surprise as she watched him glance nervously around and grab a book from a shelf.

He was definitely disturbed about something, but what? He hadn't been like this earlier. To be safe she had to pretend everything was normal.

"Miss Campbell, just take these books and leave! I, um, I have to close the shop."

He was practically pushing her out the door.

"But what do I owe you?"

"That's all right. Accept them as a gift."

The Voodoo Museum door slammed in her face and the shade was rolled down, blocking her view. She shook her head. That man had been scared, badly. Was it the phone call?

She had her books and her gris-gris bags; whatever else she needed to know she'd have to find out from one of these books.

She hurried onto Royal Street. It felt good to put some distance between herself and the Voodoo Museum. No wonder rational people could be caught up by that stuff—even she had felt a little intrigued. She would never believe voodoo actually exercised power over people's lives, but there had been something compelling in that museum, something that had made her very, very uncomfortable.

Now she needed an open café so she could sit and read the books on Maria Laveau's life and voodoo. She'd always believed in the power of knowledge. When she taught her teenagers she encouraged them to get the facts first, and that's what she was going to do.

She could go back to one of the bars on Bourbon Street, but she decided she would rather be outside in the sun.

The police station was ahead. She checked her watch. She had hours until the appointment with DeSable and her decision had to be made. She walked two blocks further down Royal Street without finding a suitable restaurant, then stopped suddenly. A small red hand-painted sign hung over a clear glass door: Evangeline Paris, Tarot Readings. Excited, she rushed to the door and rattled the handle, but found it locked. A wave of disappointment washed over her. Apparently everything opened late in the French Quarter, maybe because places were open most of the night. Kim cupped her hands around her face and leaned against the window, peering inside. All she could see was a red carpeted stairway leading upward.

She glanced around and realized she wasn't far from the Café du Monde.

The table at which she and Shane had sat was taken, but she found another even more secluded, tucked away in a corner. The sun warmed her back as she hunched over, reading. When the waiter appeared, she hastily ordered. To her annoyance, he came back three times. Once to refill her chocolate, the second time to whisk away the empty plate of *beignets*, and the last time to present her with the bill. She wasn't finished reading, so in desperation she ordered more. After bringing a fresh cup of chocolate and another plate piled high with sugary doughnuts, he finally left her alone.

The sun was hot on her neck, but she shivered. Shane hadn't even scratched the surface of voodoo beliefs. But it was all here in the books: rituals with snakes, black cats, animal bones, zombies, conjuring the spirits of the dead, and Maria Laveau.

The voodoo queen had come to prominence during an outbreak of yellow fever in New Orleans. Many believed she was the best yellow fever nurse in town. She rose to become the most powerful voodoo queen in New Orleans's long history.

When Kim finally looked up from her books she realized she had consumed five *beignets* and two cups of chocolate. As fascinating as the reading had been, as much as she had already learned that morning, she was convinced there were some things she needed to see for herself. And the first was Maria Laveau's grave. On her way through the café she stopped her waiter and asked for directions to Louie I Cemetery. He hesitated for a moment, then sent her to the Park District office just half a block away.

"They'll help you there, miss. You really shouldn't go to the cemetery by yourself."

Kim wasn't surprised by his advice. She'd heard nothing but warnings ever since arriving in this historic city. Screwing up her courage, she headed in the direction the man had indicated.

When Kim reached the Park District office there were only a few tourists looking at the wall maps and tour brochures stacked neatly on the shelves. A much ballyhooed walking tour of the cemeteries was announced in several places, but unfortunately it didn't start until the next morning. That was too long for her to wait.

The woman behind the desk smiled broadly when Kim approached her. "May I help you?"

"Yes. Could you tell me where Louie I Cemetery is located?"

"I'm sorry, but that tour isn't scheduled until tomorrow morning. Nine a.m. sharp."

"I don't want to wait. I'll just go on my own."

Frowning, the woman shook her head. "We don't recommend tourists go there alone. There have been some muggings—it's located in a bad section of town."

Kim shrugged. "I understand. But I'll take a cab and have it wait."

The official favored her with a tight smile. "My dear young woman, I'm not afraid of your getting mugged *going* to the cemetery. I'm afraid of it happening in the cemetery itself. It's very quiet and secluded there."

Being a determined person herself, Kim recognized the trait quickly in others. Since there was no point in arguing, Kim simply nodded and backed away. "I see. Thank you anyway."

Outside, she hailed the first cab she could find.

SHANE STEPPED OFF THE PORCH of the St. Charles Guest House and swore softly to himself. Where was Kim? Why would she have gone into the Quarter so early? He'd arrived here an hour before she was due at police headquarters, sure that would be soon enough to catch her. He needed to talk to her, to make her understand that this was no holiday lark. She was getting involved with a voodoo cult. Although he usually kept his emotions tightly in check, he acknowledged that others often didn't. He believed Kim and so realized she was emotionally involved in this, but he had to make her understand the dangers. He would chase her down at the Voodoo Museum.

But the museum door was locked and the shades drawn. He pounded on the glass. There was no answer. Suddenly his eyes locked on a sign in the window, which read: On Vacation For The Month. Kim couldn't have been there anyway, he realized. Glancing at his watch, he swore again. Where could she be?

Of course! Maybe she'd gone to police headquarters early. But when Shane arrived there minutes later, the desk sergeant claimed he hadn't seen the pretty young tourist caught at the murder scene yesterday. He offered to show Shane to DeSable's office, but Shane

shook his head. There was still enough time left to catch
Kim to talk this through before they had to face De-
Sable again. He wanted to make sure she didn't entan-
gle herself any deeper in the case in the eyes of the police.
He wasn't sure whom he could trust. All he knew was
that he owed her—for Louise.

THE CAB DRIVER WANTED an exorbitant amount of
money to wait. Flustered, Kim paid him for the ride and
stood at the entrance to the cemetery as he drove away.
What was everyone so excited about? She'd been on
scarier streets in Chicago. This neighborhood wasn't bad
and she was only one block from busy Rampart Street,
just above the French Quarter itself. There were even a
few people carrying flowers and wandering into the
cemetery. Kim supposed the ranger woman at the Park
District office was overly cautious.

Certainly she wouldn't do this at night, but broad
daylight? Without further hesitation she walked through
the massive iron gates.

Now she understood why the cemeteries in New Orleans were called Cities of the Dead. It wasn't like any
cemetery she'd ever seen—no graves in the ground with
small stone markers. All burials in New Orleans had to
be above ground because of the marshy earth, she knew,
but she just hadn't expected these towering crypts that
sprawled as far as the eye could see.

Kim probably would never have found Maria
Laveau's grave if she hadn't been subconsciously keeping two other visitors within view. They were women,
who were mumbling words Kim couldn't quite make
out. They laid flowers at the base of a tomb and dropped
coins into flowerpots attached high up on the marble
memorial. Kim stayed at a respectful distance, hesitat-

ing to intrude. But when they left, she hurried forward, suspecting the tomb was Maria Laveau's. It was. Those women had obviously come to ask the queen to grant them a favor. It didn't make sense to Kim, but Shane was right. Maria Laveau, even dead, still exerted influence in New Orleans.

Kim walked slowly around the tomb, dismayed to find it covered with graffiti. It was high, three "stories," with the peculiar flowerpots on two sides. The graffiti was all the same—red-painted crosses pointing every which way. She moved back around to the front of the crypt and flopped down on a wrought-iron bench facing the tomb. There was no one in sight.

What could all this mean? She now knew more about voodoo and Maria Laveau than she had ever wanted to, but it still wasn't clear how all this could be used to find out why Madame Loulou had been killed. How long Kim sat there in contemplation of the voodoo queen's final resting place, she didn't know.

Then with a start, she knew why she'd been feeling slightly uneasy all morning. That man at the Voodoo Museum shop had called her by name! He had hung up the phone, been scared to death and had known her name! How?

She was alone and it was deathly quiet. No one else remained in the cemetery and for some reason, it was smothered in silence.

A hand touched her shoulder, and Kimberly Campbell, the calm and controlled woman who had arrived in New Orleans just two days before, screamed loud enough to wake the dead.

Chapter Four

Her heart in her throat, Kim leaped up, swinging around. What confronted her was the tall, muscular form of Shane Alexander. She should have known it was him, because the same palpable tension she always felt when in his presence was there now.

"Shane! You scared me to death!" she cried, fury clouding her senses.

He stood, hands on hips, and glared at her. "You should be scared. Don't you ever listen to anyone? You were advised not to come here alone."

More relieved than she would have believed possible—could all she'd read about voodoo be starting to affect her judgment?—she collapsed onto the white iron bench. "How do you know that?"

"Because I've been chasing you all over the Quarter. You told the owner of your guest house you were going to the Voodoo Museum." Shane began to pace the few short steps from the bench to the marble front of the tomb. Each time he reached the limit he whirled in fury and his voice rose a notch in anger. "It was closed. In fact they're on vacation. I got lucky. I encountered someone who gave you directions for here." He was still steaming. "So, where were you all morning?"

"What!" Kim croaked. "Shane, I was in the Museum this morning. I got these books there." Bewildered, she rose to confront him. "You have to believe me. Something really strange is going on. The man at the museum was helpful—in fact he made these gris-gris bags for me." She held out two packets tightly wrapped in brown paper and secured with tape. "But while I was wandering through the museum, something must have happened, because when I came out, he was really scared. And . . . he knew my name."

Shane put out his hand to take the bags away from her. Silently he unwrapped each, undid the drawstring, and scattered the contents in the wind.

"What are you doing! I paid money for those! They're just sort of a joke for Dr. Van Meter and . . ."

"And?" He lifted an eyebrow.

"And you!" she finished defensively. "You don't believe that man could have put something in there that would harm you?" Slowly she sank back onto the bench. "That's preposterous! Besides, they're just for fun."

"I keep telling you this is nothing to mess around with. I don't know how those bags were put together or what they meant, but I'm not taking any chances." He sank down beside her, the pulse in his jaw throbbing. "What else happened?"

"It doesn't make sense. The museum curator didn't charge me for these books. He just wanted to get me out of his shop."

"I don't like the sound of this, Kim. Someone is keeping a close watch on you. I warned you before to stay out of this, and now it's getting too late." He ran his long strong fingers through his dark curls. "Where did you go from there?"

"After I checked the time I went to Café du Monde to read. Then I came here."

"Yeah, and what did you do to that waiter? He was falling all over himself to help me."

Embarrassed, she shrugged. "I monopolized his table for hours, so I gave him a good tip." Snapping back into her usual composure she decided he had no right to question her like this. She glared at him with renewed spirit. "Why were you following me anyway?"

He stopped short, controlling his temper with apparent effort. Taking a deep breath, he slid his arm along the back of the bench, skimming her hair as he did so. "We need to talk, Kim. I'm worried you'll be a target for these people. They obviously know who you are. If I tell the police about this, they'll let you go home. Then you can forget all about New Orleans. Forget about my aunt and voodoo."

"I've already made up my mind what to do," she said. "I plan to tell Lieutenant DeSable everything I know. I think it will help them find out what really happened."

A quick frown darkened his face.

"Everything, except your aunt's message to you," she added softly.

"I'm glad." His features softened into younger, more approachable lines. "DeSable should have gotten a report by now, so you may be cleared to go home. How soon can you get on a plane?"

This time she shifted away from the hand that rested near her left shoulder. Obstinately she crossed her arms over her breasts. "At 3:45 p.m.—two weeks from Sunday."

"What! I thought you'd come to your senses."

Like combatants, they faced each other on the small bench, each with squared shoulders and head held high, staring straight into the other's eyes. The question was who would blink first?

"I decided you're right about keeping the message a secret," she admitted. "And only because Loulou begged me to tell only you. Besides, I'm not sure it means anything anyway."

"You still haven't answered my questions. Do you plan to continue this damn poking about until you get yourself hurt? Or worse?"

Kim paused as she framed her thoughts. "There's a part of me that would like to go home and be safe, but I can't. I'm as embroiled in this as you are, as heart-wrenched and upset. Look—" She reached out a hand to tentatively touch his arm. "If these people, whoever they are, are following me, if they think Louise told me something before she died, they won't leave me alone, no matter where I go."

Shane's features clouded a moment. "You're right. If they're fanatical enough they'll follow you anywhere." Her fingers momentarily brushed his, and she could feel his withdrawal from her touch. She pulled back. "So how am I going to make sure you're kept safe till at least the end of your vacation?"

Why had she done that in the first place—touched him? He wasn't the kind of man who radiated warmth and friendliness, but he was the only person she could turn to. She tried to shake off her confusion.

"I know you're going to investigate this yourself. You told me so. Let me work with you while I'm here. Maybe I'll remember something else, something important I haven't thought of." She could hear the eagerness in her voice and stood nervously to cover it. "Shane, I need this. I've got to find out why what happened, happened."

"Absolutely not, Kim!" His face was closed to her again, his eyes grim and unrelenting.

"Then we'll continue just as we are." She thrust up her chin and marched to the tomb where she provocatively traced a red cross with her finger. "With me one step ahead of you."

"My God, you're just obstinate enough to go ahead with this yourself, aren't you?" He held up his hand and she wanted to step back a pace because of the dark anger in his eyes, but she held her ground. "Don't bother to answer that. I can see it in your face."

"You agree then?" She didn't realize she'd been holding her breath until Shane nodded his head.

"You give me no choice. I owe you. For Louise. You know that, damn it!"

Yes, she knew exactly why he was agreeing: out of a sense of obligation. But she needed one more commitment from him. "There is one other thing."

"By all means, Kim, tell me what else you want," he drawled, sarcasm dripping from every syllable.

"I'm not betraying my promise to your aunt, but somehow Lieutenant DeSable has to know that Maria Laveau, or should I say someone impersonating her, may have something to do with this."

To her surprise he nodded. "You're right." He held out his hand and without hesitation gripped hers in a firm handshake. "You've got a deal, Kim."

Their hands clung together just a moment longer than necessary. Inexplicably Kim felt the cut on her palm begin to tingle. It had been healing so nicely she'd hardly given it a thought. Now, as their hands finally broke apart, she turned it palm up and studied it. Yes, the cut was fine—no infection or redness. Why, then, should it suddenly feel so warm?

THE NIGHT DESK SERGEANT, still on duty, seemed visibly relieved when they approached. He sprang up and held open the half gate to allow them into the corridor to Lieutenant DeSable's office. Down the hallway a tall, somewhat familiar woman crossed from one office to another. Kim was sure she'd seen her before. She turned to Shane. "I think—"

"You're a half hour late!" Officer Carter snapped, stepping out of DeSable's office and fidgeting with her glasses.

"Time seems immaterial in New Orleans, I've discovered," Kim snapped back, something about the policewoman's smug expression goading her into being rude.

A faint smile curved Carter's lips as she ushered them in. "Obviously, Miss Campbell feels better this morning, Lieutenant DeSable."

He was studying a file, but he rose when they entered, gesturing to the two chairs. Again, the policewoman hovered at his back while he asked questions.

"Now, Miss Campbell, I'm glad you're feeling better. Perhaps you can just tell me again what happened yesterday."

Kim carefully recited the events in the shop—an effortless job since they ran continuously through her thoughts like an old movie—except for Madame Loulou's message for Shane. It was almost scary how easily she edited that out, without a break or a pause. A teacher often used acting skills, and she was exercising hers again to the fullest.

When she finished he asked again insistently, "You're sure. Madame Loulou didn't say anything to you we could use in our investigation and you saw no one else, in or around the shop, while you were there?"

"No one. I didn't hear anything. The person who, er, the assailant must have been gone before I got there."

DeSable turned to Shane. "And you, Mr. Alexander, can you remember anything else? Anything you saw or heard that might be unusual?"

Shane's profile was stony as he sat with folded hands, his eyes mere slits. "Miss Campbell has told you everything just the way it happened. I have nothing to add."

With a deep sigh, DeSable nodded and flipped open the file on his desk. "Perhaps, Miss Campbell, you'd like to explain what you were doing in Madame Loulou's Voodoo Shop two days in a row."

Kim exchanged startled glances with Shane. Both of them had forgotten that little detail.

"A Mrs. Whitley came forward today to say she'd seen you in the shop the day before the murder." DeSable smiled blandly at her. "Is that correct, Miss Campbell?"

"Yes, I was there, Lieutenant. I don't deny it. I was buying a voodoo doll for the anthropology teacher at my high school. Madame Loulou insisted it should be in my likeness so—"

"I interrupted them," Shane cut in, his voice steady. "I was at the shop, too. Kim left, but I didn't know she was supposed to go back or about the doll."

The lieutenant straightened in his chair. "And where is this doll now, might I ask?"

"I don't know." Kim shrugged, at this point hoping she'd never see it again.

"Lieutenant!" Shane's voice was suddenly full of anger and beneath it she sensed concern. In fact he seemed desperate. "We've got to find that doll."

"I'll send someone to look for it." DeSable punched a button on his desk and gave explicit instructions.

"The doll was wearing a green dress," Kim offered, curious as to why it should be important. "And a lock of my hair should be with it."

"Damn!" Shane shook his head, leaning forward, his body tense. "Lieutenant, you've got to let Miss Campbell go home."

"Nonsense. She's a part of the investigation." DeSable's voice was precise, but he betrayed his agitation by running a finger under his collar. "I've checked you both out. And I'm checking out Mrs. Whitley. So far we have very few leads and very few suspects. Even if we clear you, you were both on the murder scene, and I can't let you go right away." He flicked them a cool glance before lifting one sheet of paper out of the file, rapidly scanning it. "I got the preliminary report from the lab today. Your aunt died of a stab wound to the chest. We have the murder weapon, but unfortunately the only prints on it were Miss Campbell's."

Startled, Kim turned quickly to Shane before she could stop herself. But he wasn't paying any attention to her. He was staring furiously at DeSable.

"What's the motive?" he asked sharply, the pulse throbbing in his jaw.

"Robbery," the lieutenant returned flatly. "The cash register in the shop was empty. Mrs. LeCarpentiers's jewelry boxes had been cleaned out, too. All the dresser drawers had been searched. We'll be asking you, Mr. Alexander, to check out what's missing. As you can see, we can't let Miss Campbell go until she's completely cleared."

Kim watched Shane nod in assent, his profile still hard and stern, his long lashes nearly resting on his high cheekbones as he studied his hands. She forced herself to relax back into her chair. Shane had given his word.

Although she barely knew him, she believed him. He wouldn't let her down.

Then he lifted his eyes to lock with DeSable's. "What about the broken juju you found in my aunt's room?"

Kim, momentarily startled, opened her mouth to speak, but a short warning movement from Shane stopped her. She could see the lieutenant was shaken, a light film of perspiration shining on his balding head. Officer Carter, however, sitting nearby, showed no reaction, managing to retain the same smug expression she'd worn throughout the interrogation. Kim realized the policewoman had probably seen a lot worse than Madame Loulou's murder during her career on the force, but still her cool attitude rankled.

"Everyone knows voodoo is everywhere in this parish," the lieutenant finally muttered. "We don't want to sensationalize it. That's not good for the tourists."

"I don't give a damn about the tourists," Shane retorted. "What I am concerned about is finding out who murdered Aunt Louise."

Officer Carter regarded Kim coolly, though she piped up and said to Shane, "I assure you, Mr. Alexander, that's also our objective. However—"

"However," Shane interrupted, leaning forward again. "I don't believe robbery was the motive. My aunt was concerned about a revival of voodoo somehow connected to Maria Laveau."

Kim's relief was all out of proportion to the situation. Up until now she hadn't been convinced that he'd taken her warning seriously. Until this very moment she hadn't been sure *she* should take it seriously. But it felt right. The knowledge she'd gained that morning had put the whole situation into a different perspective.

Voodoo! In this day and age! Her mind told her it was impossible, but her eyes and heart told her otherwise. Still, she didn't care what she'd read or felt, she wouldn't believe in it.

Shane had done what he'd promised at the cemetery. The voodoo aspect was out in the open without her direct involvement, without her betraying the promise she'd made.

Quickly she glanced directly into his eyes and found them dark with hidden secrets. But his mouth formed a reassuring smile, the first real smile he'd ever given her. It promised steadfastness, solidity. Such old-fashioned ideas, she thought. Kim's eyes fluttered down to her hands, one curled protectively over the other, where the small cut seemed to throb with a pulse of its own.

When she could finally look up, she caught Officer Carter's face set in a mask of stony coldness. Her hand rested imperiously on the lieutenant's shoulder.

"Mr. Alexander, surely you know how involved your aunt was with the voodoo community." Officer Carter spoke rapidly while pushing her glasses higher on her nose. "There's always talk about Maria Laveau's immortality. It means nothing."

DeSable lifted his eyebrows, nodding. "Yes, Officer Carter's right. Every once in a while there are wild stories about Maria Laveau resurfacing. They always come to nothing. This can't have any bearing on the case."

This time Kim didn't react. She sat quietly in her chair, her face blank.

"I see." Shane's voice was calm and crisp. "So you don't plan to investigate in that direction."

DeSable mopped his glistening head and brow with a handkerchief. "We'll aim our investigation in any direction that shows promise. I know you're in New Orleans for the summer. I'll need you to go through your aunt's belongings and let me know what's missing. Other than that I'll wait for the boys from the lab and from the field to finish their report." He stood and extended his hand to Shane. Then he turned to Kim. "Miss Campbell, we'll be keeping an eye on you until we clear you completely. I doubt we'll find anything. Our investigation on you should be finished in a couple of days, anyway. But if you change your local address let us know immediately. And we need to know your permanent address in Illinois. We'll be in touch."

It wasn't over. DeSable knew it and so did she, but she followed Shane's lead, rising slowly to her feet. When Officer Carter opened the door Kim moved toward it, giving the woman a fleeting farewell smile that was not returned.

Shane had a passing urge to tuck Kim's hand into his arm as they walked down the marble steps to the street, but instead rammed his fists into his pockets. He had a lot of unanswered questions that would need to be sorted through before he could trust Kim completely. He knew the police would clear her, but he still had a few doubts of his own.

People crowded everywhere around them. Faint music and rich aromas filled the soft summer air. Shane felt a tug of romance as the magic of the city seemed to call to him. He knew he did his best work here; he'd thought it was the familiarity of home, the unconditional love he received from his aunt, the support he'd received from his uncle, dead these past five years. Never before had he tied it to the uniqueness of the city.

Kim stepped away from him to investigate a crowd gathered at the corner. He followed her right into its center. A man was making absurdly beautiful music by rubbing the rims of size-graduated brandy snifters filled with varying levels of water. The onlookers were astonished at the full tone, the broad musical range he could produce. They listened to "Waiting for the Robert E. Lee," and something that sounded suspiciously like Bach, before he could get her to leave.

"C'mon," he said. "It's been a long time since you had breakfast. I'll treat you to lunch." The gaiety of the crowd was infecting him as he grasped her elbow to lead her across the street. Once on the other side he withdrew his hand immediately.

"They're on every corner," he explained, deliberately diverting her attention. "Entertainers. Musicians. Break-dancers. They're all looking to make a dollar from the tourists. Now if you want to really see the Quarter, you'll have to stick with me."

She gaped at him in surprise. "You know the real 'Norleenz'?"

He laughed at her approximation of the local drawl, and then stopped, surprised that for an instant the rage he'd felt had lightened. Miss Kimberly Campbell had a strange affect on him and that might mean trouble....

They crossed Royal Street and Kim wanted to donate to a performing poodle on the corner, but Shane dragged her away. "We don't encourage animals in the Quarter. It's dirty enough as it is." Midway through his complaint about the poodle he surprised an intent look on Kim's face. Then he understood why. Directly behind him, Evangeline Paris was locking the door of her shop.

The tarot-card reader turned and saw them. A wide smile creased her face. "My children, this is indeed fate!" She clapped her hands with glee, the many bangles adorning her wrists jingling like the tinny keys of an old piano. "Just this morning I read your cards and it was most gratifying to write what I learned down for you." She thrust a piece of paper at them.

Kim took it eagerly. "We both have the wheel of fortune." She grinned up at Shane. When he merely shrugged, she asked Evangeline. "What does this mean?"

"It means wealth, happiness, your heart's desire." Laughing, she wagged a thin knotty finger at them. "I told you good spirits were with you. See, I was right."

"Thank you, Miss Paris. Now if you will excuse us...." To Shane's surprise, Evangeline stepped in front of him, the hem of her bright red-and-yellow floral skirt brushing his shoes.

"The cards also told me that you need my help."

"How is that, Miss Paris?" Shane asked coolly, raising one brow.

"Soon you must see to Louise's shop. She would want her goods to go to those who need them, those who will truly appreciate their value. I know Louise's clientele. I could help you. The cards tell me I must help you."

There was some sense in what she said, even if the cards, which he could not credit, had told her. He capitulated. "Thank you. I'd appreciate your help. In the next few days I'll be in touch."

He felt Kim stir beside him and added, "I promise, Miss Paris, you'll be allowed to help distribute Aunt Louise's store merchandise."

"Don't worry, my child," Evangeline soothed, touching Kim's shoulder. "Shane always keeps his promises. The cards told me so."

With a flounce of her skirt and another jingle of bracelets, Evangeline made her way past them and down the street.

Kim's eyes were wide in wonder. "How did she know I was worried you were just leading her on to get rid of her?"

"She's a fortune-teller, remember?" He smiled mockingly, shaking his head. "Can we go now? I'm starving."

Shane had always liked the Orleans Club. As staid and dignified as the Quarter was raucous and rough, the crumbling white-pillared mansion stood for all the things that once had been: a combination of magnificence and restraint. They walked through the high-ceilinged lobby with its exquisite French tapestries and elegant leather couches to a wall of French doors that opened onto a sheltered courtyard. In one corner an ancient oak tree shaded several tables from the afternoon sun. The waiter seated them so that Kim had a full view of a fountain of fanciful mermaids. Hibiscus perfumed the air, and from an open window high above them, the tender notes of a violin completed the atmosphere.

"This is lovely, Shane."

He shrugged. "This is the closest place I could think of.... Kim, we've got to talk about this situation." He peered at her closely and leaned forward. "Tell me about the doll, Kim. Did my aunt really intend to make one in your likeness?"

"Yes, in fact I cut a lock of my hair for her so it would be authentic." She shifted uneasily in her chair. "I don't think my anthropology colleague would have known the real thing from the twine dolls, but Madame Loulou was insistent."

"Why didn't we see it, then?" he murmured.

"Shane, it doesn't matter. I didn't even pay for it."

He reached across the table to grip her hand, wanting to make her understand. "It *does* matter. Whoever has that doll has power over you."

She laughed unbelievingly. "You can't really mean that! This is the twentieth century."

"Have you been feeling okay? No sudden pains out of nowhere? No desire to hurt yourself?"

She pulled her hand away. "Stop this! You're scaring me. I don't believe in voodoo or its power. And Madame Loulou told me if I didn't believe, nothing could hurt me."

"I've seen the powers of darkness rise up so overwhelmingly that everything and everyone was swept along by them."

"Don't be ridiculous! I have a very strong will of my own...."

A waiter brought huge bowls of seafood gumbo and a basket of warm rolls. Shane wondered at Kim's ability to sit so quietly, poised and waiting for his next attack. She didn't expect him to make small talk, so he did, attempting to defuse her anger.

"My favorite. The cook here has a special way with gumbo."

Her eyes lightened to beryl in appreciation of her first spoonful. Eagerly she went along with his change of mood. "The food in New Orleans is unlike anything I've ever had in the Midwest. Creole. French. Cajun. Everyone claiming theirs is just a little better."

It was easy to see she was determined to keep the subject light. He saw it in her eyes and the tilt of her chin.

She raised the spoon to her mouth and sampled again. "And you know what? They're *all* right! Just when I think I've found the best, around the corner is a brandnew treat."

"An interesting way to look at the world—a series of treats. Most people are continually disappointed," he mused, fascinated by the play of emotions on her flushed face.

She was devouring the gumbo, relishing every bite and not ashamed to show it. She reached for a sip of wine then held her glass up in the sunlight and squinted at it. Before she could respond, a genial male voice bellowed out a greeting from across the courtyard. "Shane!"

Shane hadn't seen Claude LaCroix for more than a year, but the man hadn't changed a bit. He was still the epitome of the Southern gentleman; thin and fit, he was dressed all in white and carried a silver-tipped cane. Louise had always admired his pure white hair and immaculately trimmed mustache.

"Claude, it's good to see you." Shane stood, shaking Claude's extended hand. "I'd like you to meet a friend, Kimberly Campbell. Kim, this is one of my neighbors, Claude LaCroix."

With a charming smile, Claude swiftly raised Kim's fingers to his lips. "Delighted, Miss Campbell." Kim's eyes flew in pleasure to his face.

Shane felt a spurt of jealousy. What was this? He'd known Claude since he was a boy and seen him greet women this way a hundred times, but today he found it . . . distasteful. Irritated with himself, after all, Louise and Claude had been friends for years, Shane pulled out a chair, urging him to join them. "Have a glass of wine with us, Claude."

"Oh, no, really, I wouldn't dream of intruding."

Even as he protested, Shane motioned to the waiter and a glass quickly materialized.

"Just for a moment then." Claude sank into the chair, running his fingertips over the pristine pureness of his mustache. "Shane, I just heard this morning about Louise. My deepest sympathy. She was quite a girl. And a friend. I'll miss her."

Claude's hand shook ever so slightly as he raised the wineglass to his lips. He was an emotional man, so Shane dreaded what was coming. Other people's emotional displays always embarrassed him. He knew why, of course, because he kept his own so tightly hidden away. Even when he wrote, the only emotions he portrayed seemed to be disappointment and anger. Powerful emotions. Powerful plays. The critics raved and the audiences flocked to see them. Only his aunt had challenged the emotional content of his work.

His eyes settled on Kim. He couldn't keep from looking at her. She'd come into his life and suddenly he was examining his work, reassessing his beliefs—becoming involved, by trying to protect her. This was absurd! Louise's death must be affecting him more than he realized.

She was staring in innocent amusement at Claude. Sunlight filtering through the leaves dappled her soft cheeks and lightly haloed the honey-colored hair curling about her forehead and throat. A yearning came over Shane, and he had to forcefully set it aside. The feeling seemed ludicrous, considering the circumstances.

"Such a charming woman, Louise." Claude was chatting easily with Kim. He shook his head. "Although she was rather unorthodox, her heart was always in the right place." He drew a handkerchief from his pocket, patting lightly at his face.

Shane murmured syllables of agreement, uneasiness making him fidget with his wineglass. He caught Kim watching him and quickly stopped.

"Don't know what we'll do without her," Claude continued sorrowfully. "She was planning our fundraiser you know, for the historical society." He turned to Kim. "All the large home owners are trying to preserve as much of our heritage as possible."

"I can certainly understand your feelings," Kim said, smiling at the older man. "I've never been anyplace like New Orleans, where the past seems so interwoven in your daily lives."

Claude's thin aesthetic features came to life. "Miss Campbell, you are very poetic and perceptive. The past cannot ever be wholly dead, for it lives in us, in our blood, in the things we've inherited." His eyes suddenly widened, taking in both of them. "I have a wonderful thought. There is a meeting at my house on Friday. Shane, you and Miss Campbell should attend. I know it is soon after Louise's . . . passing, but this was a cause dear to her heart, and we could use the owner of Belle Rêve behind us."

Before Shane could respond, Claude was on his feet and stepping away. "I'm sure Miss Campbell would enjoy the meeting. I sense she has a true appreciation for what we are trying to do here. And of course she would have the opportunity to see The Pointe." By now he was halfway across the courtyard, refusing to take no for an answer. "Dinner at seven-thirty."

Shane watched Kim's eyes grow wider as Claude disappeared through the French doors. Expelling a soft laugh, she looked at him expectantly.

"Don't mind Claude. He's a preservation nut. But he's right about Louise. She would expect me to carry on in her absence."

"But don't you have to own one of those houses or be connected?"

"I do own one of those houses. Even though my aunt didn't live there it's her house. She continued the restoration and was constantly researching the lives of past inhabitants." He could see Kim was flabbergasted by his explanation. "Actually, Uncle Jerome inherited the place. Belle Rêve. It means beautiful dream, although it was nothing but heartache for him and Louise."

"But why didn't your aunt live there? Why don't you? If you own a plantation house why do you live in town?" She was totally confused.

"The painters have been there for the past week. In fact they finished yesterday. Would you like to see it?" He stopped himself. Had his voice really sounded as eager as it had to his own ears? "That's what I was going to tell you before Claude interrupted. Belle Rêve really started everything. I told Louise I thought voodoo rituals were taking place in the bayou and she started looking into it. Whatever she found—"

"May have killed her." They fell into silence. "Do you feel guilty? Responsible?"

He shrugged his well-set shoulders. "I never knew— didn't suspect—"

"And Louise could take care of herself," Kim supplied. "Look. The bayou's the perfect place to start. Is it too late to go there now?"

"No, we could be there in no time. If I call ahead, I can get a little expeditionary force together. Equipped with lanterns, we can make a nighttime visit."

Somehow Kim wasn't sure she could stand this part.

"IT IS DANGEROUS to talk like this here." It was said to irritate and it had the desired effect; a redness flamed in the queen's cheeks. Jackson Square was full of tourists sampling the food vendors' wares. If anyone saw them at the fountain together they would look the same as dozens of other pleasure seekers. No one would be any the wiser.

But it was good to keep the queen on edge. At times she forgot where the true power lay.

"This is important! At least here no one can eavesdrop on us. What are we going to do about Kim and Shane?" the queen asked, flustered.

"There is no need for concern. Yet. We must watch them."

"How, without arousing their suspicion?"

"We have friends. Many friends. They will help us do what is necessary."

The queen picked nervously at her sandwich, throwing pieces of bread at a sparrow just landing on the edge of the fountain. "I don't like this. That sniveling girl has a knack of being in the wrong place at the wrong time. What next?"

"Think! Think and be calm. We must use our wits." The queen's excitable nature worked well in the voodoo rituals, but in other situations it acted as a detriment. That was something to consider. Carefully. "If you wished to discover why Louise was...eliminated, where would you begin? That's where we must be—one step ahead of them."

Chapter Five

At the end of a long tree-lined drive Kim saw it: Belle Rêve—Beautiful Dream. And so it appeared. The house was surrounded by a natural paradise—a profusion of trees, vines and flowers; from magnolias, to poplars to honeysuckle and wild jasmine. When she stepped out of the car she was welcomed by a veritable feast of scents.

Shane waited patiently while she stared at the house. This was one of the reasons she'd come to New Orleans. To see history preserved; the remnants of gracious Southern living. For the first time she felt all of it was real, and not some Hollywood movie set. Shane urged her toward the front door. Carefully she reached out her hand and stroked one colonnette wreathed with ivy. Wide-open galleries wrapped around the house on two levels. Instantly she thought of beautiful young girls in hooped skirts and courtly Southern gentlemen sipping mint juleps.

"Shane, it's wonderful!" She couldn't keep the excitement out of her voice, even though she knew this was not a social visit and he was not the congenial host eager to show off his home.

He looked almost embarrassed; his lashes hid the expression in his eyes, but a rueful smile tugged at his poet's mouth. "Uncle Jerome loved the place. Come on in. You might find it interesting."

Directly facing the entrance, a mahogany staircase rose to the second floor. It dominated the central hall, which ran the width of the house, dividing the rooms into two distinct sections.

"This isn't all quite original," he offered, surprising her by the note of pride in his voice. "It has the basic floor plan of a Louisiana colonial house. Four rooms on each floor. But sometime in the 1840s, or so Uncle Jerome thought, someone added extra rooms to the back of the house."

Gazing around in awe, Kim nodded. She and her father had always lived in apartments, and she, later, in a ranch-styled house with her foster family. This was the kind of house she sighed over in magazines. Such fine woodwork detail couldn't be bought any longer; it was all hand-turned. Even the ceiling medallions were of carved wood. At the end of the long wide hall sunlight streamed through three lovely fan transoms with delicate muntins developed from a flower theme.

Sighing now in admiration, she whirled, smiling. Behind Shane, silhouetted by the light from behind, stood a man. She stopped in surprise.

Shane glanced over his shoulder, following her gaze. "Leonard! I was wondering where you were off to."

A slight man with graying curly red hair and a sun-baked face walked toward them. When he smiled, a network of fine lines seamed his eyes and mouth. "I've been checking the dovecotes," he said, and his voice had a lilting accent she didn't recognize.

Raking long fingers through his hair, Shane nodded. "Fine. I wanted to go into the bayou tonight and we'll need some lights. We'll go with you to check out the dovecotes.''

Leonard stared pointedly at Kim.

"It's all right. This is Kim," Shane answered quietly.

Leonard's weathered face split in such a wide smile his eyes were mere slits. Grabbing both her hands, he held them for an instant. "Shane has told me all about you, Kimberly Campbell. A fine thing you did, helping Louise, God rest her soul. Now I understand you'll be helping us find the son of a . . ." Mumbling under his breath, he stepped away. "Pardon me, lassie, but it fair makes my blood boil." Looking to Shane, the welcoming smile dissolved. "The summer storm's growing. The lights'll be ready whenever you're ready."

"That's why Kim is here." Shane lifted a dark brow in question and she nodded encouragingly, despite the faint flutterings in her chest. In the few moments they'd stood talking, the hall had grown increasingly darker. No sun beamed through the windows any longer. She felt a momentary chill.

As Leonard disappeared through a door at the left, Kim couldn't contain her curiosity another moment. "Who is he, Shane?"

"Leonard Hamilton. He's a distant cousin who came from Scotland when my father and Jerome were boys. Leonard was into genealogy long before it became trendy. He lived with the family for a while until he found another branch and then went to live with them in Cajun country. When Jerome inherited Belle Rêve, Leonard came back to help. He's looked after Belle Rêve for as long as I can remember."

"His accent—I can't quite place it."

"Part Scottish. Part Cajun. All Leonard. You'll get used to it." He pointed her to the back of the house.

"Come on. He's right. There is a storm coming." Perhaps noticing her sudden lack of enthusiasm he asked, "If you've changed your mind...?"

Forcing the flutters in her chest to subside, Kim laughed softly. "No way. We have a deal. Remember?"

They stepped through the center of three great doors onto a gallery facing the deep yard, which was ringed by oaks larger than any she'd ever seen. They were hung with veils of Spanish moss, which blended with the semi-darkness of the gathering storm to give the day a funereal cast. Not even the bright patches of flowers left in what had once been a formal garden could wholly dispel the gloom. Kim shook herself mentally. She couldn't back out now. This was what they had come for. She'd have to conquer her terror of darkness sometime. And this seemed like an opportune moment to at least try.

The fluttering in her chest changed into a tightness that gripped her throat, but nonetheless she followed Shane down the path to where Leonard awaited.

Leonard handed Shane a large battery-operated lantern, then Shane said, "Leonard will go in first. Then you, Kim. I'll bring up the rear. The bayou is a few hundred yards beyond this stand of trees."

With a gentle hand on her back, Shane propelled her in front of him. Faint light flickered down through the foliage, but not enough for Kim. If she'd been alone she couldn't have continued. The darkness closed in around her. She was beginning to feel trapped. But with Leonard in front and Shane behind there was no way she'd be a quitter.

Both lanterns played their yellow beams against the unfamiliar landscape. It was hard to keep pace with Leonard's surefooted journey through the dense trees.

The light from his lantern grew fainter as he hurried forward, moving away from them. Fainter and fainter, until it disappeared completely.

Ahead the darkness seemed to gather, strengthen itself, and wait for her. As a child she'd thought the darkness had a personality of its own; in the closets she'd hidden in, it had first mocked her, then taunted her, finally it had bullied her into submission. She'd carried her terror into her adulthood, somehow learning to cope. She supposed it was why she preferred an urban environment to the country; New Orleans to the Rockies. She'd always hoped her unreasoning terror would subside, the memories fade. But here! The night was all-enveloping. She could hear her heart begin to pound, pulsate in her ears.

Each step was an act of will. Her hands were curled into fists and her jaw was clenched, but she forced herself to keep moving. Finally they were out of the trees.

Kim breathed a sigh of relief. She'd been through the darkness and it hadn't gotten her. And after all, she wasn't alone. Shane was with her. Even without him, she believed that her need to find the truth was greater than her fear. Her rational being was converted; now she just had to convince her emotions.

A slight drizzle had begun, which they hadn't been able to feel while under the shelter of the trees. Now it veiled the grassy marsh in front of them. Leonard hadn't waited. Ahead more trees presented an impenetrable curtain. Kim suddenly stopped, the terror consuming her again. Shane ran into her.

"What is it?" he demanded, holding the lantern aloft to peer into her face.

She stared back at him. It was at moments like this, when all her self-possession vanished, that she felt vulnerable. To her utter disgust she could not set one foot in front of the other to go further toward the darkness of the dead gray leafless trees and hanging curtains of moss, which was the bayou. The nameless terrors of her childhood rose in her mind. Vainly she tried to explain them away. Vainly she told herself she was not alone. She reiterated her need to enter the bayou, to find the truth—to no avail.

He pushed her, gently at first, then more forcefully. His dark hair was beaded with drops of rain. In the murky light she could see his eyes narrow and darken to chocolate.

"You've got to keep up with Leonard, Kim. I'm pretty secure around here, but if we get more than half a mile from the house I'll be as lost as you. It's been years since I've been out this way, and one tree looks pretty much like another to me."

"I can't," she breathed desperately.

"Okay." He accepted her refusal matter-of-factly. "Here," he said briskly, shoving the lantern into her cold hands. "I'm glad you've come to your senses. Go back to the house and wait for us."

With that he quickened his stride to catch Leonard and left her holding the lantern.

"No, Shane..." she began, but he was gone, obscured by the dark and the mist and the rain.

She turned to go back to the house just as the sky opened and the drizzle became a pelting rain. Except for the tiny island of light cast by her lantern, the darkness was complete. There was no way she could go back through those trees alone. Shane had misunderstood. She was unable to move and the blackness seemed to press against her. Taking a deep breath she fought for control. There was nothing to be afraid of, she told herself firmly. All she had to do was follow the path back through those towering oaks, back to Belle Rêve—alone.

Swinging around, she stumbled after Shane, although he was already out of sight. "Shane!" she shouted, desperately trying to keep the mindless panic out of her voice. "Shane, wait for me!"

Oozing mud sucked at her shoes as she ran through the marshy grass. Rain whipped against her face, blinding her. But none of that mattered, for her enemy was the darkness.

A dark shadow looming in front of her in the blackness made her freeze. The lantern slipped from her limp fingers. She sank to the ground. A voice bellowed above her.

"Kim, what's wrong!" Suddenly warm arms wrapped around her, pressing her face into a strong shoulder while smoothing back her wet hair. "There's nothing to be frightened of," the gentle voice coaxed. "It's just a thunderstorm."

Somehow through the fog of her fear she realized she was in Shane's arms. He was holding her, comforting her. For a moment she could barely comprehend her escape. Then, sighing, she sank into him, allowing herself this instant of weakness. She was shaking not only with fear but with cold, and he was so very warm. She could feel her heart pounding in her chest, and she could feel, too, the pounding of his, as if he were also frightened.

Her instant was over. Pushing out of the warm supportive arms, she blinked up at him through the downpour. "I'm not afraid of thunderstorms. I . . . I thought I heard something." She hoped he hadn't caught the quiver in her voice.

"Of course. It doesn't matter. We won't see anything now anyway." He picked up the lantern. "Come on.

We'll both catch pneumonia. Leonard's just up ahead."
With one hand he held the lantern high to guide them.

Perversely, now that she had stepped away from his comforting arms, she wished he would offer a hand to guide her. Just the thought of holding his hand brought a hot tingling in her injured palm. Strange, it didn't look infected, but the sensation spread right up her arm and into her chest and stomach. Odd, but it was almost—no, it was—a pleasurable feeling.

DAMP FOOTPRINTS TRACKED across the carpet in the library to where Kim and Shane warmed themselves at the crackling fire. Water pooled on the hearth where they stood. Kim trembled, whether from cold or some unnamed fear he couldn't be sure. At least Leonard had run ahead when he was sure the two could find the rest of their way home, and lit the fire. He'd also set a tray of brandy and glasses on the mantel before retiring.

As Shane reached for the decanter he saw Kim brush her heavy hair back from her face. The thin wet material of her clothes clung to every revealing curve of her body. For an instant their eyes met, hers wide, unaware of the urgency the sight of her gave him.

Back on the edge of the bayou when he'd instinctively offered her comfort he'd been surprised at how natural she'd felt in his arms. But before he could fully explore that feeling she'd broken away. He'd been oddly grateful. Then, although he'd felt an impulse to take her hand to lead her back toward the house, all the old barriers had risen, forbidding that oh-so-human contact.

"You can't go back to town in those clothes." He turned away, pouring both of them a brandy. When he handed it to her he again studied her face, dewy and fresh from the rain. "Take this and go upstairs. Bathroom's the first door on the right. There's a robe there. I'll put your clothes in the dryer.''

"I don't want to be a bother." Shaking her head, she cupped the brandy between her palms and shivered.

"You'll only be a bother if you catch pneumonia. Go on," he urged, feeling another little stroke of pleasure when she tilted her head, smiling, and a lock of shining honey-blond hair fell forward.

"You're right. Thank you. I'll be right back."

A long deep swallow of brandy burned all the way down as he leaned against the mantel and watched her leave the room. Against common sense and his own will he felt a tug for Kim. He shouldn't; not now, not when Louise's death lay so heavily on his mind.

He banked his emotions, because emotion made one careless. If there was one thing he'd learned in life it was the idea that commitment meant heartache. With each death, his mother's and father's in an accident in the Australian bush, Uncle Jerome's five years ago, and now his aunt's, his detachment from humanity's greatest frailty—love—had grown. But the emotional repression haunted him, turned into anger. It suffused his work, his plays. He had cut himself off from all outsiders, hardly allowing himself to acknowledge even the love and loyalty he'd felt for his own family. Louise's death was one more loss that reinforced his alienation.

He channeled the emotion, used it. He needed a clear head to get at the truth. Kim and this unwanted attraction for her would have to be forgotten. He would concentrate all his thoughts and energy on finding his aunt's killer. Through no fault of her own, Kim was now a part of the puzzle. She was a beautiful intelligent young woman. And he had already admitted to himself that he admired her spirit. Under normal circumstances he might be attracted to her. But these weren't normal circumstances, which made the unfamiliar feelings he felt when he'd watched her this evening even more unsettling.

KIM LOCATED THE BATHROOM easily. The vintage Victorian tub looked big enough for two people. The pedestal sink was also oversize. Larger than life. The whole house gave her a feeling of bygone times when expense wasn't a consideration and houses were built to last forever. Had Louise LeCarpentiers decorated this room? The white wicker dressing table with a pale mauve and robin-egg blue cushioned chair certainly showed a woman's touch. Matching striped wallpaper and curtains completed the decor. Only a woman would have hung the oversize mirror framed by ornate gilt and long ropes of flowers.

All this charm and she was tracking in muddy water. She glanced down at her ruined shoes and noticed for the first time what must have been obvious to Shane; she had put on very little underwear that morning. Quickly peeling off her soaking clothes she rung them out in the sink, then slipped into the navy terry robe she found hanging on the back of the door. It hung nearly to her ankles and the sleeves required several rolls to reveal her fingertips. The soft warmth soothed her damp cool skin, and the enveloping smell was clean and fresh. It smelled like Shane.

Catching sight of her own flushed face and dreamy smile in the mirror, she stared at her reflection in disbelief. Her hair was darkened to ash-blond by the rain and her eyes glistened like emerald chips beneath her wet lashes—could this be Kimberly Campbell? For an instant she looked like a woman absorbed by longing. Longing for Shane Alexander? This was crazy!

Although he had been surprisingly understanding in the bayou, she didn't even like the man very much. His overall aloofness chilled her. His single-minded determination to find his aunt's killer frightened her. Revenge was the only emotion she sensed beneath his civilized veneer. If life to him was truly as bleak as he seemed to think, well she truly felt sorry for him. She for one, was looking forward to the day she could leave this city, unhampered by police or haunting memories.

When she descended the stairs again carrying her wet things, Shane was standing at the fireplace helping himself to another brandy. Somehow he had already changed into a crisp blue shirt and tan pants. Leonard stood to one side, a glass in one hand and a cigar pincered between the fingers of the other. To Kim's surprise he quickly threw the cigar into the flames when she entered the room, as if in consideration of her.

"There's the lassie. Hand me your things to dry."

"Oh, no, really, I can..." With a chuckle, Leonard whisked them from her hands and disappeared.

"Don't look so distressed. Leonard's a part of everyone's life in this parish. He's a real care-giver." The crisp waves of Shane's thick hair had dried in disarray. But instead of looking unattractive, it made Kim want to run her fingers through its richness.

Quickly she dropped into a wing chair facing him. What on earth was the matter with her? Absently rubbing her thumb across her injured palm, she stared blankly into space. The warm tingling sensation was becoming familiar now. Maybe she should see a doctor.

She'd had cuts before, but none of them had ever felt like this.

"Kim, are you all right?" Focusing her eyes she realized he had moved to stand directly in front of her. A frown pleated his black brows. "Kim, did you hear me?"

"What were you saying?" she asked, distractedly brushing a hand over her forehead. "I . . . I think I'm coming down with something."

"Do you have a fever?" Reaching out his hand, he nearly touched her cheek, but stopped a fraction of an inch away.

Had she flinched? Kim didn't think so, but then why had he stopped? A cleared throat caught the attention of both. Leonard was standing in the wide rectangle of the library door. His sun-baked face had crumpled into little sags and hollows.

"The parish coroner called. They'll be releasing Louise's body to us for burial."

Shane tipped the entire contents of the brandy glass down his throat. Because she was watching, she saw the shifting dark thoughts in his eyes before he could veil them.

"All right. Let's get this over with. Tomorrow afternoon. Notify some friends, will you, Leonard? You know best who will expect to attend."

Kim didn't see Leonard leave because she kept her gaze on Shane's face. The veneer had cracked, and for a heartbeat she had sensed something beyond revenge. He had paced like this before, like a caged animal desperate to escape. She needed to say something; she wanted to say the right words, comforting words. "I'm sorry, Shane," she said at last. "I know how hard it is to lose someone you love."

He stopped pacing and there was a shocking quiet in the room. It seemed almost that he'd ceased to breathe.

She rose to her feet, wishing she could lend comfort. But nothing had prepared her for the cold mask of his face stripped of every emotion. She stayed rooted to the spot.

"I suppose you'll want to attend the service." His voice was a study in coolness and his gaze held her numbly silent. She simply nodded.

She had to be at that service as much in respect for Louise as to see who else attended. She wondered if the murderer would come out of a sense of perverse satisfaction, the way it always happened in detective novels. At any rate, Louise's friends from the Quarter would most likely be there, and perhaps one of them would be able to tell her something about the voodoo revival.

"Fine. I'll bring you out here myself tomorrow."

"Here?" she finally whispered.

"Of course, here. All these plantations had their own family burial plots. Louise will finally be coming home."

Mumbling something about her clothes, Kim left the room, deeply saddened by the bitterness she heard in his voice.

ALL THE WAY into New Orleans Shane had every intention of apologizing, but didn't. He could write award-winning plays, but he couldn't find the words to tell this woman that he was sorry he had behaved badly...that he usually didn't burden others with unwelcome emotion. In fact, he never showed his emotions to others. Obviously he was tired, or he would have been more careful. He would be from now on, especially with Kim. For some reason, which he decided he must at the first opportunity dissect and understand, she was causing him to behave strangely.

They were in the lobby of the guest house before either of them finally broke the silence. "Kim, about tonight..." he began.

"Yes, I'm sorry I acted so foolishly in the bayou. I promise you it won't happen again." Her softly rounded chin thrust forward and her eyes glittered aggressively.

"Yes, today was...difficult for both of us." That was as close to an apology as his chaotic thoughts allowed.

Nodding, she smiled, as she absently rubbed her hand. He remembered she had done the same thing in the library at Belle Rêve.

He took her hand, turning it palm up, the delicate fingers slightly curled. With one finger he stroked the cut. "Does it hurt...?" His voice faltered as a warm sensation coursed through his body, and with it the desire to touch with his lips where his finger had been.

They both stepped back awkwardly.

"No, it's fine. I'll see you tomorrow morning," she said quickly. With a nod, she hurried up the stairway.

Shane watched her turn into the second-floor hall. Cursing under his breath, he paced around the small lobby. What was the matter with him? He'd never lived a celibate existence, but neither did he constantly need to have a lover. And right now that should be the furthest thing from his mind. Maybe once he'd laid Louise to rest he'd be able to get back to reality. He'd forget about the attraction he felt to this stranger and get on with his life.

A piercing scream drove all other thoughts away. Taking the steps two at a time he reached her open door in the time it took to take four harshly drawn breaths. She was pressed back against the wall, both hands trembling at her mouth.

On the snowy white bedspread lay a decapitated rooster, a crimson stain spreading in ever-widening circles.

Chapter Six

"Kim, look at me!" He stood, blocking her view of the bed, his fingers gripping her shoulders. "Kim, I'm getting you out of here."

She shrugged his hands away and peered at him. Shane's skin had lost its healthy hue and his eyes were as black as she had ever seen them, but they were filled with kindness.

"What does this mean?" she asked, proud of how calm her voice sounded. Years of practice had made this possible; outwardly calm and in control, while inwardly shuddering with fear and rage.

"It's a warning, Kim. And we're going to listen to it. First, I'm calling the police. Then I'm getting you a room close to mine at the Orleans Club."

"No, Shane, I—" She was interrupted by a horrified gasp from the open door.

"Why are they doing this? I've paid!" Mr. Charles nearly shouted, standing in his robe, his disordered hair and whiskers attesting that he'd made a hasty exit from a sound sleep.

"What? Paid what to whom?" Shane bit out coldly. All the gentleness she had sensed a moment before had disappeared.

Mr. Charles lifted his hands as if to ward off a blow. "Nothing! Nothing! I...I don't know what I'm saying."

Giving the older man a disgusted look, Shane reached for the phone beside the bed.

Despite her brave front, Kim couldn't look at the creature on her bed or the crimson stain. Warding off a wave of nausea, she turned to Mr. Charles who looked as pale as Shane. Did she look like that, too? As if all the blood had been drained away, leaving the veins beneath blue and exposed.

"Mr. Charles, I'll need a new room."

"I...I'm sorry, Miss Campbell," he stammered, wringing his hands. "But there is nothing left here at the guest house."

The frightened whine in his voice rubbed on her already raw nerves, but she forced a smile. "Then what do you suggest?"

"I don't know, Miss Campbell. I really don't." His whine grew more pronounced. "I told you not to go to that Voodoo Museum. If this gets out, it will be bad for business."

"Mr. Charles!" The tone of her voice widened his eyes and his hands fell to his sides. "Mr. Alexander is calling the police. They will handle this. In the meantime I need a place to sleep. If not here, then surely you can find me another guest house."

The anger in her voice must have gotten through to him, for he nodded and stepped away. "I'll call someone I know at Oak House. I will see to it now."

"Where's he going?" Shane questioned from behind her right shoulder.

"He's finding me another guest house."

"No, Kim, I'm taking you to the Orleans Club."

"I can't afford the Orleans Club."

"Don't be ridiculous, Kim. I'll take—"

"No, you will not!" she exploded, thrusting out her chin, glaring at him.

He glared back, the pulse throbbing in his jaw, but she ignored it. "What did the police have to say?"

"DeSable wasn't there. But I spoke to Carter. They're sending a squad car to investigate this mess. Tomorrow DeSable will get in touch with us."

"I'm surprised Officer Carter didn't demand we stay here for questioning."

"Actually, she was fairly understanding. Maybe she's not as bad as she seems." Threading impatient fingers through his hair, he shot her a cool look. "But that's beside the point, Kim. Quit being so damn stubborn. Just admit that in this particular situation I know best."

"Maybe you know more about . . . that." Gesturing toward the mess on the bed, she met his eyes steadily. "But I know what's best for me. I'll find my own room."

The manager returned. "Miss Campbell, the owner of Oak House is expecting you. Here's the address."

Shane snatched the paper from a startled Mr. Charles. "Let me see that. This is on the wrong side of Rampart Street, out of the Quarter. You can't stay there."

"I assure you, Mr. Alexander, Oak House is a fine old establishment." Mr. Charles's mussed whiskers quivered in indignation. "I know the owner personally."

Smiling, Kim edged him out the door. "Thank you. I'll pack and be out of here in a few minutes. Is my bill up-to-date?"

"Miss Campbell, please!" He held up his palms in protest and she saw that he was trembling. "Your bill is taken care of. I regret this horrible incident. If only—"

"Thank you again, Mr. Charles," she interjected quickly, slowly shutting the door. "You've been most helpful." Helpful and scared. Just like the owner of the Voodoo Museum. But she couldn't think about that right now.

Taking a deep breath, she turned back to the room. Shane had used those few moments to throw the ends of the spread up over the bed so that all she could see was an oddly shaped lump in its center. A wave of relief washed over her and she went limp for just a moment. But then she pulled herself upright. She wasn't going to let him see how much this had affected her.

"I'll leave while you pack. I want to make some phone calls downstairs. I assume it *is* all right if I drive you to Oak House," he asked with mild sarcasm in his voice.

"I'd appreciate it. I'll be down in fifteen minutes." As soon as the door clicked shut behind him, she fell into the small plaid corner chair and tucked her head down between her knees, breathing deeply. As she recovered her senses, she reviewed recent events. On one level she floundered in waters too deep for safety, but on another level, she knew she couldn't do anything but see things through to the end.

Acknowledging that, and feeling more clear-headed than moments before, she got up and began to throw her belongings into her suitcase, forsaking her usual neatness.

The sooner she got out of here to a new room, the sooner the sick churning in her stomach might subside.

Once in Shane's car she did feel more in control, and she noted the similarities between Mr. Charles's behavior and that of the curator of the Voodoo Museum. "Mr. Charles knows more about this than he's telling us," Kim said. "He mentioned money. A pay-out."

Shane nodded, flicking her a sidelong glance. "Yeah, he's terrified. A lot like you said the curator of the museum was acting this morning."

"Remember what you told me about Maria II, Shane? How she used fear to control people in New Orleans? Maybe that's what this voodoo revival is all about." She paused a moment, puzzled. "But to what end?"

"Louise told me what she thought was behind it. Extortion," he said flatly. "That's probably what he meant by a pay-out."

Stunned, she stared at him. "That's it! What are we going to do? Go to the police with our suspicions?"

"Not yet. They might be involved." His mouth a hard firm line, he pulled to the curb and turned to her. "Tomorrow several shopkeepers from the Quarter will be at the funeral. One of them might be willing to tell us something."

The rage had returned in full force; it was evident in his every fiber. Tomorrow he was burying his beloved aunt and at the same time searching for her killer. There was nothing Kim could say to his cold facade. She nodded, then followed him out of the car.

Oak House might be on the "wrong side" of Rampart Street, but as Kim checked in she could feel its haunting charm. A faded Aubusson carpet lay on the small sitting room/office floor and a solid oak staircase curved gracefully up two flights. Kim could almost hear the swish of silken dresses on those steps, hear the soft drawls of the elegant guests, smell the perfume of roses. No, the scent of flowers was real. Somewhere in the house, a potpourri was simmering.

Room key in hand, she returned to the entryway where Shane was waiting and grinned at him. "I like it. I'll be just fine here."

He shrugged. "I guess it will be all right. I'll pick you up tomorrow at ten. What room are you in?"

Looking at the key, she smiled. "Maybe I'm in the third-floor turret in the east wing. The room is 302."

"Fine. Sleep well, Kim," he said briskly, and was gone.

She watched from the long narrow window as he got into his car and pulled away. He had been so set against her coming here at first, and she had been prepared to argue with him. Why had he given in so easily? That surprised her. But she shouldn't be surprised, for he had other, more important things to think about. She understood, and besides, she could take care of herself. She'd been on her own a very long time.

KIM HADN'T BEEN on her own at all the previous night. She fully realized that when she and Shane were driving away from Oak House the next morning. A police car sat across the street. She stared at Shane's stern profile. "They've been there all night, haven't they? No wonder you gave in so easily."

He barely flicked her a glance. "I don't know what you mean. I'm happy to see the police doing their job."

She left it at that, turning to stare out her window as a smile tugged at her lips. Although she was fully capable of taking care of herself and had done so for most of her life, she felt cherished, special, that he had taken the time to make sure she was protected last night.

Surprisingly, the dark hours had passed more quickly than she would have believed possible. Maybe it was just exhaustion because she had stayed up for some time reading the voodoo book. Shane had been right again; the rooster had been meant to frighten her. But she had eventually slept, dreamlessly. She remembered what

Madame Loulou had promised her—without belief the voodoo could not affect her. But truth to tell, her resolve was a bit shaky this morning. Nevertheless, she would control it. Otherwise how could they piece together the puzzle and find Louise's murderer?

The moment they entered the wide central hall of Belle Rêve, they heard voices in the library. Kim hesitated. It was beginning.

Then Leonard appeared, closing the mahogany doors behind him. "It be Judge Rudolph and his wife." He smiled gently at her, his weathered face creasing into soft sad lines. "I'm glad you're here, lass, to see all Louise's friends."

Raising one dark brow, Shane glanced at his watch. "They're early. Did he say why?"

"He be Louise's lawyer." Leonard's small watery blue eyes glistened with unshed tears. "Everything is ready. I set up a buffet in the dining room for afterward."

Kim stood, uncertain, as Leonard walked slowly away. The old man seemed burdened this morning, yet he had taken the time to welcome her.

Pushing open the library doors, Shane glanced around, nodding. "It's all right. Come in with me."

A heavyset man with a mane of steel-gray hair looked up from the tea tray and his wide ruddy face broke into a welcoming smile. "My boy!" Gripping Shane's hand with both of his, Judge Rudolph shook his head. "I'm most sorry to see you again under such circumstances. Louise will be sorely missed by her friends and neighbors."

"Thank you, Anton," Shane spoke quickly, stepping back to urge Kim closer. "I'd like you to meet a friend, Kimberly Campbell."

"Miss Campbell, it is indeed a pleasure." The judge bent over her hand and for an instant Kim thought he would kiss it. Instead he merely held it, perhaps a moment longer than necessary, but then she was feeling pretty edgy this morning. "Marlena, meet Shane's friend, Miss Campbell."

Marlena Rudolph was an older faded version of the Southern belles Kim had imagined at Belle Rêve. Certainly she had never done anything so foolish as sunbathing. Her parchment skin was so beautifully painted that from certain angles one might think she was a much younger woman. It was her raspy voice that gave her age away.

"Miss Campbell." She nodded coolly, then smiled up at Shane. "My dear, my heart aches for you. Is there anything Anton and I can do to help?"

Shane took her thin, beautifully manicured fingers and did indeed carry them to his lips for a fleeting kiss. "Thank you, Marlena. I'm just glad you were well enough to be here today. Louise would be honored."

Clearing his throat, Judge Rudolph reached into his pale blue jacket to pull out an envelope. "We came early to give you this. You know what Louise's will contains, but this was something more that she gave me not too long ago. She wished you to have some extra instructions in the case of her death."

Shane studied the slim white envelope on his palm, his eyes hidden by a sweep of thick dark lashes. "I see." Finally he looked up. "Thank you."

"Well, Marlena and I will leave you in private and wait for the others on the back gallery... Miss Campbell."

At a loss, Kim waited until the heavy doors shut behind them. Despite her brave act around Shane, she was still badly shaken and confused. She opened her mouth to speak, but stopped, realizing Shane had forgotten her presence. He stood where he was, slowly opening the unsealed envelope and carefully unfolding the single sheet of paper.

"Instructions . . . ?" He read swiftly, then looked up, his expression bewildered. "She wants me to give a ball! A Mummer's Ball to celebrate her life."

A vague suspicion that there was more behind Louise's request than met the eye flickered through Kim. Setting the feeling aside for the moment, she walked slowly toward him. "I'll help, if I can," she offered, once again the need to comfort him overwhelming her.

The sudden change in his expression—sadness to anger—struck her like a blow. It took her every ounce of control not to whisper words of comfort; not to try to make him feel as warm and safe as he had made her feel. Instead she stepped away, allowing him the privacy she knew he needed to mourn in his own way.

"I heard some other people arriving." She kept her voice deliberately neutral. "Don't you think it might be a good idea if you greeted them?"

It appeared she had finally said the right thing. The cool facade returned as he carefully placed the envelope into his pocket.

"Yes. Let's get this over with." Striding to the doors, he flung them open and allowed her to pass through.

To THE QUIET AND SECLUDED old cemetery of the Alexander family they came to lay Louise LeCarpentiers Alexander to rest. An iron fence bedecked with honeysuckle and wisteria surrounded the graves. Friends and neighbors crowded around the simple square vault beside a huge raised family crypt dated 1812. A great stone angel surmounted the tomb, looking over the green of the trees and the family laid to rest there.

Kim found herself standing beside Claude LaCroix. Somehow in the walk from Belle Rêve she had lost sight of Shane. Now Claude leaned close. "All plantation families had their own private cemeteries. Many of them have been swallowed up by the swamps." His thin lips tightened beneath his white mustache. "Leonard has let this go. At The Pointe, our gardeners regularly tend our family cemetery."

Nodding absently, she tried to look interested in what he was saying, but her eyes were scanning the gathering. Leonard was standing near Judge Rudolph and his wife. Marlena, she thought, must have felt miserable wearing a long-sleeved dress in this heat. Even at this distance she could see the beads of perspiration on her flawlessly made-up face.

Evangeline Paris was here, too, her orange hair tied neatly back with a blue scarf. She wore a plain long blue skirt and blouse, and she was talking to a group of people—perhaps Louise's friends from the Quarter. And there was Mrs. Whitley, the woman Kim had run into at Madame Loulou's shop. Twisting to look behind her for Shane, Kim sucked in too sharp a breath.

"Are you all right?" Claude inquired politely.

Again she nodded, turning back to him. Frantically her gaze searched for Shane. DeSable and Carter were there, just outside the iron fence, watching and listening.

At last she spotted Shane beside the crypt. He was about to speak; she couldn't just push her way forward to his side. He was stretching out his arms to silence the crowd. His voice rang out in the sudden quiet.

"All of you here today were my aunt's friends and neighbors. So you know she was a unique woman with a view of the world many did not understand. Whether we understood her or not, we could not help but respect her for her courage to live life as she saw fit. Today we are here to honor the integrity of her life. She would not wish us to mourn her, but to celebrate in the joy her presence gave us."

Even from where she stood, Kim could see Shane's dark eyes dissolve into amber. The breeze that swung the curtain of moss above the group didn't cool the air or freshen the sudden close heat.

"Although Louise was my greatest fan and my most severe critic, she never really approved of my work." He paused as a rustle of soft amusement filtered through the crowd. "Except for one piece, which she has requested I read."

Shane took the white sheet from his pocket, holding it in front of him, but Kim could tell he didn't need to read the words; he knew them by heart.

"Linger with me in this golden time
When the sun's brilliant flame extinguishes all the strength of the earth
To be reborn a silver caress of moonlight.
Find with me...
Phantoms of impossible happiness in buried shadows.
Time without measure is ours."

He refolded the paper carefully. "Most of all, Louise would not wish us to forget her."

A strange emotion filled Kim's heart. She was looking into the face of a man she could love. But, she mustn't, a small voice inside her cried. Just as she couldn't stop the hot tears streaming down her cheeks, she couldn't understand Shane—his aloofness, his cynicism. Yes, he had shown her kindness, even concern, but always his detached side as well. Just like the characters in his plays. Whatever darkness filled Shane wasn't, however, reflected in the lines he had just spoken. They were quite different indeed. How long ago had they been written? The man who wrote them had not been filled with rage.

It was at that moment she realized her tears were not for Louise, not for the beauty of the words, but for herself... and for Shane.

SHANE FELT NUMB, utterly detached from the mingle of well-wishers who filed past him on the front porch of Belle Rêve. It was finally over—the service, the food and drink, the words of condolence. He hadn't even minded DeSable and Carter being there. They had apologized for intruding on the service and then had left promptly after questioning Shane and Kim about the previous night at the St. Charles Guest House. Again, he had seen Kim's strength, her determination to see this through to the end.

Afterward, they separated to speak quietly with several shopkeepers from the Quarter, to carry through their plan to get as much information about an extortion ring as possible. But after an hour, he still had no new clues. He wondered how Kim was doing.

Kim. Strange how he could instantly find her even in this press of people. After the moment in the library that morning she had not tried to comfort him again. Instead, she had assisted Leonard with the details of the day, instinctively knowing what to do.

Deep within him he felt an urge to touch her lovely soft skin, a yearning so strong he had to look away. Evangeline Paris was standing by his side. He noticed her dress and makeup were less theatrical than usual.

"The tarot tells me you wish to settle things in Louise's shop soon."

Startled, he realized she was right, even though he always resented the fact that her tarot could predict his wishes. The sooner he got the task over with the better. Besides, there might be something there that he had overlooked, something that might be a clue to help him identify Louise's murderer.

He glanced around; the crowd was thinning out. "You're right. It's only a little past one. I'll meet you at the shop in two hours."

With a nod, and an almost ladylike swish of her skirt, Evangeline walked away.

Shane didn't recognize the raw-boned, tall woman standing before him now.

"Mrs. Whitley?" Kim asked, suddenly beside him. Startled, he met Kim's gaze.

"Mrs. Whitley and I met at your aunt's shop." Kim smiled, holding her hand out to the woman. "Thank you for coming. May we ask you a few questions before you leave?"

"I told the police everything I know!" The woman stepped back quickly, glancing nervously behind her. "There's nothing else I can tell you."

"Mrs. Whitley, don't be frightened." Shane forced his voice to be quietly steady. This could be the lead they desperately needed. "We can help you."

"You couldn't help your aunt!" the woman whispered, her wide face drained of all color. "You know what the cult can do. Please, just leave me alone!"

Kim would have followed Mrs. Whitley as she fled down the stairs, but Shane held her back.

"No, leave her. She won't tell us anything more now. She's too scared."

Shadows of vulnerability haunted her eyes as Kim stared up at him. "Your aunt was right, wasn't she? These people are being threatened."

"Yeah, and paying money to protect themselves from unfortunate incidents. Like the rooster."

"What are we going to do about it?" Kim asked, her voice firm.

The strong urge to touch her came again, but he had to ignore it. "We're going to Aunt Louise's shop and search it. There must be something there we overlooked. We have nowhere else to go at this point."

A couple of hours later they arrived at the shop. Evangeline Paris was waiting for them in the courtyard. The shop was dark and stifling when they entered. Memories of that afternoon flooded back to Kim, but she managed to quell them.

Suddenly Evangeline pushed Kim and Shane to one side, and flung out her arms to embrace the shop.

"Louise," she breathed, "I am here, *ma chère*." She spun about to face her stunned companions. "Her spirit is here. I feel it."

Shane snorted impatiently.

"She is content, Shane, and so should you be."

He reached the corner and flipped on the light switch. Matter-of-factly he rummaged through the jars on the shelves behind it. "Everything seems to be here. The lieutenant wants me to look through her personal stuff. See if I can spot any jewelry or other valuables missing."

"Now that's a job for me, Shane," Evangeline insisted. "I suppose I know better than you the trinkets your aunt possessed."

Kim could see Shane visibly relax. Rummaging through his aunt's drawers was not a task he relished, she knew.

They were really here to search for clues. And while they were here, she hoped to find the doll his aunt had been making for her. After all, everyone seemed concerned about the silly thing.

"Shane, this case is locked," Kim said. "I remember your aunt wore the key on a gold chain around her neck." Her voice shook a little, memories of that afternoon filling her with new sadness. "Was...was it with her things?"

"No, it must be with her jewelry," Shane muttered, still methodically sorting through Louise's receipts. "Nothing here. Damn. I was sure... Kim!" His head shot up, his eyes narrowing. "Is that doll in the case? The one that Louise was working on for you?" He moved quickly across the room.

"It's hard to say. There are lots of dolls in here." Kim stepped back as Shane took a pen knife from his pocket and began to pry open the case.

"Don't do that." She stopped him. "Maybe the key's in the other room. I'll be right back."

Quietly, Kim parted the purple beads. "What have you got there?" Kim asked.

Evangeline Paris was studying a picture. Spread around her on the floor were items from a large wooden treasure chest: scraps of lace, beads, a hand-painted antique lace fan, a rubber-banded stack of letters and an open picture album.

"I don't know. It fell out of the album. Looks like a picture of a voodoo ceremony. Just like Louise to keep this in the family album." She thrust the book at Kim. "There are quite a few pictures of Shane in here."

"Yes." Kim closed the album without even looking at it. Then put out her hand. "May I see that?"

The photo appeared to have been taken with a Polaroid camera, and the picture was blurry. But to anyone who had visited the Voodoo Museum, it was obviously the Dumballah ritual. A woman held a coiling snake above her. Even with her head thrown back, Kim could see the resemblance—to Maria Laveau. It was almost uncanny, the similarity to the portrait that Kim had found so mesmerizing.

"Shane!" The urgency in her voice brought him beside her in an instant. Wordlessly she handed him the photo. Recognition hardened his face.

A door slammed.

"What's going on in here?" Officer Carter stood amidst the tinkling purple beads. "Oh it's you, Mr. Alexander. I thought the police still had this shop sealed. I'm sorry for interrupting."

"My time here is finished." Evangeline rose from the floor. "I will make a list for you, Shane. If I'm needed, I'll be at my shop."

Carter stepped aside as Evangeline swished past. "I'm sorry again, Mr. Alexander. I'll be going now."

"Wait. You might want to report to DeSable that we haven't discovered anything valuable missing. But there is something that supports my theory." He handed her the picture. "Does this look familiar?"

Pushing up her glasses, Carter studied the instant photo. "What is it?"

"It's a Dumballah ritual. And the woman bears an uncanny resemblance to Maria Laveau."

"I'm not familiar with voodoo, Mr. Alexander," Carter stated coolly. "But I will certainly give this picture to Lieutenant DeSable."

"No," Shane took the photo from her, slipping it in his pocket. "I'll keep it myself."

Raising one eyebrow, she shrugged. "As you wish. We'll be in touch. Good day."

Jeanne Carter had completely ignored Kim's presence. Was that why she found the policewoman so offensive?

No, it was something else. Something Kim couldn't quite put her finger on.

"Come on, Kim. We've got to go through these drawers." He was prowling the room, pulling open bureaus, rifling through the contents.

"What exactly are we looking for?"

"That doll for one thing!" he said furiously, slamming a cabinet door. "Anything that might help us!"

In silence they methodically searched the room. Half an hour later Kim found the diary in a small trunk tucked away beneath a table. A tablecloth of cream Belgium lace had hidden the trunk from view.

Sliding to the floor, Kim placed it on her lap and opened it. She hesitated for a moment, reluctant to intrude on the old woman's privacy, but then decided their need was greater.

Carefully she turned the pages. "Shane, I've found something!"

She didn't even glance around when he knelt beside her. "Shane, listen to this— 'I can feel the old evil being resurrected. The people are afraid. I will fight it with all my strength.' That was two months ago!"

Kim leafed through the remainder, quickly scanning the entries. "Here, this must be a part of it. 'Maria Laveau did have another child. Perhaps that line is the vehicle for this revival of the darkness. I can feel the malevolence directed at me, but I'm stronger now and can repel the evil, but I don't know how long I'll be able to hold out. Leonard came today. Rituals are being held behind Belle Rêve. He wants me to stop them. My beloved Shane also came. I must keep him safe. The darkness has already scarred his soul too deeply....'"

Shocked, Kim peered up at Shane's face for the first time, but his expression was hidden.

"Is there more?" he asked.

"Yes. 'My customers have dropped off. Evangeline says she has noticed it, too. There's trouble brewing in the Quarter. I'm not sure why, but I can feel it. Claude's invitation arrived. How fond I am of him! He has a real appreciation of the past. That committee might be a place to start. Their help would be invaluable. There is much power and influence in that group.'"

Kim paused to flip through several blank pages. "Ah, she starts again. 'I've been searching the parish records. Obviously someone has been before me and removed the evidence I need. The evil is becoming more powerful. There is more than one. I have my suspicions. I MUST go to Claude's dinner. Despite the personal secrets they hide most of the committee are good people. Perhaps I'll be able to unmask the power behind this growing menace.'"

Kim stared up into Shane's stony face. "There's one more page."

"Please finish it."

Taking a deep breath, she pressed the pages wider. "This is dated the afternoon I first came here. 'Shane came today and I told him some of what I knew. I fear for him in this. The darkness has long held a fascination for him, and although he would never be a part of it, I worry that he might get lost in it. A very sweet girl came into the shop today. A poignant reminder that innocence still exists. I felt a bonding with her, an understanding. I yearn for my Shane to be drawn to such goodness. I took great pains with her doll. I am quite pleased.' That's the end,'' Kim said quietly.

Again, as when she had read the love-potion poem, the words seemed to echo in the room and bring a tingling of fear that pulsed in the cut on her palm. She wouldn't look at Shane, determined not to show him how much Madame Loulou's words had affected her. She refused to feed the growing fascination for a man she could never understand. *The darkness has already scarred his soul too deeply....* How? Kim wondered.

Shane rose slowly to his feet as she closed the diary and placed it safely back in its hiding place.

He went to his aunt's desk and stood, fingering a heavy cream card—the engraved invitation to Claude's on Friday for the historical-preservation meeting.

Finally he spoke. ''Louise even circled the date in red on her calendar. Look.''

On the desk was an appointment calendar with a note about the party circled several times in red ink.

''What do you think it means?'' Kim tried to still her racing pulse, and she could hear fear in her voice.

Shane turned and her breath caught, as it had before, at his look of anguish. ''It means we're going to that meeting to find a murderer.''

Chapter Seven

Kim had thought Belle Rêve beautiful and charming, sitting contentedly in its fragrant garden. But even its magnificence had not prepared her for Claude LaCroix's plantation home.

The Pointe, at the end of a very long drive, seemed lost in time. Enhancing the beauty of the approach was a row of Carrara marble figures of Greek and Roman gods and goddesses mounted on pedestals.

Incredulous, she turned to find Shane smiling at her, one dark brow raised. "Wait until you see the house," he said.

Its tremendous mass rose up on a huge brick foundation. Arches over twelve feet high graced the facade. Two temple-like wings extended on either side of the main house, somehow managing to combine vastness with delicacy and grace.

When Shane opened the car door and she stepped out, their eyes met. His were lit with a wry humor she had never seen or expected, considering they had come to uncover Louise's murderer. But the possibility that Claude could be even remotely connected to voodoo seemed ludicrous to them when confronted with all this splendor.

"I feel as if I've stumbled onto a movie set." She laughed nervously.

"The theatrical magnificence doesn't end here. Prepare yourself," he murmured, casually taking her arm.

A great flight of marble steps under four towering fluted pillars led them to the front door. Kim noted with awe the silver knob lock and hinges.

One servant had taken the car, and now another admitted them to an enormous hall with the most spectacular spiral staircase Kim had ever seen. Beautiful Corinthian columns supported the vaulted ceiling. Kim glanced up at Shane's stony profile as they were ushered across the polished black marble floor to another set of oversize carved doors. The hint of humor on his face had vanished.

"Miss Kimberly Campbell and Mr. Shane Alexander," the servant announced soberly before stepping back to allow them to enter.

When Shane had picked her up he'd been wearing a white dinner jacket, and she'd been glad she'd chosen the fanciest dress she'd brought with her—a strapless emerald green gown. To that she had added the only piece of good jewelry she owned—a string of pearls. Now, she was doubly glad.

Claude, again all in white, his evening clothes complemented by an enormous diamond stickpin, swept forward and took her hand, carrying it gracefully to his lips. "My dear Miss Campbell, you look especially lovely this evening." He beamed and led her toward a distinguished-looking couple standing in the middle of the room. "Allow me to present the Honorable Philippe duNumours, our state representative, and his wife, Elise."

Kim extended her hand, her heart beating rapidly. Everyone she met tonight could be a lead or a suspect. She mustn't forget that. "I'm delighted to meet you." Her voice sounded quavery. She would control it.

"Phil, Elly, I didn't know you'd be here this evening. Nice to see you again." Shane sounded natural, at ease.

Even though Kim knew what he was thinking she could find nothing but urbane friendliness on his face. She was somewhat surprised by the warm way the older couple greeted Shane, as if they were truly delighted to see him again. They eagerly drew him into conversation about Belle Rêve, but when Elise turned to include her, Claude pulled her away toward an enormous chair facing the fire.

"You must meet Madame LaForge, one of Louise's oldest friends."

Resigning herself to the inevitable, Kim plastered a smile on her face. That's why she was here—to question as many people as possible.

Dwarfed but certainly not overpowered by the tapestry wing chair was the tiniest woman Kim had ever seen. She sat ramrod straight, one veined hand resting on an ebony cane. Silver hair pulled severely back into a bun looked natural and flattering on her. Sharp gray eyes assessed Kim. "And who is this child?"

"Madame." If anything Claude appeared more formal. "Allow me to introduce Miss Kimberly Campbell of Illinois. This—" he paused dramatically "—is Madame Virginie LaForge, the driving force behind our historical society."

"Miss Campbell. The young lady who was with Louise when she died. You, my dear, have had a harrowing time of it. When Claude finishes his introductions—" here one slim brow rose expressively "—do come and sit by me. I'd like to talk to you."

Kim smiled shyly, a little in awe of this grand lady who nodded her dismissal like a queen. Strange to think of this woman being one of Madame Loulou's oldest friends. They seemed so different. Louise had had the same fragile smallness and translucent skin, but Madame LaForge possessed a haughty regalness uniquely her own. Kim could not in her wildest flights of imagination see this woman involved in voodoo or extortion. So far everyone she'd met appeared charmingly normal and friendly. Perhaps she and Shane had read too much into the diary entries and the date circled in red on Louise's calendar.

Or, someone in this room was a very good actor. Behind one of these smiling facades a killer lurked.

The thought sent an icy finger down her spine. She drew back a little, but Claude didn't seem to notice as he led her toward three people seated at the far end of the room near another fireplace, this one unlit. They were deep in conversation, but Claude coughed discreetly to gain their attention.

"Ahem. Judge and Mrs. Rudolph. Mrs. Stuart. Miss Campbell, who has accompanied Shane Alexander to our gathering."

Judge Rudolph took her hand, giving it a warm squeeze, and Kim relaxed. She knew these people and could let down her guard for a moment. "Of course, Kimberly is known to us. We are delighted to see you again, aren't we Marlena?"

Marlena Rudolph managed one of her usual greetings, a cool curve of her thin, carefully painted lips, but Mrs. Stuart gave her a real smile.

"Miss Campbell, welcome to our ranks. I hope we won't bore you too dreadfully with our talk of restoring Louisiana to its former glory."

Amidst the friendly laughter Shane strolled up, but to her surprise, Claude again drew her away. Short of being rude, Kim didn't have any choice but to go with him. Besides, she needed to get closer to him. It was easier for her than Shane to be objective about Claude, for she didn't have the history Shane had shared with him.

"While we're waiting for Mr. Ralph Stuart to arrive I'd like the honor of showing you my home, Kimberly. All the others have been here before and they know each other, so I'm sure they'll excuse us."

A maid entered with a plate of hors d'oeuvres while a waiter stood by patiently to serve her a drink. Claude hovered solicitously beside her, an eagerness animating his thin face.

"Here, we'll just take our gin fizzes along with us as we go. You all make yourselves at home," Claude announced to the room. "I'm giving Miss Campbell the tour."

Kim met Shane's eyes across the room and easily read the shifting thoughts there. Her nearly imperceptible nod reassured him and he gave her a faint smile. She realized the tour was considered a great honor, so she would graciously do her part—and question her host unmercifully in the process.

As they crossed the wide black marble hall, Claude placed her hand in the curve of his arm. "Let me start by telling you The Pointe was once the greatest house in the entire Mississippi valley. Guests visiting from Europe in 1861 looked forth from the belvedere and called the view with its great fields of cane and corn, its four sugar houses, its miles of roads and drainage ditches, the most striking in the world. It is my goal to restore The Pointe to that previous state of glory."

The fervent passion in his voice struck a chord, and Kim stared up into Claude's flushed face. She taught her drama students to understand their character's ruling passion, life's chief motivating force. Restoring The Pointe was obviously Claude's.

Kim could only guess at the titles of the various servants preceding them, throwing open doors and switching lights on and off. One servant pushed open paneled cypress doors with hand-painted enameled knobs and hinges, which led into the library. Low flames burned in the fireplace of white marble, the light reflecting off the glass doors of the bookcases lining the walls from floor to ceiling.

"These mahogany cases were made in France especially for this room." Claude explained. He slowly circled the library pointing out the rare books, an old set of Shakespeare, nineteenth-century portfolios of engravings, and a collector's edition of Audubon's *Birds of America*. So many priceless possessions in this one room alone.

"This is unbelievable. These things should be in museums," she breathed, running her fingertips lightly over a glass display case.

"Many have been. But thankfully I was able to buy them back."

Self-satisfied smugness had replaced the passion in his tone. Kim thought she had to remember to ask Shane the source of Claude's income. Could money be behind the revival of voodoo? Was there real money to be made in extorting protection from the small businesses in the Quarter? Surely that would only be a trickle of the funds necessary to sustain this life-style.

Quickly she refocused on Claude, realizing she hadn't been paying attention. "I'm sorry, what were you saying?"

He patted her hand. "I know, my dear, it's hard to take it all in. I was just describing this next room."

He had led her to the downriver parlor, which was similar to the upriver parlor where they'd started the tour. Here the Irish lace had been replaced with Belgian linen so fragile it was almost transparent. The furniture was less sturdy, Louise XV, she guessed. A rosewood grand piano dominated one end of the room. Kim ran her fingers lovingly over the keys.

"Do you play, my dear?" Claude asked.

"Only a little and never on so fine an instrument as this. Do you play, Claude?"

"No." He laughed. "I was given lessons as a child, of course, but my instructor informed my mother I was tone deaf."

"Any other hobbies?" she asked innocently, keeping her smile firmly in place.

"No, I'm afraid The Pointe takes all my time. Speaking of which, we must press on. There is still so much to see."

They peeked into the dining room, already beautifully set for dinner. The carved English oak table had been brought from Canada by a branch of the family, he carefully explained. "Note the ceiling—the faces of the nymphs were said to be portraits of my ancestor's daughters."

By the time they ascended the spiral staircase, Kim was exhausted. Claude had spent the time showing off his possessions and Kim had spent her time in careful probing. Fortunately he hadn't caught on that she was spying, but unfortunately he had taken it as interest in him personally. He was an outrageous flirt—Kim assumed that was what he was doing. Why else the soft pats to her hand still tucked firmly in the crook of his arm, and the sly little smiles as he stroked his mustache.

But when they stood in the entrance to the master bedroom and he ran his fingertips down her bare arm, Kim realized it was time to take another tack.

"How long have you known Shane?" she asked brightly, pulling her hand away as unobtrusively as possible and stepping back out into the hall.

Charming as ever, he smiled, waving his hand for the servant to open the next door. A sitting room, it was obviously a man's domain, and it had painted murals of stags in various poses depicting the four seasons.

"Since he was a boy," he answered. "I was a friend of Jerome's and Louise's for years. I was terribly shocked by their divorce."

Knowing she would never have the nerve to question Shane and at last seeing an opening to ask about Louise, she said, "Why did she leave Belle Rêve? It's so beautiful."

"Louise was a unique woman. A free spirit, you might say. Jerome was a conventional man. Finally their differing views of how to live became insupportable."

A sadness for Madame Loulou halted her steps outside the door. With piercing clarity Kim understood how the woman must have felt loving a man who did not share her vision of life. "How tragic for both of them," she whispered.

"My dear, don't look so distressed," he said quietly, again taking her hand. "They had a special relationship—living separate lives, but still very much devoted to one another."

"But what about Louise's interest in voodoo? How did he react to that?" she asked, looking up into his face. Was there the merest tightening of those thin lips? In the dim light of the upper hall she couldn't be sure.

He shrugged. "When you are reared in New Orleans, voodoo doesn't seem bizarre, my dear." He patted her hand again, a gesture she was beginning to find very irritating. "Come, let me show you the bedroom of the mistress of the house. That'll brighten your spirits."

A few seconds later, light flooded one of the most beautiful rooms Kim had ever seen. Done all in white and shades of gold it seemed to glimmer, as did the huge fruitwood half-tester bed.

"With your coloring, my dear, you would look perfect in this room," Claude enthused, raising her fingers to his lips.

It was definitely time to change the subject. She broke away from him, stepping around the room to briefly touch some of the porcelain figures on the dresser. He followed, a rather intense look in his eyes. Frantically she tried to divert him. "How many rooms does the house have?"

"Seventy-five."

"Seventy-five!" she said, aghast.

"Yes. Although many of them are in the two wings that are not completely restored." A complacent smile lit his lean face. "But I will soon be able to complete that stage of the restoration, too."

A servant approached and stood quietly until Claude turned to him. "Yes?"

"Mr. Stuart has arrived."

"At last. Well, Kim, I hope you've enjoyed this tour as much as I have." He watched her expectantly.

Kim knew he was expecting her admiration. "You have a lovely home, Claude. Thank you for showing it to me. I learned so much." Not enough, she thought, but something. There was more beneath Claude's gentle Southern gentleman facade than she had at first thought. He was fanatical about this house, about re-creating every authentic detail. Did that tie into the voodoo extortion ring?

After several gin fizzes the formality of the group had evolved into a congenial party of friends. Philippe was holding forth on the difficulty of getting a restoration bill he had sponsored through the House without having a lot of inconsequential riders added to it when Kim entered the room.

Shane was waiting for her. He stood near the door, a smile tugging at a corner of his mouth. He had told her to prepare herself, but how could she have imagined such ostentatious opulence in this day and age? Claude must be fabulously wealthy to afford the upkeep.

"Now that we're all here," Claude interrupted firmly, "Miss Kimberly Campbell, Mr. Ralph Stuart, our parish's lobbyist for historical preservation." He paused only momentarily for them to acknowledge the introduction. "I have a real treat for you all tonight." A knowing smile softened his usually severe expression. "I have instructed my staff to prepare for our dinner the exact menu that was served General Pierre G. T. Beauregard when he dined here before the war."

"The Civil War," Shane whispered conspiratorially, his warm breath feathering her left ear and sending little shivers down her neck.

Without thinking, because it felt so right, she smiled up into his dark eyes and leaned closer to him.

To her surprise Judge Rudolph stepped between them. "I believe I am to escort you in to dinner, Kimberly."

Shane merely lifted one brow as he turned to Marlena. There was nothing for Kim to do but follow the lead of the other woman and place her hand on Judge Rudolph's arm as he led her into the dining room.

She did feel ridiculously relieved when Shane was seated on her right. And when their legs touched momentarily under the table, she felt another funny little shiver. Could one gin fizz have made her tipsy? Or was it because they were allies; partners, here under false pretenses, which in itself lent a certain excitement. She must, however, stop dwelling on the way he made her feel and concentrate on dinner and the guests. They all fitted perfectly into the old-world opulence of the house—beautifully gowned women with charming manners and powerful men relaxing with their friends. Where were the dark secrets at which Louise had hinted in her diary?

"This dish was named for Count Louis Philippe de Roffignae," Claude announced importantly as a plate of oysters was set before her. "You will remember he was mayor of New Orleans from 1820 to 1828."

The wine was poured and Claude turned to Shane. "I believe a toast to Louise is in order. Will you do the honors?"

Kim's eyes flew to Shane's face, but she couldn't read his expression as he pushed back his chair and stood. Lifting his glass, he said, "To my Aunt, Louise LeCarpentiers. In honor of her love of history, her remarkable zest for life, her devotion to the preservation of our past. To Louise."

Virginie LaForge beamed her approval from the end of the table. She drank from her glass, encouraging all at the table to join her. "She will be missed, Shane."

Murmurs of approval went round the table. The judge set his glass firmly back in place. "Louise was a good friend to our cause. Perhaps we should do something to honor her memory."

"A lovely idea, Judge." Elise pursed her lips thoughtfully. "I'll give it some thought, and at our next meeting I'll have a recommendation."

Kim watched Shane's reaction carefully. She could see that now, unlike during the funeral, he was firmly in control; his eyes remained a soft, almost warm, brown. Obviously he didn't really believe anyone in this room was a murderer. Not these people who spoke so warmly of Louise. Kim hoped he was right.

Shane turned to talk to Marlena and the next course arrived—escargot soup flavored with Pernod. It was delicious, but Kim noticed that Shane only ate about half of his. She looked pointedly from her bowl to his. He smiled so good-naturedly that Kim's heart did a funny little flip-flop. Had he decided this was a wild-goose chase and he was actually starting to open up to her, here among friends where he could relax and enjoy himself? In all the time they'd known one another there had never been one relaxing moment. She caught herself, suddenly remembering that it had only been a week. With everything they had shared it seemed much longer.

"This dinner will go on forever, Kim," he leaned closer, his eyes teasing her. "You'll never make it unless you start cutting back."

He was right. Crawfish *étoufée* was followed by broiled red snapper, veal rolls and olives embellished by mustard greens and turnips, spiced stewed okra, and *maquechou*, a kind of Indian corn and tomato dish. Kim didn't refuse a thing, but learned to take very small portions.

The conversation flowed around her: stories of the cream of New Orleans society, historical tidbits; even Shane contributed some Broadway anecdotes. But nothing offered any clues as to why Madame Loulou had written so cryptically about this party, these people.

There was a choice of desserts: *gâteau de sirop* or *bananas foster*, flamed at the table. Kim sipped champagne and followed Shane's lead throughout the evening. Background music by a trio of string musicians floated in on breezes from a closed courtyard outside the French doors. This was the life Louise LeCarpentiers had left behind to live in the Quarter; this comfortable existence had been hers and she had turned her back on it. Would Kim ever have that kind of courage? To completely alter her life on a principle?

Three hours after they'd sat down, Claude stood. "We won't adhere to tradition. Let's all repair to the downriver courtyard for coffee."

It felt good to move around a little; Kim wasn't used to such an elaborate meal and she had been so tense throughout it her nerves were on edge. She hadn't been enjoying these people's conversations; she had been analyzing and dissecting their every word.

The courtyard held the requisite fountain, its soft tinkle soothing in the velvety night. Flickering candles and lanterns illuminated every corner, helping to douse Kim's fears of the dark. Night-blooming jasmine perfumed the air. They settled into strategically placed wicker chairs, Shane next to her. Claude offered a choice of absinthe or Creole coffee as a waiter passed pralines and macaroons on porcelain plates covered with real lace doilies.

Another waiter poured green liquid into tall glasses of ice. When he carefully placed a slotted spoon with a sugar cube over the top of each, Ralph said playfully, "We'll have to hope the judge looks the other way."

Kim watched the waiter slowly pour water over the sugar cube. The drink in the glass became cloudy.

"Madame LaForge?" Claude offered her a glass from a small silver tray.

"No, thank you. I shall have coffee."

Kim leaned forward anxiously, not understanding the slight undercurrents she suddenly sensed. Was this the first crack in the facade?

Shane turned toward her. "Don't take it," he commanded. "That's the real thing. It's been outlawed since 1912 because it's so addictive. I can't think what Claude's doing."

"Probably following the menu for General what's-his-name." Kim didn't think it was strange at all that Claude would insist on this detail. Evidence of his obsession with authenticity was everywhere in the house. Apparently, regardless of cost, Claude was determined to re-create the past.

"Shane, do you think your aunt suspected Claude?" Kim whispered, leaning closer to him.

He tilted his head, casting her a sardonic look, but she didn't retreat, although they were so close anyone watching might think they were lovers.

"Claude and my uncle played chess together. They were close friends."

She did sit back then into the protection of the wicker chair to consider. She noted that Claude and Marlena Rudolph were the only ones drinking the forbidden liquor. And Madame LaForge was the only one who appeared visibly upset. Still, although her lips pursed in disapproval, she said nothing aloud.

The rest waited for the coffee as small conversational groups formed naturally, with Louisiana historical preservation being the dominant subject of discussion.

When Philippe monopolized Shane for fifteen minutes about a bill, Kim excused herself, catching his eyes before wandering over to the fountain. She perched on the rim and dipped her fingers into the clear water, watching the tiny goldfish swim around them. She had never experienced the life-style of the rich and powerful before. Perhaps if you had enough money, you could get away with . . . anything.

"So what do you think of Claude's home?" Shane asked quietly from over her shoulder.

Light from the hanging lanterns shone in the rich mass of his wavy hair, and she had an urge to push her fingers through it. Instead, she took her hand from the water and folded it with the other in her lap. "I think it's unbelievable. An incredible attempt at living life the way it was over a hundred years ago. And about as far from voodoo as you can get."

"Right on all counts," he observed.

Glancing up at his shadowed face she wondered what he really thought. "You really can't see any connection between these people and your aunt's death, can you? Shane, there is something here in this house, something about Claude's obsession with it, that is wrong."

"Time is a dream, one of our greatest poets once said. Here at The Pointe, that is doubly true."

She swallowed hard against the odd lump in her throat. "Very prettily said," she murmured. "Even poetically brilliant, but I don't buy it."

"I beg your pardon?" One black brow rose over suddenly darkened eyes.

Refusing to back down, she faced him. "I can be more objective about these people than you. Your aunt's diary entry was pretty clear. Someone here is involved with voodoo and extortion. My instincts tell me it has to be Claude. But I haven't the slightest idea how to prove it."

He stood, and his face was completely lost in shadow. "Come. It's time to get back to town. We can't talk here."

Their goodbyes stirred others to their feet. Several guests joined them on the front marble steps to see them off.

Shane's sports car was very intimate after the vastness of The Pointe. When he mentioned that the last car ferry had already crossed the river for the night so they were going to take a back road to a bridge, she simply sighed and sat back, relaxing for the first time that night. Even the pitch blackness outside the windows roused no fears. She felt safe here with Shane.

She could sense his growing anger, however. "You're angry with me, aren't you?" she finally asked his stony profile.

The pulse throbbed in his jaw. "I know these people. You don't," he stated flatly.

"Then why did we even go tonight?" she demanded, stung by his cynical tone.

"Because we haven't gotten anywhere in this damn investigation and neither have the police! Any clue has to be followed, Kim, but—"

The car engine suddenly spluttered and died. Kim sat bolt upright.

"What the hell?" Shane muttered, steering the coasting car to the shoulder of the road. "Kim, hand me the flashlight in the glove compartment."

She could see instantly the compartment was empty. "It's not here."

"What do you mean it's not there?" Leaning across her, he groped into the small space. "There's always a flashlight there. Stay here while I check the trunk."

He slammed the door and she resisted the urge to lock them all. Instead she turned, watching him open the trunk and a moment later slam it shut. He gestured for her to pop open the hood and flip on the headlights. She forced herself out of the car, leaving her door open so the light could push the darkness back. Thankfully there was a full moon in the cloudless sky. Her heels sank into the grass. Even if he was angry with her, it was better to be with him in the half dark than in the car alone.

Across the road an enormous man-made dike held back the Mississippi River. On this side, gray trunks of dead trees, tangled undergrowth and tall marsh grass merged into the bayou.

Shane was half-turned from her, peering under the hood, his white dinner jacket straining across his wide shoulders as he fiddled with the engine. In the glare of the car lights their shadows stretched out behind them. She could feel her fear rising.

"Shane, what's wrong?"

"I don't know...damn! Stand back, Kim. You're blocking the light."

Taking one step away, she stared into the darkness. There were no other cars on this road, no one to stop for help. The full moon cast eerie shadows across the landscape. Suddenly the moonlight glistened off something at the top of the dike. Frowning, Kim stared at it, wondering what could be up there. A road sign perhaps. But the light showed something long and narrow. Strange, it almost looked like—

"It's a rifle!" she gasped. Without thinking, she flung herself at Shane, pushing him down just an instant before a bullet slammed into the open hood. Shane yanked her to him as another bullet flew by.

As they fell he folded her into his arms and together they rolled off the shoulder of the road into the bayou. They stopped finally in a slight hollow, his arms wrapped around her. Her breathing was ragged, and her heart thudded painfully in her chest.

"A rifle. I saw a rifle on the dike," she whispered hoarsely.

Shane's face above her was intense, his eyes narrowed as they searched the darkness. Suddenly he pulled away to get a better position, but she reached out and pressed closer to him.

Finally he lifted his head cautiously. The danger that had hung heavily around them seemed to fade away. Kim felt Shane's body relax next to hers.

"It's all right. Whoever it was is gone," he breathed.

She stared at him wide-eyed, terror retreating before something stronger. They were so very close. But Kim needed to be even closer. Some ancient, primitive force inside her welled up out of fear and yearning with a pounding sweetness. She tangled her fingers in the waves of his hair and pulled him to her. The same force called out to him and he answered it, his eyes lightening to amber as he searched for and found her mouth.

The shattering kiss entwined them closer and closer, the sound of their mingled breath shutting out the night.

Chapter Eight

Kim was sinking. Down, down into an abyss from which there was no return. Her fear was forgotten in the overwhelming sensation in which she floated. She knew she was safe. He was here. And his arms surrounded her, supported her. As long as she could feel close to him she could feel safe. But suddenly he pulled away. "I'm sorry."

But before she could ask why, they both heard the sound at the same moment. Another car. Reinforcements for whoever held that rifle? Or rescue?

She squirmed away. Without ceremony, he clapped a hand over her mouth, shaking his head. Her eyes widened, glistening like gems in the moonlight.

He watched the headlights approach and stop, illuminating the abandoned car. A door opened and slammed. A flashlight played around the scene. She could feel his muscles bunch in readiness.

"Shane. Shane Alexander!"

Shane recognized the voice. The menacing presence fled before the light. It was safe now. Relaxing, his body seemed to go limp as his voice adopted a sternness. "It's the judge," he said. "Anton Rudolph. We're safe now."

"Anton!" he called in response, pulling Kim up from the damp ground. "Someone was shooting at us."

"What! Shane, Kim, are you both all right?" Anton rushed to them, shining the beam of his flashlight over their faces. "Are you hurt? Did you see who it was?"

Shane could feel Kim begin to tremble in delayed reaction at his side. "No. It happened too fast. Did you see anyone?" Without thinking of the consequences, he slid his arm around Kim's shoulders and she sank against him.

"No, no, nothing. Just your car. What do you want to do? The police must be notified...."

"I know, but I want to take a look around here first. Then could you drive us to Belle Rêve?" Shane walked Kim carefully toward the car. When he would have taken his arm away he felt her fright, saw it in her vulnerable green eyes. He opened his trunk and produced a blanket, wrapping it around her shivering body before urging her into the back seat of the judge's car. Marlena sat in front.

"You're safe now, Kim." He assured her and himself at the same time. They were both safe. For the moment.

He really didn't want to let her out of his sight, but he had to try to figure out what had happened. He flashed the beam of light all around the ground by his car.

Breathless with fear, relief and something curiously close to joy, Kim pulled the blanket more tightly around her shoulders.

Marlena turned. "Can I do anything for you, Miss Campbell?" Her beautifully painted face was empty of anything but polite concern.

Kim shook her head, gazing out the window at the two men, who were talking in soft tones. They paced the area, flashlight searching the ground. Kim saw Shane suddenly stoop to pick something up. A moment later he slid in beside her, but didn't touch her. He had withdrawn, back behind the cool detachment. How could he? After everything they had been through together…hadn't he felt it, too? Something inside her had reached out to him, and he had responded. There in the moist grass he had shared her feelings.

Now he was all business, leaning forward to converse with Anton. She caught something about the police, about alligator poaching. Marlena, like Kim, sat in carefully controlled silence all the way to Belle Rêve.

At last Shane touched her, helping her out of the car. Judge Rudolph let his window down and poked his hand through the opening.

"Give it to me, my boy. I can get it to the police tonight. I'm going to the city."

Shane dropped a small metal casing into his palm. "Make sure I get the results," he said.

Hearing a noise, Kim whirled around, then sighed in relief. It was only Leonard, hurrying toward them from the veranda.

"What's this?" He seemed surprised to see them, his watery blue eyes opening wide. "Where's your car?"

"Back on the Bayou Road. It died." Shane patted the older man's shoulder. "Perhaps you could arrange to have it towed for repairs. But for now, could you just take Kim into the library? We've had quite a night."

Kim could hardly move. Every muscle in her body was reacting to the damp chill of marshy earth. She wasn't even going to protest Shane's autocratic manner. She knew at this point it would do no good, so she simply smiled at the judge and his wife and did as she was told. It had been obvious in the car that Shane was rigid with anger. This was not the time to question him. That could come later, when they were alone.

Leonard clucked like the mother hen he was purported to be, settling her into the chair by the fire and turning to pour her a brandy. His muffled cough brought her to her senses.

"Leonard, aren't you feeling well?" She stood and dropped her blanket to the floor. "You go on to bed. I can pour my own brandy and one for Shane. It's been quite a night, as Shane said. I think we could all use some sleep. We'll talk about it in the morning. Shane will explain it all to you then, I promise."

"All right, lass. As long as you and the lad are all right, I suppose I might as well retire. Use the blue bedroom. The sheets are aired out. Shane can show you." Another raspy cough shook him as he walked slowly away. Tonight he seemed older, less robust.

A sip of brandy warmed her. She kicked off her shoes and let the fire toast her toes. Here at Belle Rêve she felt safe again. No matter what Anton said, she knew it hadn't been alligator poachers on the bayou tonight. Someone wanted them out of the way. The diary had been right. Madame Loulou had pointed them toward that dinner meeting, and somebody hadn't liked it. They must be getting closer to the truth.

She absentmindedly took another sip of brandy, then almost choked as a thought hit her—someone who'd been at Claude's tonight might have tried to— No! Try as she might she couldn't imagine Madame LaForge, the state representative or his wife, or any one of those distinguished guests trying to kill them.

But someone had taken a shot at them. She knew it. And so did Shane.

She sighed softly. Shane. She knew what he made her feel, what that kiss had meant to her. What she didn't know was what it had meant to him. She started out of her daydream as he entered the room, throwing off his dinner jacket to reveal a damp shirt clinging to his chest and shoulders. Mud stained his trousers. She could still feel where those strong thigh muscles had pressed her flesh.

"What a night!"

"I sent Leonard to bed. He was coughing. Shane, I think he's coming down with something." She handed him a snifter, laughing shakily. "I never had brandy before I met you. It has the most incredible ability to warm you from the inside out."

Like your kiss. The unbidden thought confused her. She sat back into the chair by the fire, fingering her glass carefully.

"You do know what happened out there tonight?" she asked quietly.

"For starters, you saved my life." He tipped the brandy down his throat, then paced to the decanter, pouring more before turning to look at her. "Someone at the party tried to kill us."

Her insides quivered a little at the intensity in his eyes, but she lifted her chin. "Claude?"

"Damn it, I don't know!" His fingers ran through his already mussed hair. "But why? Why would any of them be involved in voodoo and the extortion ring we suspect is at the heart of the matter? It doesn't make any sense. We need more to go on."

"We have the picture of the new queen. If we can find out who she is maybe that will be the tie-in." Rising to her feet, she placed her half-empty glass on the tray. "What do we do now?"

"Keep you safe." The harshness of his voice surprised her. But when his hands lifted toward her shoulders, she felt herself sway toward him. *Yes. Hold me. Kiss me again.*

"I wish you could go home. I wish this was all over." He spoke firmly, finally. He moved away and drained his brandy glass.

"I can't leave. Not now. They think I know something. You said yourself they would follow me. We'll be safe only after they're caught." More upset than she believed possible—how could she think of kisses at a time like this?—she challenged him. "Our deal is to work together, remember?"

He snapped on the desk lamp and sat in the swivel chair. "Yeah, that damn deal may get you killed." He unlocked a drawer, took out the blurred picture of the queen and studied it.

Something about that picture bothered Kim. Maybe it just reminded her of the painting in the Voodoo Museum. Or maybe there was something else. She held out her hand.

He thrust it at her impatiently. "Got any ideas?"

"If only we could see her in person, maybe even catch her during one of these rituals. The lighting would be better..."

"Sure. We'll ask them to schedule a special showing for us." He pushed the papers on his desk to one side. "They've been so careful, constantly moving their site, we'd never be able to find them." He ran his fingers gingerly over the calendar that had been hidden beneath, before slapping his palm against the hard surface. "Tomorrow is the Eve of St. John," he continued wonderingly.

She couldn't believe the change in his voice. "What? What's that got to do with anything?"

"St. John's Eve. Maria used to hold visuals in the bayou on St. John's Eve. Don't you remember, I told you about her?"

"Oh, yes, Maria II. She extorted a lot of money with those rituals. But what's that got to do—"

"It's tomorrow!" He stared at the calendar in disbelief. "I can't believe we almost missed this. The queen will have to be performing tomorrow—they wouldn't ignore this day."

"We have to be there, Shane. At that ceremony. We'll be able to figure out who she is!" Excitement warmed her cheeks and animated her voice.

"I don't want you to go." He stood, carefully placed his hands on the desk and leaned over to glare at her to intimidate her.

Without her shoes on, she barely reached his shoulder. Regardless, she glared back at him. "We are in this together. You promised, remember? And Evangeline Paris says the cards told her you always keep your promises."

"Kim, this is not a lark! It's dangerous. You should finally realize that after tonight," he growled, the pulse along his jaw throbbing as he prowled the room. "I'm not taking you into the bayou to a voodoo ritual."

"Fine," she snapped, "I'll go by myself." She wouldn't of course. Not even for him could she face that living darkness alone. He had no way of knowing that, however. She took perverse satisfaction in watching him struggle. He should, after all, because he had given her his word and she had believed him. She still believed him.

Her faith was rewarded with a long-suffering sigh. "You are the most exasperating woman I've ever met. All right, we're in this together—but just us. Don't mention anything to Leonard. I should have noticed earlier that he didn't look well." He rammed his fingers through his already disordered hair. "But you will be staying here tonight. No arguments."

She was so exhausted she could have slept propped against the wall, but she'd never let him know that. She nodded graciously. "Fine. You know, Shane, I'm not an unreasonable woman. There's only one problem. How do we find out exactly where the ritual will take place?"

"I'll find out if there's a traditional place for the Eve of St. John ritual."

"And I'll spend the day in the Quarter, talking to people."

His smile warmed her. "Good idea."

"See, don't we work better as partners?" she teased.

His only response was a grunt.

ACCORDING TO PLAN, Kim left Shane behind in the leather-goods store and wandered off to go window-shopping. About a block away she found her real objective—Mrs. Whitley's Potpourri Emporium. How ironic that her shop should be on Dr. Van Meter's "street of dreams." It had all started from here, the day Kim had gone searching for the voodoo shop. Now, however, she was searching for a killer.

Deliberately she stopped at a lace shop, examining the merchandise carefully. At a Mardi Gras shop she bought a feather mask. If anyone was following or watching she wanted to make sure they were convinced she was shopping.

She knew Shane was somewhere behind her. That was part of the plan they'd formulated in the car on the way into the city. They had to question Mrs. Whitley without putting her into any danger. If Shane saw anyone following her he would try to divert them.

Surreptitiously Kim scanned the street. She couldn't see anyone who looked familiar, but then she couldn't see Shane, either. After studying the window display for a few moments Kim entered Mrs. Whitley's store. The mingling scents of hundreds of dried flowers, herbs and spices permeated the room.

There were three customers ahead of her so Kim took her time, slowly circling the counters, sniffing large glass containers of potpourri. She finally decided on Elizabethan Rose and filled one of the plastic bags provided.

Mrs. Whitley recognized her over the shoulder of the customer she was waiting on. Her fingers trembled as she made change.

"What do you want?" she hissed when Kim reached the counter.

"We want to stop what's happening to you," Kim said softly. Then in a louder voice she asked, "How much do I owe you?"

For a moment the shop was empty of all others. Mrs. Whitley's face paled.

"You're going to make trouble," she whispered, taking Kim's money, desperately trying to make it appear a normal transaction.

"No. We're going to stop the trouble. Help us. Tell me where the voodoo ceremony is tonight."

"Please. Leave me alone."

"I will leave when you tell me." Kim was determined.

Her breath caught at the look of terror in Mrs. Whitley's eyes. A new customer entered the shop. Kim thought all was lost. But Mrs. Whitley surprised her. With trembling fingers she scribbled on the back of the receipt, then put it and Kim's potpourri into a bag.

She thrust it into Kim's hands. "Thank you, miss." Quickly she turned to another customer. "May I help you?"

Kim clutched the bag in suddenly trembling fingers. Across the street Shane lounged on a park bench, seemingly unconcerned. She darted through traffic and fell triumphantly onto the seat beside him. Her smile was so infectious he lifted one eyebrow expectantly.

"Well?"

"I've got it! Mrs. Whitley wrote it on the back of the receipt." She dug into the bag and casually read the message. "Lefitte Plantation. Do you know where that is?"

"Absolutely. Are you sure you want to go through with this, Kim? It's not too late to back out." His eyes were warm, as she had seldom seen them. And somehow she knew he wanted to reach out to take her hand, though he didn't. There was no need, for his gaze was as powerful as a touch.

In defence she thrust up her chin, something she did with alarming frequency around him. "I'm going. If it wasn't for me, you wouldn't even know where to start looking." She stood impatiently. "I want to see all this over with as much as you do. Maybe tonight we can end it."

THEY DECIDED TO START in the Lefitte graveyard. Shane had gone to the courthouse and pulled the old records, so he knew exactly where it was situated on the property.

It was in deplorable condition. Either the vegetation had grown in overwhelming abundance, or the tombs themselves were sinking into the mire. An unearthly light filtered through the trees. The sluggish water at their backs seemed thickened with menace. They could hear the soft beating of a drum not far away. Shane had no need to caution Kim to silence.

She crept closely behind him, struggling to hold her fear of the dark in check. Moss, damp and stringy, brushed her face. Everything she touched was cold and clammy. He stopped abruptly and she stretched her neck to peer around him.

Ahead, a makeshift altar of broken marble had been erected. Near a small fire, three men were softly drumming. Standing in a semicircle, half-hidden by the shadows, a large group of people swayed as one. The drumbeat increased in loudness and tempo. Women dressed in white starched petticoats separated from the group and formed a small circle. Swaying and spinning on their toes, they dipped and curtseyed in a graceful dance. The rhythm accelerated and the women moved faster until their skirts flew, forming a swirling vortex of white.

Suddenly the drumming stopped and the white circle became still. Kim held her breath in anticipation, shivers coursing through her. The circle of women fanned out, leaving one woman alone. Unlike the others, she wore a loose-fitting red top and skirt. She was beautiful. Her skin glowed in the firelight and her thick black hair cascaded down her back.

Kim grasped Shane's arm, pulling him down so she could whisper into his ear. "It's her—Maria. The queen. Just like in the picture."

He nodded without taking his eyes from the slowly unfolding scene. The drums began again. The woman in red undulated with each pulse, slowly circling the group, her movements sensual, provocative.

A man in a shapeless white robe brought a basket to her and stepped back reverently. She lifted the lid, reached in and drew forth a large striped snake.

Kim's grip tightened on Shane. She'd read about this, seen the pictures, but still she couldn't believe it was happening. Her gasp of shock and fear was drowned out as the worshipers began to chant.

"Dumballah ye' ye' ye t'a blam kom an mawr jeevah m'on dir du moovel . . . Dumballah ye' ye' ye' t'a blam kom an mawr jeevah m'on dir du moovel . . ."

The chanting and drumming built, louder and more powerful, until Kim could feel the beat pounding through her veins. The queen twined the snake up one arm, across her neck and down the other arm.

Appalled yet fascinated, Kim tried to make sense of the scene. Then suddenly the fire exploded into a high white pillar and the woman swept the snake triumphantly over her head. The dancing, the chanting, the drumming stopped abruptly.

The woman stood still in beautiful pagan splendor, and a smug satisfied smile curved her lips. At that moment Kim noticed the fine gold chain that hung between the queen's breasts. At the end of it dangled a gold key—Madame Loulou's key to the doll cabinet.

Suddenly she recognized some of the queen's artfully disguised features. Terror swept over her. She knew who this woman was. This was the woman in the Polaroid. This was Jeanne Carter!

Stunned, she didn't notice what happened next. Shane stepped in front of her, blocking her view.

"What?" she mouthed, before the drumming resumed, echoing through the darkness.

"Let's go," he whispered. "We've seen enough." He pulled her away, gripping her arm so tightly she couldn't resist.

"Wait," she cried, staring intently into his face. "I know that woman. So do you. Look carefully, Shane. It's Jeanne Carter, the policewoman. And that gold key chain she's wearing—I think it belonged to your aunt."

"Stay here," he commanded before turning back a few steps to look.

His face was a granite block, lips compressed to a thin line, when he returned. "You're right. If you pull the hair back and add glasses, it's Jeanne Carter. How could I have missed that before?"

"Shane, that means that Jeanne . . ."

". . . murdered Aunt Louise." Involuntarily he started forward but this time she gripped his arm.

"Shane, there are too many of them. And we've been here too long for safety. Follow me." She pulled him in the direction of the road.

If he hadn't been right behind, she would have been overcome with terror. All of her worst nightmares had found a permanent home here among the moss and oaks, where a living darkness gathered. In her haste, she lost her footing, tripped over a cypress root and let out a squeal.

Clasping a hand over her mouth, her eyes widened in fear. Quickly she turned to look behind them. Even in the darkness she could sense him shake his head.

"Don't worry, I've been watching," he whispered. "No one is following and I think we're far enough away. Are you all right?"

"I'm fine, or I will be." Ignoring the pain in her ankle she peered at him anxiously. "Could we just get the hell out of here?"

She glanced back when they were free of the swamp. The darkness still hid all its secrets, taunting her.

Chapter Nine

Kim closed and locked her bedroom door, then leaned back against it, shutting her eyes. The image of Jeanne Carter dancing in the firelight with the snake flashed across them. She forced her eyes open, trying to eradicate the vision. But she could still feel the throbbing of the drums. The beat was inside her, pulsing through her veins. Hugging her arms to her body, Kim stared at her reflection in the mirror; her green eyes flashed and her cheeks were stamped with color. No wonder people got caught up in voodoo. It was powerful, hypnotic.

They'd certainly need their wits about them. It wouldn't be easy accusing one of DeSable's staff, especially since all the evidence they had was the blurry photo and their word as witnesses to the voodoo rites.

Would it be enough? So far every lead they'd provided for DeSable had been discounted. He'd let them know he didn't need or appreciate their help. This time, she determined, they would make sure he followed through even if they had to go to the police chief himself.

She shed her clothes and climbed into bed. Even though it was stifling hot outside and the small air conditioner didn't quite do its job, a shiver ran down her spine. She pulled the covers tightly beneath her chin. Tomorrow it would all be over. What would happen then between Shane and her?

A single tear slid down her cheek and she tasted salt at the edge of her mouth. Everything was all mixed up in her mind—Madame Loulou, and Shane, and feelings she didn't understand. From the first moment she'd seen him in his aunt's shop a bond had formed, an attraction neither of them could control. Just as they'd had no control over that desperate, shattering kiss in the bayou. Now what would happen to them? And what did she want to happen? Explore these feelings even further, or let them go?

Sleep came slowly, fretfully. As she slid into its depth she kicked her covers off against the oppressive heat of the room.

IN THE EARLY HOURS of morning Shane woke suddenly. A vague image niggled at the back of his mind and wouldn't let him return to sleep. He finally gave up. After pulling on jeans and a ragged I Love New York T-shirt, he padded barefoot down the stairs to the library.

His typewriter beckoned to him. He hadn't really been able to do anything productive for days. Neat pages of script, held in place by an amethyst crystal paperweight, rested on the rolltop desk. He figured if he re-read them he'd get enough inspiration to carry on. This play just wouldn't come to life for him. He skimmed the pages, then throwing the manuscript down in disgust, he closed his eyes.

There it was again. A shadow, a shape just on the edge of his consciousness. He settled into his chair and deliberately focused on the image. Vague sounds came to him, chants, a scream of ecstasy. A flickering flame...

His mind played with images from that scene on the bayou earlier. He concentrated on recalling details.

Several of the remembered watchers seemed familiar. But try as he might, Shane could not force his mind to recognize them. It'd been too dark, and he and Kim could not get close enough to discern features. Jeanne Carter had been easier because she stood directly before the fire.

Jamming his fingers through his hair, he swore softly. This was important! If he could identify some of those worshipers on the bayou he could develop more leads. There would be real people to question about Louise, and somewhere in there, someone would make a mistake. Then he'd have them. The fuzzy Polaroid of Jeanne Carter might not be enough to convince DeSable. After all, the lieutenant would only have their word about what they'd seen at the voodoo ritual.

Involuntarily his fists clenched, but his mind would not bend to his will. It refused to recognize any of the watchers. He got up and strode around the room. Already it was warm; the day would be a scorcher. Tiny beads of perspiration formed on his brow.

Shane's inner alarm went off.

Something at the altar. Something there had caught his attention during the ritual. Then he remembered. A doll in a green dress, a beautiful formed voodoo doll with one honey-blond curl, had been at the foot of the altar. The doll they hadn't been able to find at the shop.

Why had Jeanne Carter taken it with her the day of the murder? He considered carefully. Obviously Kim hadn't seen it last night. That was lucky. She'd been shaken enough just witnessing the ritual and recognizing the queen.

What should he do? His first impulse was to go to the police. But DeSable was Jeanne Carter's immediate superior. Could he be in on it, too?

The alarm inside his head was at full throttle now. He never should have left Kim alone, unprotected. He'd taken her away from the ritual as quickly as possible and dropped her at her guest house because that was what she had wanted. But now he sensed something was wrong. They had her effigy...and they had met last night. What were they planning to do?

The time to think was over. Now he had to act. He had to get to Kim before they did. The car skidded down the driveway, its roar shattering the dawn's peace. Disregarding every stoplight and speed limit, Shane raced frantically toward New Orleans and Kim.

About halfway there a news bulletin interrupted the station's "easy early morning listening" program. "This news just in. A police officer has been found shot to death in the French Quarter. Identification is being withheld, pending notification of relatives. This is the first fatal shooting in the Quarter since 1972 when—"

Shane snapped the radio off. He'd known something was wrong—he'd felt it—from the moment he'd awakened. He had to get to Kim in time. His sense of urgency grew with each passing mile.

When he reached the city limits he switched the radio back on. "The officer has been identified as Jeanne Carter, a three-year member of the force. Her career was marked by distinguished—"

A fire engine cut Shane off. His car swerved into the curb, but luckily there was no one about this early. Sirens screamed from every side.

His heart was pounding like a hammer as Shane finally realized why. The fire department had closed off two city blocks surrounding Oak House. A wall of flame completely covered its west wing. Charred paint showed where the fire had been extinguished.

Where was Kim? He searched the huddled crowd but when he couldn't find her, he pushed his way through to the chief.

"Is everyone safe?" he demanded.

"Look, the fire's under control and there are no fatalities." The chief barked, barely sparing him a glance. "Now get back. I have work to do."

"But the east wing with the turret, are you sure everyone's out of there?" Shane insisted, refusing to be pushed away, sick fear grinding in his stomach.

"That was the first place we looked, because the manager said it was the only side occupied." He drew a blackened hand over his sooty face. "Listen, if you're a reporter you'll get your story later. Just let me do my job." He strode away, pointing out a new position for the hook and ladder.

Shane searched the crowd again, weaving through it. "Have any of you seen a blond-haired woman, very pretty? She was staying in the hotel."

Several people shook their heads. No one had seen anyone who resembled Kim coming out of the burning building.

Then he broke free of the throng and noticed the ambulances ahead. Paramedics were working over several stretchers. On one of them lay a diminutive figure. Shane raced to it and even before he reached the stretcher he could see the golden locks of hair spilled across Kim's face.

"I know her," he cried out.

"Oh?" one of the paramedics said. "We'd like to. Brave woman. She managed to crawl out of that—" he pointed to the smoldering building behind them "—before it collapsed."

Shane was barely listening. He leapt into the ambulance with the unconscious Kim and the paramedic, then he hunched over the stretcher, willing her to wake up. His fingers stroked her shoulder gently while he encouraged her to breathe. The oxygen mask was bringing color back into her face. Only then did he notice one of her hands remained fisted. Gently he uncurled the slender fingers. There on her white palm lay a smooth black stone.

It was marked with the symbols of death.

He took it until he could dispose of it properly. He would keep Kim from any more harm.

They rolled her into an emergency room where he watched through the curtains a few minutes later. Two doctors and a nurse worked over her.

"Mr. Alexander."

Without removing his eyes from Kim's white-draped figure, Shane nodded. "DeSable. You got my message."

DeSable came to stand beside him. Shane flicked him a quick glance and was shocked by the strain evident on the man's jowly face.

"The fire was caused by one of those electric potpourri machines they had going night and day," the lieutenant muttered. "Sorry about Miss Campbell. It's been rough for her."

Shane opened his fingers, revealing the hex stone. "The fire was caused by the same person who left this in Kim's room."

Perspiration ran down the side of DeSable's cheek and he wiped it away with his palm. "What the hell is that thing?"

"C'mon, DeSable. You've been in the Quarter long enough to know a voodoo hex when you see it." Shane spat out the words. "Jeanne Carter put it in Kim's hand, sentencing her to death before she set fire to Oak House."

"What the hell are you talking about! Officer Carter was killed last night in the line of duty! I should haul your ass to the station—"

"Recognize this?" Shane interrupted, pulling the Polaroid photo from his pocket. "It's a picture of Jeanne Carter cleverly made up to look like Maria Laveau."

"Let me see that!"

Shane knocked DeSable's outstretched hand away with his fist. "I think I'll take this to the police lab myself. Jeanne Carter has been posing as Maria Laveau. She killed my aunt. I know it. I may not be able to prove it yet, but I will. Jeanne Carter was behind this voodoo revival. Kim and I saw her perform a voodoo rite in the bayou yesterday. She was using it to extort money from shopkeepers . . . for whatever reason we don't know yet. She mesmerized the superstitious in town and made them her minions. They must have been the ones to threaten local shopkeepers to get money from them."

"Nonsense! Jeanne Carter was a police officer. I trained her myself!" DeSable's face was scarlet, the veins standing out in his neck. "None of this had anything to do with voodoo. You're as obsessed with the damn stuff as your aunt was!"

Shane resisted the impulse to slam his fist into DeSable's face. Where was the detached observer? The uninvolved man resigned to the world's overwhelming evil? Stepping back, Shane drew a deep breath to keep his voice level. "I'm going to make sure everyone involved in my aunt's murder pays, Lieutenant. Everyone. Jeanne Carter was obviously not working alone. From now on Kim is out of this, but not me. I'll stick with it to the end."

"What are you saying?" DeSable snapped. "Let the police handle this."

Shane gave him a stony stare.

The lieutenant shook his head in resignation. "Christ, I think you're crazy, but Miss Campbell deserves some consideration, I admit. I'll put a police guard on her hospital room."

"Don't bother." Shane's mouth twisted in a sneer and his voice was like ice. "I'm staying with Kim all night and then I'm taking her home with me to Belle Rêve."

"Listen here—"

"I have nothing else to say, Lieutenant. And if you persist, I'll slap a harassment charge against you so quick it'll make your head spin. Now stay away from both of us!"

Shane strode off down the labyrinthian hospital corridors to the private room where Kim had been moved. When he reached it, he went in and sat on the hard chair next to the bed. It was just the two of them now.

Opening his fingers, he studied the stone again, reexamining the ancient hex marks. He was positive Jeanne Carter had done this. Somehow she knew they'd seen her in the ritual. They'd been targeted for elimination just like Louise. His aunt must have gotten very close to the truth, whatever it was.

But why had the queen been sacrificed? Because he and Kim could identify her? And now someone very powerful was watching them, waiting.

He wrapped the stone in his white handkerchief and shoved it deep into his pocket. It had no power to harm Kim now.

"KIM?" THE TONE in Shane's voice was new to her.

She opened her eyes and grinned weakly. "Hello." Late-afternoon sun flowed warmly into the blue bedroom. Vaguely she remembered being discharged from the hospital and Shane insisting she come to Belle Rêve. She hadn't possessed the strength to resist. Everything seemed to have happened in a fog, with everyone around her moving through it in slow motion. She'd still been awake when he carried her from the car to the bed. Now she felt as if she'd been asleep forever.

He was sitting on the bed close to her. One thing was certain—he hadn't been napping, for fatigue deeply lined his eyes.

"You should be the one resting. You look awful," she whispered through her raw throat.

"Flattery will get you everywhere. How do you feel?" His long graceful fingers swept her hair off her forehead. "Can I get you anything?"

Feeling awkward and light-headed, Kim nodded. "My throat still burns and it's parched. I could drink a gallon of water."

"That's the smoke inhalation. Your throat membranes are swollen and inflamed. Here, the doctor gave me something to give you." He slipped an arm under her shoulders and helped her to a sitting position. "It will be a while before you can clear all the smoke out of your system. Until then you have to be particularly careful."

Dutifully she swallowed the liquid and when she finished, Shane set the cup down and plumped up her pillows. She eased gratefully back onto them. Funny how exhausted one became after nearly suffocating.

Strange she couldn't remember much. She just knew she'd awakened suddenly, gasping for air, and had barely been able to grab a wet cloth, hold it to her nose, before she escaped the smoke.

"Shane, what are we going to do about Jeanne Carter?" she whispered.

"Jeanne Carter is dead, Kim," he said flatly.

"What!" She struggled to sit up, but with a gentle hand he urged her back onto the pillows.

"Just relax and I'll tell you all about it. She was killed last night, supposedly in the line of duty."

"But you don't think so," she asked, watching his face carefully.

"No. I think she was killed because we could identify her. They know we saw the ritual last night."

"Who are *they*, Shane?" Suddenly she was cold with fear and yearned to be close enough to him to feel his warmth.

"I don't know, Kim. But I'm going to find out if it's the last thing I do."

Now fear for him turned her blood to ice. "Where will all this end for us?"

"It's already ended for you," he stated emphatically. "I told DeSable so in the hospital—"

"Shane, we have a deal!" With effort she struggled to her elbows.

"Kim, lie back. I'm sorry. I'm taking unfair advantage, I know. So we won't fight it out until you feel better, okay. Deal?"

Exhausted, she slumped back, nodding, and fought a sudden urge to sleep again. What was in that drink anyway? Later, when she felt more herself she would make him see reason. She wouldn't allow him to face this danger alone. "Shane..." She yawned and fell promptly asleep.

As she drifted into the depths of a peaceful sleep, he watched from the door, rubbing his tired eyes and the rough stubble of his beard. No wonder Kim thought he looked awful.

When he took a shower he turned the water on full blast. The sting against skin and scalp shocked him wide awake. A quick shave and a change of clothes made him feel almost human again.

He went to the library and settled into an easy chair to think. Again he forced himself to think about what he'd seen in the bayou. Kim had been concentrating on Jeanne, and she hadn't noticed the voodoo doll. After what had just happened he was glad she was unaware of its presence at the ritual. However, his top priority now was to search Jeanne's apartment and try to find that doll before any more harm could be done. He could imagine what they were planning. Besides the hex stone which had been placed in her hand, and which Kim forgot about finding before her collapse, the doll indicated they planned further mischief. It, too, had probably been hexed; fortunately Kim didn't believe in voodoo. It might save her. He sighed and leaned into his hands.

He couldn't force his mind to recognize the figures at the ritual. They were probably just local citizens in town; people he passed every day.

The typewriter beckoned him. Yes, he reasoned, he could try to step back from this puzzle, leave it alone and perhaps something might surface in his mind, the missing keys. At least he could finish outlining the last act of his play.

An hour later the wastebasket was brimming with wadded-up sheets of paper. It wasn't going right. Work, usually his only refuge from the world, failed to distract him. In disgust he abandoned the pages of manuscript, scattering them over the polished surface of the rolltop desk.

He paced the room furiously trying to sort through his thoughts. Why hadn't he taken this more seriously from the very beginning? Why hadn't he foreseen the danger to his aunt? Why had he stupidly left Kim alone last night? Shane was an expert at guilt. He had been drowning in it for years. Now he was sinking to bottomless depths under the weight.

Kim might have been killed. In fact, her life was still in danger and all because she had shown compassion to a stranger. She'd gotten involved without thought of herself. His aunt had sensed that goodness in her. Since that first day when he wrapped her cut palm with his handkerchief, there was something that linked them together. Some bond he couldn't, wouldn't, define.

But now he should be concentrating on tying Jeanne Carter to his aunt's murder. Jeanne had certainly not acted alone. She wasn't clever enough to have put this scheme together. There were others out there waiting. He could sense the evil directed toward them.

Kim suspected Claude. Maybe, just maybe, he should respect her intuition. But could someone who had known and cared about his aunt really be involved? Right now he'd better be prepared to suspect anyone. Whoever it was had all the right pieces in this game, knew right where they were, and held the ace in the hole—the voodoo doll of Kim.

A part of Shane still believed in the power voodoo could weave over one's mind and body. He wouldn't allow it to harm Kim. He would do everything within his ability to keep her safe.

Chapter Ten

There was no doubt about it, Leonard was hovering. He stood over Kim in the sunny breakfast room as she ate the light lunch he had prepared. He brought her iced tea when she wandered out onto the back veranda to sit and admire what remained of the formal garden, now a colorful tangle of rosebushes, azaleas, sweet olive and camellias.

He followed her into the library where she'd decided to sit and read. "Leonard, is something wrong?" she finally asked, looking up quickly to catch him watching her guardedly from the doorway.

A slow smile seamed his weathered face. "No, lassie. My job is to keep an eye on you. I promised Shane you'd come to no harm whiles he's in the Quarter at Judge Rudolph's office."

"As you can see I'm perfectly fine." She sent him a placating smile. "Please don't worry. I promise I'll stay right here in the library until Shane gets back."

"Aye, lass, I understand. Just give a holler if you need me." Slowly he pulled the library door closed, shutting her in.

A crack of sunlight through the window warmed her. She leaned her head back against the chair dreamily. It just didn't make sense. In the midst of this horrible mess, with her very life in jeopardy, she had never felt so secure. And Shane made her feel that way.

He hadn't told her very much about the night of the fire. That had been two days ago. She didn't need to know the details.

She got up and wandered around the room that in her mind was so totally Shane—polished and orderly. The roll-top desk was open. Resisting the urge to pick up the scattered sheets strewn across it, she knelt instead, gathering discarded wads of paper that had missed the already over-flowing waste basket. As if she'd somehow willed it, a few sheets slid from the desk, drifting to the floor beside her. The temptation was too great. She picked up the papers and scanned them. It must be his latest play.

With each word she read, warm thoughts of Shane dissipated. She'd thought she'd sensed a softening in him which might have something to do with her.

Fool! It must have only been wishful thinking. The words of this play were the same as always, a brilliant but tormented struggle against evil...destined to have another unhappy ending. Art mirroring life?

Rocking back on her heels, the pages still clasped in her hands, Kim made a decision. Somehow, out of his aunt's death, Kim would change his philosophy. Justice would triumph over this evil, if she had anything to do with it. Life had taught Kim tenacity and she embraced it with gusto. They were well on their way to exposing this frightening voodoo revival that was destroying lives. Sitting down, she reviewed the facts.

They'd already learned so much. The missing key and the picture tied Jeanne Carter irrevocably to Madame Loulou's death. But Jeanne Carter had not been at

Claude LaCroix's dinner party and Madame Loulou had specifically directed them to that party. She'd felt someone there was directly involved. If Shane couldn't fully accept that because of his close ties to those people, she would have to keep guarded, her eyes open.

How long Kim sat ruminating, she didn't know. But when eventually she rose slowly to her feet a pain stabbed at her temple. She gasped, and though she gently massaged the area, there was no relief. This pain was worse than a migraine. It must be the aftereffects of the smoke inhalation, she thought. After replacing the papers on the desk she staggered back to the chair. If she just sat quietly with her eyes closed, maybe the sharp jabbing pain would go away.

"KIM. KIM, WAKE UP. It's time for dinner... Kim...." came to her.

She opened her lids, her eyes still unfocused, and lifted unsteady fingers to her temple. "I have a headache."

Shane seemed to flinch. "Do you want me to call the doctor? He said this would probably be an aftereffect."

"No, I'm sure it's from the smoke inhalation." Her voice sounded shaky to him. "Maybe I'll feel better when I eat something."

Her back was ramrod straight as she walked with him to the dining room. He noticed she looked tired, strained, but she smiled, complimenting Leonard on the centerpiece of camellias. She always thought of others first. It was one of her traits that he admired most.

Leonard smiled appreciatively. "Aye, lass, the scent is pleasing. And we have enough in garden to give every lady at the Mummer's Ball."

Her eyes widened in delight but a frown marred her smooth forehead. "That's right. The ball's in a few days. Shane, what should I do about my clothes? As comfortable as these are I don't think they're appropriate."

He took a sip of wine before answering her. He had done something this afternoon after leaving Anton's office in the Quarter that he'd never done before. "I stopped by Oak House and picked up your things. I brought your cosmetic case, but everything else is at the cleaners. They're attempting to get rid of the smoke damage...." To his chagrin he felt embarrassment warm his neck. "Anyway, I bought you some new clothes. They're in your room."

Two pairs of eyes stared at him; Leonard's narrowed and watchful, Kim's incredulous.

"You shouldn't have done that!" she protested. "How did you know my size?"

Shrugging, he simulated innocence. "I just looked at the labels. Kim, it's no big deal. Just a few things to tide you over." Attuned as he was to her, he understood her unspoken distress and neatly changed the subject. "But the Mummer's Ball is another matter. Any ideas, Leonard?"

"Aye, lad, there be the trunks of clothes in the attic."

Shane's gaze flicked over Kim's intense face, a spark of interest igniting her eyes which were unusually dull tonight. "I'd forgotten about the trunks. Would you like to look through them tomorrow, Kim?"

"Yes, I would like that." He could see her smile was forced and she was working hard to keep her tone light. He noticed how carefully she pushed herself up out of the chair.

Rising quickly, he moved to help her, but stopped as she stepped forward. "Kim, are you sure you don't want to see the doctor?" With effort he held himself in check and kept his voice neutral. "Maybe we should drive to the emergency room. Just to be sure."

"No, no, I'm fine, really." She smiled weakly but her slender fingers rubbed urgently at her temple. "All I need is a good night's sleep. I'll take some pain-killers." Slowly, without her usual grace, she climbed the steps one at a time. "I'm reimbursing you for the clothes. And tomorrow we should plan what we're going to do next...about...your aunt...."

He struggled with himself, wanting to help her, unable to make the offer. This time if he took her in his arms he wouldn't be able to let her go. So he followed closely behind her up the stairs, fearful that she might lose her balance. She looked ready to drop from fatigue.

"Get some rest, Kim," he said, closing her bedroom door. "Tomorrow we'll decide what our next move will be."

He walked downstairs considering whether to call the doctor. The small coil of fear inside him had developed into something stronger. Could this really only be an aftereffect of the smoke inhalation? The doctor had said it might be, and had given her medicine to combat it. But she looked so sick, so weak. Concern for her filled every thought and lessened his urgent need to find out if anyone else beside Jeanne Carter had been responsible for his aunt's death. For the first time there were other emotions flooding through him than the need for revenge.

THE NEXT MORNING, she felt a little better. But by the time she and Shane finally made it to the attic in the afternoon to hunt for clothes for the Mummer's Ball Shane was holding, the ache had started again at her temple. She attempted to ignore it as she discovered all the wonders left by past generations. The great attic of Belle Rêve was supported by heavy beams held together with huge wooden pegs. Over the years cobwebs had formed over the abandoned treasures.

But the delights that spilled out of the two trunks Shane propped open distracted her. There were long white kid gloves, each with tiny pearl buttons; gilt-painted fans; fawn-colored men's breeches which she laughingly held up for Shane's inspection and he just as quickly rejected. There were also silk dresses with yards and yards of material in their skirts; and dozens of petticoats.

She finally pulled out a man's blue frock coat and thrust it at Shane. "Here! You could wear this to the ball."

His expressive eyes were bright with amusement. He was propped against an old dresser, his arms folded across his well-muscled chest. In one fluid movement he straightened, taking the coat from her fingers. "All right. I'll wear this. If you'll wear that ivory silk dress."

The gown he referred to had a tantalizingly brief bodice and sixteen petticoats. She wasn't sure it would fit.

Shane's smile was so young, so *free* that Kim's breath caught. She could feel her blood pounding to every extremity of her body. For that moment her headache was forgotten.

"Yes. I'll wear it, if I can get the corset laced tight enough without help," she said, laughing gaily.

Here she could enjoy Shane and forget everything that had gone before. Since the fire, they hadn't discussed what Jeanne Carter's death meant to their investigation. Some instinct that Kim hadn't known she possessed, but that was finely tuned where Shane was concerned, told her he was deliberately avoiding the issue. He had not wanted her involvement from the beginning and now he was determined to pry her loose. But she couldn't, any more than she could deny her aching need to be close to him. She needed to see his smile again and again.

She turned to another trunk in confusion. She shouldn't be forming any attachment to Shane. It was obvious he wouldn't welcome it.

This trunk she soon learned was full of junk, as if someone had taken the contents of a desk and turned the drawers upside down. Quill pens and ink pots, penknives, yellowing scraps of paper, were jumbled together. The bottom was lined with leather-bound books. She picked one up. It was an old account book. Beneath it was a cook's record of menus and recipes. Kim laid it to one side, thinking it might make interesting reading. Then she spied a maroon cordovan-leather journal whose gold letters were practically worn away. It was dated the turn of the century and had belonged to Abigail LeCarpentiers.

When Kim opened it, two creased sheets fell out. They were brittle with age. Hardly containing her curiosity, she carefully unfolded them.

"Shane!" Eagerly she motioned him closer. For another moment she forgot the insistent throb in her temple. "Look at this. It's a genealogy. I recognize some of the names—Rudolph, LaCroix, even your aunt's name, LeCarpentiers. This must be someone's attempt to tie all the old families together."

"Let me see that." Shane peered at the spidery writing. "It's more than that, Kim. DeSable and Carter are tied in here, too. What's on that page?"

Kim was staring in horror and fascination at the page she held. It was a genealogy, all right, and it started with Maria Laveau. "All of those families are descendants through various lines to Maria Laveau."

Shane twitched the page out of her unresisting fingertips. "These must have belonged to Louise's great-aunt. They were her trunks."

Standing on tiptoe, Kim peered over his shoulder. "How can all these people be related?"

"That's not uncommon down here. Families inter-married all the time." He carefully refolded the papers. "Practically everyone at Claude's party is in here."

Unsaid between them was the shared thought that they were completely surrounded by people who had a direct connection to the old evil; any one of them could be involved in the present one.

Suddenly the pain at her temple could no longer be ignored. Perhaps the heat or the dust in the attic was making it worse. The air seemed to close in, making her perspire, although she wore only a light cotton sundress.

"It's gotten awfully hot up here, hasn't it?"

He frowned, stepping closer to her. "Kim, you look pale. Is it another headache?"

Even nodding made the pain worse, but she tried not to show it. "It's probably just the heat. Let's take these things downstairs. You said Leonard knew all about genealogy. Maybe we should show this to him."

"I will, as soon as he gets back. He went to the market. He's cooking you something special tonight. Let's go on down."

It was much cooler on the lower floor, less like a slow baking oven, and she imagined she felt a little better. When Shane suggested she lie down for a nap before dinner, she quickly agreed. She hung the ivory dress with all its petticoats on the closet door. It was the last thing she saw before her eyes closed.

THE HEADACHE, however, wouldn't go away. She nibbled at strawberry shortcake, but hadn't been able to eat any of the delicious dinner Leonard had prepared to tempt her. It required a major effort just to remain sitting upright.

Leonard had studied the yellowed pages, pouring over them with awe. "Someone did a right fine job of researching these families. These were the papers Louise wanted me to find. See you can follow her line all the way back to Maria's eldest son. Many of the locals are tied into this family. Madame LaForge was a Petouche before her marriage. Her line is here, too." He pushed his coffee cup away. "But there's one line started that stops after one generation. Must have died out, or records couldn't be found."

"But what does it mean, Leonard?" Shane hunched over his plate, his fingers stroking the stem of his wineglass. "How can it help us?"

"Don't know, Shane. Except it gives us more suspects. More people linked to old voodoo." Leonard shrugged his narrow shoulders. "That doesn't mean much. Most of Southern Louisiana is probably just the same."

"Then what secrets could the people at that party be hiding?" Kim asked carefully, using all her strength to appear as normal as possible. She wasn't sure she fooled Shane, for his eyes suddenly narrowed.

"The only thing I can think of, lass, is that Marlena Rudolph might be an alcoholic."

That brought Shane's head around. "I've thought the same thing. When I was younger, I wondered about her unexplained illnesses."

"Aye. But no one knows for sure. And the Judge, he'a a sly one. Never has said a word."

Kim suddenly thought of Marlena standing in the heavy moist heat of the cemetery. Strange that she had chosen a long-sleeved dress. It was inappropriate in this heat. And she had done the same at Claude's party. That night she had also drunk the forbidden green liqueur.

"Maybe it's not alcohol. Maybe she's a drug user."

Both men stared at her. Shaking his head, Shane laughed softly. "Marlena Rudolph? Kim, she's the epitome of the old idea of fragile womanhood. If she pricked her finger, she'd probably go into a swoon."

"Aye, lass, Shane's right. We'll have to bark up another tree."

She listened to their responses, but their voices faded in and out. She couldn't seem to hold onto any thought long enough to voice it and answer them. The chandelier's light burned her eyes and even the slight shuffle of Leonard's heavy shoes across the wooden floor as he got up hurt her ears.

"... Kim." She suddenly realized Shane was speaking to her and she couldn't remember what they had been discussing. To preserve a slim illusion of control it seemed important to disguise her lapse of attention.

"Shane, if you don't mind I'm going to bed early tonight," she interrupted, pushing herself away from the table.

His response came quickly. "Kim, I'm calling the doctor. Or better still, I'm taking you to the hospital."

Retreating before him, she shook her head. She moaned involuntarily, then bit on her lower lip to stop it.

"Quit being so damn stubborn!" There was anger in his voice and his mouth was a hard line. "You obviously need some medical attention."

"I'm getting medical attention. I'm going up to my room to drink some more of that vile liquid the doctor prescribed."

They glowered at each other. Her determination was a last effort against the sluggish dictates of her body. She must get upstairs quickly. "Shane, tomorrow if I'm not better we'll go to the doctor," she sighed, desperate for privacy where she could give in to the pounding pain at her temples. She needed to bury her head in the pillow with a cool cloth across her burning eyelids.

By midnight the wet cloths were useless against the hot pounding inside her head. She sat up and the room swung sickeningly around her. Shane was right; she needed help. Making her way to the door, she whispered his name and reached out, fumbling awkwardly with the knob. There was a faint light burning on a cherry chest in the hallway, but more shone up from the first floor. The library, Shane was always in the library. She found the stairway and clung to the banister. It helped her descend the steps on wobbly legs.

She found Shane sitting at his desk, his head bent over papers, his long fingers absently threading through the heavy waves of his hair. How often had she wanted to bury her own in that richness?

His dark eyes discovered her instinctively. "Kim?"

Leaning her throbbing head against the door frame, she closed her eyes. "I can't stand it anymore."

When she slowly opened her lids she found him standing only a foot away, with light shimmering all around him. She blinked several times, trying to clear her vision.

"Why won't it go away?" she asked desperately.

"Kim." His voice was a soft plea. She felt him find her shoulders and hold them, trapping her between his lean body and the wooden door frame. "Kim, tell me exactly where it hurts."

Trying hard to concentrate on his words, she directed her hands to her temple. "Everywhere...here...it feels like a thousand pins jabbing inside my head."

Why had his eyes darkened so?

"Kim, I'm going to help you," he said quietly. "Don't be afraid. I know you're weak. Let me carry you back to bed."

Using every ounce of what little strength she had left, she lifted her hands around his neck. It didn't matter that she had let her guard down. She needed him and, mercifully, he was there to help her.

Strong arms caught her, holding her tightly. She moaned softly at a new stab of pain, rubbing her cheek restlessly back and forth over his chest. His shirt was rough against her oversensitized skin.

He remained silent as he swiftly mounted the steps, elbowed open her bedroom door and placed her carefully upon the bed.

"Here, take the last of this medicine from the doctor," he urged, his voice hard, almost angry.

Was he angry with her? Why? Because she was clinging to him, not standing on her own two feet as always? Couldn't he understand it just wasn't possible at this moment? The only possibility was allowing him to support her as she drank the last of the dreadful concoction.

His arms were powerful. Quickly but impersonally, he undressed her. She sighed in relief as a cool cloth sponged her heated body before he pulled a nightgown over her head. Would he ever hold her again with urgent desperation as he had in the moist grass of the swamp?

"Kim, you must go to sleep now. I promise in the morning the headache will be gone," he said slowly, patiently, as if to a child.

She believed him. Through the pain reddened haze of her mind she focused on one solid fact; nearly from the first moment in Madame Loulou's shop, when he had offered his handkerchief to stanch the flow of her cut, she had believed in him.

He laid her carefully back onto her pillows.

"You always keep your promises, Shane." She sighed and closed her eyes.

Shane sat for a long time at her bedside assuring himself she was finally asleep. The firm chin was tucked into the pillow with one small fist clenched beside it. Her cheeks were flushed with too much color. Could this be more than smoke inhalation? Even though Kim didn't believe in voodoo, he still did, somewhere back in his subconscious. And she might, as well, without knowing it.

Could evil be working here? He longed to gather her in his arms, to comfort her, to protect her. By pulling the sheet up around her shoulders he was able to ward off the desire to touch her. Each time he won the battle, the next skirmish became more difficult. What could these barely controlled feelings for Kim mean? Reluctantly he backed away from her bedside.

He couldn't stand by and watch her suffer when he could do something. The medicine would help her. Logically he knew it—he also recognized that what he was about to do was illogical and of little value. Except for believers.

Rushing downstairs he made his way to the library and clumsily searched the bookshelves. Somewhere here, Shane knew, were the voodoo books his aunt had collected. As much as his Uncle Jerome had detested them, he hadn't brought himself to discard any of the belongings she had left behind. Suddenly he found what his fingers clamored for. It was hidden away on a top shelf, a slim black volume of spells. Quickly he found the right entry, and knew that he needed a talisman.

The right configuration drawn on parchment in blood would attract favorable spirits. He found the right design, the one powerful enough to overcome any hex that might have been placed on Kim.

He assembled everything he needed in front of the fireplace in the library. He lit a small fire, then took the candles and held them one at a time over the flames. Taking his penknife he sliced his left index finger, and made his talisman. To make it more powerful he began to chant in a low tone—words he'd thought he would never be able to speak again. They came back to him quickly, as well-remembered as if he had used them yesterday—the supplication to the power of light he'd learned long ago as a boy in Africa.

Chapter Eleven

The headache was gone. No pinpoints of pain stabbed at her temple, no red haze clouded her vision. Kim blinked several times, gazing up at the ceiling. The relief was immeasurable. Rising, she looked around. The blue bedroom, like the rest of Belle Rêve, had been decorated with excellent taste. Sunlight peeked through those windows, enticing her. After several days of headaches she felt so healthy; she desired some action. Humming softly to herself, she leapt up and scurried around the room, gathering up her bath things.

The bath, following the night's rest, was the last dose of medicine. When she headed back to her bedroom, she felt refreshed. Shane was standing in the hallway outside her room. He needed a shave, badly. He looked like he hadn't slept at all. The little song she'd been humming stopped abruptly.

"How do you feel?" he asked with such urgency it surprised her.

"Good...great! Actually, I've rarely felt better."

She stood absolutely still as he moved toward her, and reached out to slide one finger through a strand of hair that had fallen on her cheek. His face was so gentle. She was so close to seeing beneath his facade she dared not move. She didn't want to break the spell weaving in the air between them. This was not the cynical playwright, full of bitterness and disillusion. What had changed him, if only for these few moments? And, how could she keep this Shane?

His face bent down to her and she froze, afraid even to take a breath. But he stopped, pulled his hand away, then himself.

She could breathe again, but only with regret.

"Shane?" she questioned softly.

"I'm glad you're OK, Kim. Very glad."

"You look exhausted," she said quietly, hoping he couldn't see how affected she was by this glimpse of gentleness.

"Yes. I can sleep now," he replied cryptically. He turned away to his room. "I'll see you later."

Only when he swung around did she realize she was clutching her towel to her. What did he think? He hadn't seemed disturbed by her unconventional attire, but then . . . he had undressed her. Embarrassment flooded through her as she remembered the events of the previous night. Gently, she turned the knob of her bedroom door, feeling as mystified as ever by the man.

AMAZED AT WHAT A FEW HOURS of sleep and a hot shower could do, Shane eagerly entered the kitchen, anxious to find Kim. To his surprise and disappointment it was empty. But there was one place setting on the service table with a note propped against a small bouquet of garden flowers. Leonard's touch. The note said Kim and Leonard had gone into the bayou that morning to the honey tree. What could they be thinking of? Kim felt well enough to tramp around in the swamp behind Leonard? He could hardly believe it. Automatically he moved around the kitchen fixing himself a breakfast snack. The talisman had been effective. Or the medicine had finally kicked in, the rational portion of his mind insisted. She was safe and well and that was all that mattered. But he knew he had to find that voodoo doll. It held too much potential danger. A rational, clear-headed man might not believe in powers beyond what could be scientifically proved, but with Kim, he couldn't take chances. She might be more psychologically vulnerable to voodoo than she was willing to admit. It was all a mind game, potentially lethal.

Maybe it was time to explore where all these feelings were leading him. Already he had allowed her to become too involved, and she'd had several close calls. Perversely, he never thought of sending her home... away... anymore. He only thought of protecting her. In the hall this morning with her skin glowing and the faint scent of her perfume in the air, he'd been unable to resist at least one small touch. He knew what the bath towel concealed. He'd seen it all clinically while he'd been helping her to get to sleep last night.

But now, and this morning, his thoughts were far from impersonal. He wondered how she would look as he brought her body to life under him....

The teapot whistled. He poured boiling water onto coffee crystals, stirred once and drank without thinking.

The searching heat matched his state of mind.

He prowled through the first floor. They'd been gone an awfully long time. What if something had happened? Lots could go wrong in the bayou. What if Leonard had lost her...? He had to stop these destructive thoughts.

Better to use his brain more productively. Like inventing schemes to find the doll before it psyched them both out in its mysterious ways again.

Noises from the kitchen informed him they were finally home safe. Kim rushed into the dining room, her face glowing with enthusiasm.

"Leonard showed me the most amazing thing! And I figured out what our next move should be."

"What would that be?" he asked. She had never looked so beautiful, although she carried about her the faint aroma of burning cypress.

"First, Leonard says to tell you there is a pot of honey in the kitchen . . ."

"Took you to the Three Sisters, did he?" Shane said, remembering years ago when Leonard had taken him to three ancient cypress trees in the bayou. In their hollows, bees had created nests. About half the bayou residents had at one time smoked out the bees so their honey could be collected.

"Yes, it was incredible. What a story, and honey, to take home to my students. I've already had some on toast. It's delicious." She dropped down in the chair next to him. "But I want to tell you my idea. That's really what's important." She looked at him expectantly. "The trail ended with Jeanne's death, right?"

He nodded.

"Well, then, it's obvious that's where we have to pick up a new lead—at her apartment or house or wherever she lived." Kim rested her chin on her fist resolutely. "Well, what do you think?"

"I think we should do it." He could foresee only one problem. "It will be easy enough to get an address for Jeanne Carter. But how do we get in?"

She sprang up with such a playful look lighting her face that Shane wanted to hug her close to him.

"Shane! Haven't you ever seen any old *Remington Steele* reruns on television? We're going to break in with a credit card."

IT WASN'T AS EASY as it looked on television. Thank goodness, Jeanne's townhouse had its own private little courtyard. There were no curious neighbors threatened to interrupt them. Kim was surprised at the location—a beautifully maintained building in the heart of the Quarter. It looked expensive.

The lock finally clicked beneath Shane's inexpert fumbling; he pushed the door open.

"Wow!" he gave a low whistle. "The police department must pay better than I thought."

The living room was straight out of the best of the glossy home-decorator magazines. Oversize cream couches with pillows of teal and rust surrounded a large glass-and-brass coffee table. Lush green plants in terracotta and glazed crocks were placed in strategic locations around the room. Everything was coordinated and elegant.

Shane lifted one dark brow and turned to Kim with an ironic smile. "Officer Carter had surprisingly good taste."

"Yes, didn't she?" Kim agreed, peering into a dream kitchen, all hanging copper pots and quarry tile. "Expensive, too," she continued thoughtfully. "Why don't you look down here and I'll go through her bedroom. I have a better idea of where women stash their private things."

With that rueful smile still tugging at his mouth, he nodded. But his voice stopped her as she began to climb a narrow wrought-iron spiral stairway.

"Glad to have you back, Kim."

"I beg your pardon?" Their eyes met and for once his were free of shadows. A secret pleasure filled her.

"I just meant, it's good you're feeling better," he said quietly, and to her delight color flushed his lean face.

To cover her surge of feeling, Kim answered him teasingly. "You should have been a doctor. It was your bedside manner that did it." With that she ran up the remaining steps so he couldn't see her expression. It was getting harder to control her feelings when he was near her. But she turned to the task at hand.

Jeanne's bedroom was as neat as a pin. Almost too neat, as if someone had been through it already and set everything to rights. The brass bed was piled high with pillows, had an English printed coverlet, and a white dust ruffle. Kim dropped on her hands and knees to peer beneath it. A vague sense of uneasiness filled her. Fortunately there was nothing but a few dust balls. She felt much better when she stood up again.

Her eyes immediately fell on the walk-in closet. Discovering its door refused to stay open on its own, she propped a box of heavy shoes against it, then within seconds was inside rummaging through the assortment of clothes, bags and shoes. Enough light came in from the bedroom for her to manage—good thing, since the overhead bulb seemed to be burnt out. She stretched as far as she could to reach the high shelf for a box. It was heavier than she'd anticipated and she lost her balance. Stumbling back, her foot dislodged the box propping open the door. Before Kim could reach out, it slammed shut.

She was shut in, in complete darkness. Suddenly she was ten years old again and locked in the upstairs hall closet. Her heart seemed to stop. Then her breathing. She'd never survive—there were too many monsters here in the dark who could get her. For an instant she could feel them surround her—

No! She was an adult now and there were no monsters that could hurt her. She groped frantically for the doorknob. "Shane!" she yelled. "Get me out of here!"

Frustration replaced panic and in her search she struck out in blind fury. Wood paneling gave way beneath her fingers at the same moment light blinded her.

Shane stared aghast at her from the open door. "Kim! What is it?"

Her eyes slowly refocused. "Shane. Thank God you came. I thought I was trapped in here. In the dark."

She stepped toward him as he pushed all the clothes remaining on one rack to one side. "What is this fear of the dark that you have?"

She fought to catch her breath, and noted the serious look on his face. Something told her she should tell him. "When I was younger—" she said hesitantly, gaining confidence as she went along "—my father would drink too much. I'd hide...in the closet until I knew he'd fallen into a stupor. You see, he could be rough."

"Oh, God, Kim! I'm sorry. It's all right. I'm here with you," Shane said, pulling her closer.

She savored his warmth before glancing up and resuming. For some reason she felt impelled to tell him it all. "It felt as if I was locked in there—for good, at times. Sometimes I'd have to spend hours until the coast was clear. For years I had nightmares. Foster homes and therapy helped. But my phobia about the dark has never gone away."

He pulled her back into his arms. "Kim, I wish I could protect you from all the hurts and pains of the past."

Kim was about to lift her face to his to satisfy her impulse to kiss him, when she noticed the surprise in his eyes.

"What's that?" he asked.

She twirled around. In her desperate attempt to escape she had opened a secret compartment.

There was room enough for them both to enter, although Kim insisted on propping the outer door open again first.

"Oh, no," Shane muttered, softer than a whisper.

"What is it?" she asked, her voice a thin reed of sound.

"It's an altar room. If there had been the tiniest doubt about Jeanne Carter this would clinch it." He picked up a wooden shaft carved in the body of a serpent. "This is Dumballah, the snake, used for the joining of male and female spirits." His fingers pushed aside some bones that didn't bear explanation and lifted out a photograph that had fallen face down.

"It's Claude!"

Kim peered over Shane's shoulder. Smiling out at them from the photograph was Claude LaCroix, dressed all in white, standing in an unfamiliar room with a juju on the wall behind his left shoulder.

"What does this mean, Shane?" She could feel his back stiffen under her breasts and she stepped away while he slid the picture into his shirt pocket. He seemed to be looking for something else; his hands were searching under and around the altar base.

"Shane, what...?"

"Get back, Kim. There's nothing else here, damn it! Let's get out of here. Now!"

When they reached the courtyard, a strong breeze bent the trees, the shadows of their leaves distorting Shane's face. She had never felt such a sense of foreboding. He had not spoken a word since dragging her from the apartment.

"Shane, Claude is involved somehow, but why?" she ventured, still unable to rationalize how Claude LaCroix—social lion, throwback to Old South chivalry—could even know Jeanne Carter—voodoo queen...extortionist...murderer.

"That's a good question, Kim. One I plan to find the answer to."

"Shane, I'm sorry you had to find out this way. I wish it could have been different."

Her offered sympathy was accepted blankly, coldly, and she felt him pull back into himself.

"I'm not sure how I'll do it, but I'm going to force Claude to admit the truth. And then I'm going to kill him!"

"I TELL YOU, I saw them leaving Jeanne's apartment." Claude's hand was shaking with fear.

It had been foolish of him to call this meeting. Coming here in broad daylight, where anyone could have followed them, was madness. But it would do no good to reprimand him; he was way beyond that.

"Claude, get a grip on yourself. Tell me exactly what you saw."

His silver-tipped cane tapped rapidly across the floor while he paced. "I was walking from the Orleans Club through the Quarter when I saw them coming out her door. I kept out of sight." His voice lowered dramatically, "What if they found something there that incriminates me?"

"If Kim and Shane got in, they broke in. Very resourceful of them. But hardly earth-shattering. What could they find of yours at Jeanne's apartment, Claude?"

Amusement was difficult to hide at Claude's offended look. He was actually trying to be chivalrous.

"The queen...favored me with...special attention," he said carefully.

That fool Jeanne Carter had aimed high. Just as well that she had been eliminated before her own interests endangered them all. Claude would have to be reassured. He was too valuable to be left in this state of mind. But first more information was needed.

"Tell me quickly. How did Kim look? Did she seem ill?"

"Ill?" Wringing his hands together, he shook his head. "She looked fine." Understanding dawned. "Ah! Your power has failed this time."

"My power never fails!"

The doll still lay on the altar, with the black-headed pin protruding from beneath the honey blond curl. "Shane must have called upon the spirits to help him. But his puny knowledge need not concern us, as long as we have this." The doll was held up and Claude again saw Kim's likeness.

"How is that going to help us now? If they found something..?"

"You need not worry, Claude. I was there myself and removed everything that would implicate any of us."

Even his cherished mustache drooped in relief. "Thank goodness. I was quite worried, you know, or I would never have called you."

A shake of the head stopped him. "This is in no way over, Claude. It won't be over until we stop Kim and Shane."

"But how? I can't—"

"You can! And you will!" The doll was thrust into Claude's trembling hands. "Feel it, Claude! Know we have her in our power!"

The doll was put back on the center of the altar, surrounded by black candles, a broken bone across its stomach.

"You will be attending the Mummer's Ball. Watch for your opportunity, Claude. It will come."

Chapter Twelve

Shimmering sunlight filled the library as Kim tugged at the immodest bodice of the antique ball gown they had found in Belle Rêve's attic. It was a dress meant for beautiful parties and romance. Tonight would hold neither.

Tonight one of the guests at this Mummer's Ball would be exposed as a killer. It was still hard for Kim to believe Claude's involvement, although there was little doubt after finding the picture. But what she couldn't understand was why. Tonight she and Shane would put it all together. Their plan was clever, tailored to Claude's weakness.

Coldly, calculatingly, too much so for Kim's taste, Shane had set the scene. Kim was to be the official hostess. Somehow she had found the courage to remind him that this ball was also in memory of his aunt. There'd been a slight softening then, but his determination was ironclad.

Shane spared no expense in his aunt's honor. A large oil painting of Louise, done over fifty years ago, was moved at Kim's suggestion from his uncle's room to the place of honor in the ballroom where she could preside over the festivities. Ivy festooned the doorways and the ballroom walls where the eleven-piece orchestra would play. The anteroom behind the main dining room had been opened to accommodate a huge buffet. All the traditional delicacies of New Orleans would be set out later. Five chefs presided in the kitchen, each with his own specialty.

Downstairs, in the upriver parlor, a Cajun band would play for the young "hip" group. Evangeline Paris had picked the darkest corner of the downriver parlor to set up her tarot card booth, separated from the room by a Chinese screen.

Shane had planned an entertainment for ten-thirty in the garden. Jugglers and acrobats would perform, then offer to teach any willing participants.

Every detail had been thought of. Shane said he expected over three hundred guests—from the elite of New Orleans society to some Quarter residents who had been Louise's best customers.

Yes, the stage was set.

At the appointed hour Kim would make sure Claude was on the back veranda to discover the pictures of Jeanne Carter and himself. Shane would have all the others there, everyone who had been on the genealogical chart. Once Claude was exposed everything else would follow. Shane thought Claude would break down and spill his guts, as he so indelicately put it. And if any of the others were involved, they, too would be unmasked. Then, at last, the nightmare would be over.

The grandfather clock on the second floor began to strike.

It was time. She picked up an ivory lace fan, hung a small lace and satin bag on one arm, and fastened a slide bracelet onto her other wrist. It was so large that if she wasn't very careful she would lose it. She knew it had belonged to Louise and each slide, or piece, held a particular memory. The same bracelet was in the portrait.

At the last chime, Shane appeared in the doorway. His shoulders looked even broader, his body more muscular in the tight breeches and blue frock coat. He was already in character, seemingly relaxed—the charming host. His gaze slid over her like a caress. Was this all part of the playacting?

"You look ravishing. Come. Our guests are arriving." His hands took hers lightly.

Outside, on the front veranda, she needed to pinch herself to make sure she wasn't dreaming. A line of torches lit the driveway. All the guests had left their cars off the highway and were either riding in carriages Shane had provided, or walking up to the house. The grounds were alive with fanciful costumes, brightly colored hooped skirts and dashing dinner jackets.

The night air was soft with music. A slight breeze carried the scents from the flower gardens which surrounded Belle Rêve inside.

She was almost afraid to look again at Shane. The backdrop of the evening was awakening a fantasy she couldn't allow. This, the party and Shane's charming demeanor, was all staged for a reason.

He pulled out a deck of cards from his buff breeches, and shuffled them with one hand.

Drawing a breath, Kim laughed, trying to get into the role she must play. "Do they allow riverboat gamblers at these society dos?"

He laughed. "Well, ma'am, they won't be able to keep me away," he drawled, "not with you looking like that." He returned the cards to his pocket and she caught a glimpse of a small pistol in his inside pocket.

"Shane!" she gasped. "What are you doing with a gun?" A ludicrous vision of him confronting Claude with it raced through her mind.

"Kim, it's not loaded," he said softly, his expression grave, obviously sensing how upset she was. "It was in the frock coat with the cards."

"Give it to me!" she demanded.

"Kim, what's the matter with you? This little thing couldn't hurt a fly."

Moving in front of him so it appeared she was adjusting his cravat, she slipped her fingers inside his jacket.

"What the...?"

She dropped it into the purse hanging from her wrist. Stepping back, she smiled sweetly.

"I'll keep it, if you don't mind. Now, Shane, be charming. Here come your guests."

Shane's presence beside her made it possible to smile and greet the dozens of guests streaming into Belle Rêve, as if the shock of seeing that gun hadn't filled her with dread. Shane was in danger. The threat against them both was very real. No matter how he tried to explain it, that was the reason he carried the gun.

An hour and a half later her face ached from smiling, but Kim was determined to do her part. It fascinated her how adroitly Shane handled the light superficial exchanges, the flattery. She was frightened by how detached he could be in the midst of all this. She longed to see beneath his facade. She yearned to see it crumble away like the walls of Jericho. But she had very little time left.

He turned to her, lifted one dark brow, and placed his hand on her arm. "They're all here now."

Everyone who had been at Claude's party and who appeared on the genealogical chart had arrived.

She nodded. "I'm ready."

He leaned over, his breath warm on her neck. "Phil's beckoning me to that group of state senators in the corner. I won't subject you to another evening of preservation. Just mingle and try to look like you're enjoying yourself." To her surprise, he raised her fingers to his lips. "We'll meet later and go over the timing once more."

Doing what he suggested, Kim wandered through the house, smiling at the guests, checking to see everyone was comfortable and everything was going smoothly. But she couldn't relax; the clock seemed to rush to the appointed hour.

Downstairs a surprisingly large group waited for a turn with Evangeline Paris. In the room with the Cajun music, Leonard was sitting by the fireplace. She heard someone request "The Alligator Princess" as she walked by. Outside, couples strolled through the gardens oblivious to everything but each other. Kim envied them. The party was a success.

Where was Shane? She reentered the ballroom in the middle of a Viennese waltz. Claude, in a white frock coat and pants, was leading Marlena Rudolph onto the floor. She was wearing a red silk hooped skirt that didn't allow him within two feet of her. A black lace purse dangled from her wrist and a black orchid was tucked into her bodice. Again tonight, she had chosen a gown with long tight sleeves.

How were the others at this party who were on the chart connected? Shaking her head, she chided herself for being ridiculous. Next thing, she'd be suspecting Leonard! She'd already been foolish enough about that gun. The weight of it tugged on her wrist. It might be ridiculous, but she felt easier about Shane with the gun in her possession.

A little jolt of pleasure went through her. There he was, still deep in discussion with the men from Claude's dinner party. Kim wove her way through the dancers to Madame LaForge who was holding court in a far corner.

She finally reached Madame LaForge.

"I saw you coming, child, and sent the others away." A knowing smile formed on the thin aristocratic lips. "I see poor Shane has been captured." She patted a needlepoint chair. "Sit here and we'll have that talk we never got around to the other night."

"It's nice to see you again, Madame. Your costume is magnificent." Kim couldn't help but admire the gown. The white satin and empire waist created appealing clean lines.

"Not a costume, my dear," Madame explained simply. "My wedding dress. Fifty years old."

"It's really beautiful," Kim sighed.

"A beautiful dress with beautiful memories," Madame reminisced, her eyes clouding with memories. "Louise was my junior bridesmaid, all in pink. We held lilacs and lavender and it rained the whole day."

Kim's chest tightened. What would she give to be able to have cherished memories like Madame LaForge's? She preferred not to remember the past. Her childhood had been full of trauma. Up to now life had been hard work—to build normalcy, to regain control.

"Shane is coming to ask you to dance. Doesn't he look dashing this evening? Reminds me of Edward, my husband."

"Madame," Shane bent over the older woman. "You won't mind if I claim Kim for this dance?"

"I'd be delighted to watch you young people," she urged, dismissing them with a nod of her head.

Kim looked up at him standing so tall before her and her heartbeat quickened. Was it time already to set the plan in motion?

He extended one hand, his amber eyes glittering with rueful humor, playing his role to the hilt for Madame LaForge.

Kim fluttered her fan and batted her eyelashes, smiling shakily. "I'd be honored, sir."

The music played, but she couldn't have said what it was. Willingly, she had joined with Shane to find his aunt's murderer and it had changed her life in ways she had never dreamed. Tonight they would confront people Shane had known his whole life, people who cared about him, and accuse them of being involved in Louise's murder. How could he do it so coldly, so calculatingly? She barely knew these people, yet her insides were a tight knot of anguish. Again, Kim realized how differently she and Shane viewed life. The realization squeezed the knot even tighter.

"What is it, Kim? Can you go through with this? You look pale."

She looked directly into his eyes. They were dark, intense; shutting her out.

"No, I'm fine." She threw back her head. "I assume that's why we're dancing, so we can finalize our plans."

"Yes, I've already put it in motion. I've arranged to meet people on the terrace at the appointed hour. Dance with Claude and then ask him to take you onto the terrace for some air. I don't want him to suspect."

Instinctively, Kim stepped away from him, pulling out of his arms just as the music stopped. Shivering, she shook her head. "Do you know how cold you sound?

Claude has been your friend for years. So have all the others. We're going to destroy lives tonight."

"I know," he returned grimly, no softening in his face. "Just as they destroyed Louise." His amber eyes searched her face. "Can I still count on you?"

"Yes," she said curtly, turning away from him to escape from the ballroom.

The dining room was full of people piling food onto their plates. The noise from the parlor packed with people eating and drinking overwhelmed her. She crossed the hall into the downriver parlor, really not caring where she was as long as she was far away from Shane.

"I've been waiting for you."

Startled, Kim realized the tarot-card reader was speaking to her. They were alone.

"The cards told me you would come."

"No, Miss Paris," Kim tried to back away. "I've got to check the rooms, make sure everyone gets to the buffet."

Evangeline smiled knowingly. "The cards have a message for you."

"Really, I don't want to hurt your feelings, but I don't believe . . ."

"You don't have to believe." She indicated a chair behind the screen. "Sit. Even Madame LaForge has had her fortune tonight."

Kim hesitated, twisting the bracelet at her wrist. How could a tarot reading hurt her? And Evangeline looked so earnest, just as Madame Loulou had that day so long ago. This woman was Louise's friend.

Kim hadn't been surprised when Shane told her he'd specifically asked Evangeline to attend and do readings tonight. It might be tradition, but he had wanted to include his aunt's old friend. That seemed like the right thing to do. So did this.

"OK," she capitulated. "What should I do?"

Evangeline handed her a well-worn pack of cards.

"Clear your mind of all but one question while you shuffle the cards. When you're ready, ask the question aloud and place the deck in front of me." She repeated, "Only one question and the mind must be clear." Kim shuffled. She should ask about Louise's death or perhaps something to do with Claude. But her mind refused to clear. The cards riffled through her hands. She closed her eyes and concentrated. How could they find out if Claude had something to do with Louise's murder?

The words refused to come.

"Do I know the man I'll marry?" She opened her eyes, surprised that the cards were on the table. Where had that question come from?

Evangeline was already turning over the first card. "'The Hanged Man.' This card shows your present position. It means you are in a state of transition. Your life is set for a change but uncertainty faces you. You must make adjustments and even a sacrifice."

"The second card," she placed it crosswise over the first, "shows the immediate influence on your life. Oh, dear. I'm afraid this is not good. We show here a threat, rogues surrounding you, storms and loss of a treasured possession. Let's continue, try to find something more positive. Now this third card shows your goal."

She flipped it up. "Aha! 'The Lovers.' This is good for your question. It denotes the beginning of a romance."

Quickly she turned up the next three cards. "This is the past foundation of your life. You didn't have a happy childhood, did you? But you have overcome this adversity to build a good life for yourself."

Kim squirmed restlessly in her chair. Really, this was a little too close to the truth! How could cards tell Evangeline Paris these things? She fought very hard not to let her emotions show as the tarot reader continued.

"A cunning person capable of trickery will try to prevent your happiness." She looked up at Kim. "See, it is good you came to me; now you are forewarned."

Kim smiled wanly.

"These last four will give us a true picture of your position." Rapidly she turned each card over and placed them in a vertical line.

"This is you, Kim. See, the woman is surrounded by swords. She appears calm but she is imprisoned by her inner anguish and turmoil. You are in a state of crisis. This next card is upside down. It means that in your crisis you will face deceit and fickleness. There will be obstacles and opposition from the one that tries to trick you. But your inner self, the strong passionate you that longs for a partnership, will have to face the unknown. To receive your heart's desire you will have to overcome many divergent influences, resist unknown enemies who will mislead you."

Evangeline took her hand and turned it palm up. She traced the scar carefully. "In the beginning I told you the spirits were favorable, now the cards are giving a warning." She squeezed the hand she held. "Heed my warning."

Kim had been mesmerized during the reading, but this last was just too much for even a tolerant person.

She'd had quite enough for one night. She tapped her fingers against the final card and quoted softly, "I am the sole master of my fate...."

"Kim!" Judge Rudolph peered around the screen. "Shane has been looking everywhere for you. I thought I saw you come in here quite some time ago. The Presentation Waltz is about to begin. Awards for costumes are next and you're in the running."

"Thank you, Miss Paris. Tarot is fascinating," she continued politely, and the woman nodded, unsmilingly. "Perhaps one day you can show me more about it."

She lightly placed her hand on the judge's outstretched arm. "Thank you for finding me. Those cards . . . some of them were frightening. Do you believe in that sort of stuff?"

"Certainly not!" He looked at her like she'd just declared lunacy. "There's Shane. I'm going to find my wife."

The Presentation Waltz was a dance enabling all the costumes in the contest to be displayed. Shane was in the midst of the dancers. He didn't need her yet. It wasn't time for their rendezvous on the back veranda. Out of a corner of her eye Kim saw Leonard duck out the French doors. His prosaic view of the world was just what she needed after the tarot-card reading.

He was smoking a cigar. The moment she approached he pitched it away. "That's all right. I don't mind . . ." she began.

"Louise would have loved this party," he blurted. "She always wanted to fill this place with people. But Jerome always wanted to be alone." He shook his head. "Those two were meant for each other, loved each other to the day they died . . . they just couldn't live together."

No comfort here after all. Just a reminder that history was repeating itself.

Before Kim could respond, Madame LaForge, leaning heavily upon her cane, joined them on the veranda. "It always amazes me that Cleopatra can win a costume contest," she laughed. "The only originality in that outfit was how much you could see through it. Oh, well! Kim, are you enjoying the party?" Madame LaForge leaned over the balcony to stare at the stars. "We used to dance on these verandas during the twenties. It was the only place we could get away with the Charleston." She shivered slightly. "Leonard, could you be a dear and get my wrap from my chair? It's chillier out here than I anticipated."

"Are you all right?" Kim asked anxiously as Leonard quickly left.

"It's not me I'm concerned about," Madame patted her hand consolingly. "You were so pale in the ballroom."

Kim laughed uneasily. "I'd just had my tarot reading. It was amazing how close the cards were to real life, and scary. I guess that's what you saw."

Leonard returned and carefully draped a soft cashmere shawl around Madame's shoulders. "Would you care to stroll?" he offered his arm courteously.

"Thank you, Leonard," she smiled, leaning heavily upon his arm as they crossed the veranda.

Kim followed, listening to the Cajun band playing a lively tune below them.

Someone motioned from the dance floor and Leonard excused himself. With a deep sigh, Madame LaForge sank against the veranda railing. "I'm not sure but that I'm coming down with something."

"Can I help you?" Kim offered impulsively, noting the sudden paleness on the skin of her fine-boned features.

"Perhaps you could, without disturbing anyone else."

Kim placed one arm around the older woman's shoulders as they skirted the ballroom to the upper hall and descended the stairs. When they reached the second floor Kim opened the door to her own room.

"Thank you, my dear. If I could just have a few moments of quiet."

"Of course," Kim soothed, settling Madame LaForge upon the daybed.

"Thank you, dear. Perhaps if you could just keep me company for a few moments. Did you enjoy your tour of The Pointe the other evening?"

"Yes," Kim smiled; even ill, Madame LaForge would never forsake her party manners. "It's a tremendous undertaking, recreating all that grandeur."

"It's been Claude's life work. The family fortune has gone into it. Actually, the fortune of his former business partner, too."

"What happened to Claude's partner?" she asked quietly, excitement rising in her.

"Three months ago the poor man was out fishing and drowned. They think he had a heart attack and fell out of his boat. He and Claude had some sort of insurance arrangement between them. Claude received everything."

All doubt about Claude fled. He wasn't interested in extortion. Just as Jeanne Carter had used fear of voodoo for personal gain—just as Louise had been killed because she threatened to expose the extortion ring involving shopkeepers—Claude had used the voodoo cult to get rid of his business partner. The insurance collected would support Claude's obsession. These people weren't worshippers of voodoo, they were simply cold-blooded killers who murdered for expedience and greed. There was a certain relief at understanding this, at last.

She had to find Shane and tell him. "Madame LaForge, can I get you anything?"

"Perhaps you could ask Leonard to get my driver."

"I'll do it now." Quickly Kim went to the door. She was desperate to find Shane.

"Oh, dear!" Madame LaForge struggled up. "I forgot my cane on the veranda."

"Please don't worry. I'll get it for you."

With a grateful smile, the older woman settled back onto the pillows. "Thank you again, dear. You are most kind."

As Kim closed the door she saw Marlena go into a bedroom down the hall.

Soundlessly, Kim followed her. Shane must wait. There had been something furtive about Marlena's movement, begging to be explained.

The door squeaked softly as it opened and Marlena heard it. Swinging around, her thin face turned suddenly pasty white as her evening bag fell to the carpet. The contents spilled out across the floor.

"I'm sorry." Moving, Kim knelt. "Let me...."

"No!" Marlena insisted. "I'll get it." She swept everything up, but not before Kim had seen the syringe.

Stepping away, Kim now knew the truth. Marlena was an addict. She probably used the extortion money to support her habit. What was wrong with these people? How involved was everyone?

"What do you want, Miss Campbell?" Marlena demanded, drawing herself up proudly.

"I saw you come in. I thought I could help you with something."

Her thin painted lips formed that cool smile. "I always use this room to freshen up when I'm at Belle Rêve."

"Of course. I'm sorry I startled you." Backing up, Kim closed the door and raced down the stairs as quickly as she could in a hooped skirt. She had to find Shane and tell him about Claude and Marlena. They might not have been among the voodoo worshipers that night—but they benefited from them in some way.

The grandfather clock chimed the hour. Oh no! She'd missed the rendezvous on the veranda! Where was Shane? Was he searching for her, wondering at her absence?

She found Leonard directing the caterers in the dining room. "Mr. Alexander wants all the leftover food to go to the Quarter's community kitchen. We don't want it to go to waste." Realizing Kim needed his attention he turned to her. "What is it, lass?"

"Madame LaForge isn't feeling well. She's resting in my room. She wants you to call her driver."

"Of course, I'll see to it." He hurried away and Kim turned to go upstairs to retrieve the cane. Then she would find Shane.

Through the French doors she saw a man, all in white, slip off the back veranda and out into the darkness. Was that Claude? Maybe it wasn't too late after all.

Lifting her voluminous petticoats she hurried after him. The yard was well lit and the jugglers were just gathering up their things for the night.

Claude had gone in the direction of the maze. Strangely, when she reached its entrance no one was about. Suddenly it was too dark, too quiet. Her heart began pounding with the old fear. She turned quickly back toward the house, unable to go on alone. Tonight was not the night she would conquer her nightmares.

A couple, strangers, came out of the maze laughing conspiratorially. Relieved, she joined them to go back to the house.

Claude was standing at the steps when she returned. They were in the right place at the wrong time. Where was Shane?

"Kim!" he exclaimed. "I thought I saw you. We haven't had a moment together. Perhaps you would join me. The waiter just brought me these." He offered her a champagne glass.

"Thank you, Claude." Sinking onto the wicker settee, she forced herself to smile as her mind raced. If she could just hold him here long enough, Shane would show up. Then they could spring the trap. "A quiet glass of champagne is just what I need."

He was his usual charming self, complimenting Shane on the party, her on her dress. Shane had insisted she must not try to question Claude on her own, but Shane wasn't here. Surely it wouldn't hurt to probe just a little.

"I heard you were involved in a fire, Kim. I'm so sorry. You seem to have recovered however." He patted her arm. "Is there anything I might do for you?"

"How kind of you, Claude, but Shane has taken care of everything." She lifted her champagne flute while studying his reaction, but she didn't take a sip. "Did you hear about Officer Carter? She was part of the investigating team on Louise's murder. She was found shot to death in the Quarter. I can't help but wonder if there might be a connection."

"No, I didn't know that." He shrugged, sipping at the champagne. "I heard about the shooting, of course. But

I didn't realize she had been investigating Louise's tragic death. What does Shane...?"

"Claude, could you come help get Madame to her car?" Leonard called from the door. "She's not feeling well and she's ready to go home."

Kim rose as quickly as she could in the dress. "Leonard, I was supposed to find Madame's cane and take it to her."

"No, lassie. You stay put. Madame said to tell you you'd done enough already. She'll call you tomorrow for tea."

"Yes, Kim, stay here and enjoy this beautiful night." Claude agreed. "I'll make sure Virginie gets her cane."

Most of the guests were inside. The garden was empty now; some of the lanterns had been extinguished so that only a few pools of light pushed back the darkness. The light spilling out onto the veranda from the hall didn't reach where she stood, but it didn't bother her over much. Shane would come soon. And when Claude returned...they'd have him. They'd successfully tied him to the voodoo cult through Jeanne Carter and now they had a motive—greed.

The voodoo angle was obviously used to control the weak-minded. Jeanne Carter needed money to sustain her lavish life-style and Claude needed money desperately—it didn't matter if it came through willing contributions or extortion or murder.

From out of the darkness a smelly cloth was shoved over her face. She gagged. Ether. Struggling desperately, she kicked and twisted, but a pair of strong arms encircled her, trapping her. Before she blacked out, she had the presence of mind to slide Louise's precious bracelet from her wrist, and fling it near where a lantern stood. Her flailing masked the clinking sound as the piece of jewelry skidded across flagstone. All she could hope was that Shane could decipher her distress signal, and come searching for her.

Chapter Thirteen

When she woke, she woke to deathly silence. She could smell damp earth, and mustiness, and . . . cigar smoke.

She was trapped in a "House of the Dead."

Squeezing her eyelids tighter, she rose and willed herself to awaken. This was only a nightmare. It had to be!

But a damp chill seeped through her clothing to her bones. The chill of death. This had to be a crypt, a crypt inside the Alexander family cemetery.

Horror drove her to her knees. She rocked back and forth, her arms wrapped tightly around her body. This nightmare was real!

She mustn't lose control. If she did, she might lose it permanently.

Reality intruded into one tiny corner of her mind. Acrid smoke choked her. The smell of a burning cigar . . . her captor must have been smoking.

There was only one person at the party whom she had seen smoking a cigar—Leonard.

No! That couldn't be right. Probably dozens of men at the party smoked cigars. Evangeline Paris's words nagged at her memory: *"Rogues surrounding you . . . a cunning person capable of trickery . . . unknown enemies who will mislead you. . . ."*

Even as she rejected the idea, she remembered it was Leonard who had made sure she was alone on the veranda.

A new fear grew in her, overwhelming her fear of the darkness. First it had been Claude, now Leonard; both above suspicion, one would have thought; both Shane's friends. She feared for his safety in a sea of enemies, and they seemed to be closing in.

She had to get out of here to warn him! Without thought for herself, or her own fears, she located the door latch, took off her thin shoe, and began to pound away at it. Then she remembered the gun. She could use the gun butt to force the lock. She reached into her purse and pulled it out. If the gun were loaded, she'd be out of here in a moment. Fancifully, she aimed it toward the door and pulled the trigger. A deafening roar filled the crypt.

The gun fell from her scorched, partially numb fingers. Light-headed with relief, she pushed open the heavy metal door and stumbled out into the moonlight.

She had to find Shane! But to do that she had to make her way through the darkness back to Belle Rêve. The crypt cast a large shadow across the moonlit grass and Spanish moss in the trees. Off in the distance an owl hooted. The nightmare wasn't over.

Fleeing through the night, terror gripped her in physical pain. Yet, side by side with the terror was the conviction that she could save Shane if she could just reach him in time.

Footsteps sounded ahead of her and, with her heart pounding in her ears, she looked frantically for a hiding place. But to hide, she'd have to step off the path, indistinct as it was, and into the deeper darkness. Before she could make a decision, a large figure loomed between two trees. She recognized who it was at once.

"Shane, you're safe! I need to warn you," she gasped softly before beginning to weep. Of all the reactions she had feared this was the only one she hadn't anticipated. Through everything that had happened, she had only cried once, when Louise had died.

"Where have you been?" He grabbed her hands and she winced in pain.

"That gun was no toy," she laughed shakily. "I think my hand will never be the same."

"You look awful," he muttered before pressing her bruised hand to his lips.

Numb with shock and fear, she repeated his name in a shaky voice. He pulled her into his embrace, his fingers tilting her tear-stained face up. His eyes were so full of relief and, something else she was afraid to name, that a torrent of tenderness swept through her. In a moment, his lips were on hers, driving away her panic.

"Have you been hurt, Kim?" he breathed into her ear, not releasing her from his iron grip.

"No, I'm all right. I was locked in the crypt. They may have been planning to come back after the party. That doesn't matter now," she gasped. "It's you who needs help, Shane."

"What is it? Who locked you in there?"

"I, I think it was Leonard," she whispered, tears streaming down her cheeks. "I had to get out to warn you. We can't trust anyone."

"Don't be silly, Kim. Leonard would never hurt me . . . or you."

"But, Shane. . . ."

Disregarding her frantic efforts to convince him, he shook his head, sweeping her up in his arms. "You're in shock. Don't say anymore until we get you back to Belle Rêve and warm again.''

Leonard was waiting for them in the library, poking at the flames in the fireplace.

"Oh, no, lad ... Here, let me help you," he offered, reaching out for Kim.

With a soft cry, she flinched away, deeper into Shane's embrace.

"Kim, Leonard isn't going to hurt you," Shane insisted, lowering her onto the couch.

She struggled to sit up and opened her clenched fist. It held half a cigar. "One of the men who abducted me—and I now think there had to have been two to carry me that distance—was smoking a cigar. And this was thrown into the crypt with me." Confusion and fear had given way to anger. Kim's voice was tart. "You left me on the veranda, Leonard. And you smoke cigars."

Shane took the cigar from her palm, rolling it between his fingers, before lifting it to his nose.

"Kim, you're right, we can't trust everyone. But we can trust Leonard." He held out the butt. "Here, Leonard, you tell me," Shane said dryly.

Leonard grimaced. Kim waited for an explanation. Finally Leonard spoke up.

"Lass, this is a Cuban cigar," he said gently. "Impossible to get nowadays except for the very rich. The only person I know who smokes them is Claude LaCroix."

Kim felt astonished. And ashamed. Blindly, she flung her arms around him, and kissed his cheek as she apologized to him.

Slowly Leonard broke out into a grin. "That's all right, lass. I'm glad our Shane here has such a fierce protector."

Kim colored as Shane hurried off to bid farewell to the last lingering guests. She accepted the cup of Earl Grey tea and the quilt Leonard brought her. Slowly the chill seeped from her body and heart. She was in control again by the time Shane returned.

But his face was red with anger, and he suddenly erupted. "Damn him! I'm going to The Pointe right now and face him with this."

Kim sat up straighter, ready to stop him at any cost. She wouldn't let Shane go by himself to Claude's. Who could guess how many of the old guard were involved?

"Lad, I share your feelings. I do," Leonard protested. "But you must use your wits and not go off half-cocked."

Kim sighed, sitting back, reassured that Leonard would make Shane see reason.

Tossing down the last sip of brandy, Shane turned to them more subdued. "Well, what do you suggest?"

"Go to the authorities. You have proof now."

Shane laughed, threading his fingers through his hair. "DeSable thinks we're crazy.... Perhaps we should talk to Anton Rudolph. Tell him what we know and go from there."

"Aye, lad," Leonard nodded. "The judge is a canny one."

"Wait!" Kim struggled to her feet, the quilt falling away. "I'm not sure we can trust Judge Rudolph."

Shane's dark eyes searched her face. "Why, Kim? Did he have something to do with your abduction?"

"I don't think so...but I was right about Marlena. I saw a syringe in her evening bag. She must be part of the extortion ring. The money fuels her drug habit."

"Great!" Shane muttered, threading long fingers through his hair.

"Poor lass... I've known her and Anton all my life. She was so bonny when she was young." Leonard shook his head. "Lad, this may have nothing to do with the other. It's either the police or the judge."

Shane's eyes studied her again. "What do you think, Kim? DeSable or Anton?"

Sinking back onto the couch, she again pulled the covers tightly around her shoulders. "I hardly know these people." She shook her head. "They seem so...nice. But Claude is involved. Maybe the others are, too. Especially the judge. Marlena's problem seems tied in. So far I don't see DeSable's connection."

"Then you say DeSable," Shane muttered, pacing. "But Jeanne Carter was his partner. And he was a fool the night of the fire. Every time we've gone to him with information he tells us we're crazy. We can't trust him."

"The judge was in the genealogy," she insisted.

"But he saved our lives the night in the bayou," Shane said quietly, stopping in front of her.

Unable to deny that, she nodded, trying to dampen her uneasy feeling. "Maybe you're right. Maybe we should talk to Judge Rudolph. First thing in the morning?"

"That's my intrepid Kimberly. You'll be safe here, I promise. Go to bed and get some rest. It might be a long day tomorrow.

The smile Shane gave her stayed with her as she marched upstairs.

But two hours later she was still lying in bed staring up at the ceiling, unable to sleep. Too much had happened. Too much had changed. She needed Shane. If she talked to him, maybe some of the questions inside her would be answered. Yet they were such opposites. Too different to have a genuine relationship. This wasn't real life. Somehow Kim had stumbled into a tragedy and when it was played out she would at least outwardly have control of her life again. But would life ever be the same?

With or without Shane, Kim knew she had changed. She could not go back to what had been. Incredibly, that thought comforted her, and she fell asleep.

Chapter Fourteen

The judge stood in welcome. "Shane, my boy, and Kim. How delightful to see you again."

Anton's office was lined with heavy mahogany bookcases. In the center of the room a large, well-organized desk faced two comfortable chairs.

"I was just having tea. Here, let me fix you a cup," he insisted, motioning them to sit down before he turned away.

After handing them each a cup, he settled back into his chair behind his desk. "Now, then, Shane, what is it I can help you with?"

Over the rim of the cup Kim watched Shane as the story came out: starting with Louise's death, the blurry Polaroid, the voodoo ritual, the fire, Claude's picture on the sacrificial altar. Every detail was included, even last night's abduction and her incarceration in the crypt.

As he finished, Shane's face was granite hard and Anton's was horrified.

"Claude LaCroix! We've been friends for years. I can hardly believe it."

"I'm sorry, Anton, I knew you'd be shocked. Because of Claude's involvement I wanted to talk it over with you before I exposed him to the police." Shane shrugged, his face grim. "I'm giving him more consideration than he deserves, the bastard!"

"Of course, dear boy, I understand your feelings," Anton nodded, coming quickly to stand beside her. "And you, Kimberly." He took both her hands, holding them tightly for an instant. "What you've been through. It horrifies me. But now it's over." He pursed his lips, gazing over her head. "I think I know someone who can be trusted to help us handle this, Shane. I'll return in a few minutes."

He disappeared through the door they had entered earlier and Kim was curious. If he was going to call someone, why hadn't he just used the phone on his desk?

Shane didn't seemed concerned though. He was examining the bookshelves, then paced to the window to pour another cup of strong tea. It didn't matter that he was attempting to retreat behind his wall of aloof detachment. She gained pleasure from just watching him. Suddenly he hesitated and turned back toward Anton's desk. Without warning he stopped as if riveted to the spot. She followed the direction of his gaze. He was staring at a picture on the desk.

Puzzled, she went to stand by him. "What is it?" she asked, raising curious eyes to his face.

He merely shook his head, ignoring her, concentrating on the snapshot.

She looked at the picture. It had been taken at a golf outing. Everyone wore a sun visor. Anton, Claude, and two other men she'd never seen before were smiling into the camera holding a trophy. Behind them a long fairway stretched into the distance. Despite the obviously-sumptuous surroundings, the men looked a little ragged.

"Does this remind you of something, Kim?" Shane demanded, still not looking at her, but lifting the picture from the desk so she could see it more clearly.

"No, Shane, what . . . ?"

"Of course! Anton was at the ritual." In a blur of movement, Shane dropped the frame, shattering the glass on the floor. He grabbed her arm, twirling her around. "We've got to get out of here!"

They had taken only three steps when the door opened. "I'm most sorry, dear boy, but we can't allow you to leave," Anton said in a soft tone. He was not alone. Claude LaCroix, looking as white as his habitual suit, stood beside him, and a third man she'd never seen before. He had the biceps of a weightlifter, and he was holding a large gun pointed directly at them.

Shane pushed her behind him, holding her there with one strong arm. Fear surged through her when she saw his expression. They had been surrounded by enemies all along. The cards had been right, but she hadn't heeded their warning. And Shane had realized the danger too late.

"Don't be ridiculous, Anton! Tell him to put the gun away and we'll talk," Shane said cooly.

Anton laughed suddenly, clicking the door shut. "Shane, don't be a fool! I'm afraid it's too late for talking. You and Miss Campbell have been much too resourceful. I very much regret we must put a stop to your activities. Permanently."

Claude absorbed a hiss of air. "Why couldn't you have stopped? Why did you keep probing? Nothing like this was supposed to happen."

"Stop sniveling, Claude!" Anton commanded.

"When did the owner of The Pointe start taking orders from anyone?" Shane cried.

Claude flushed and looked away. The silver-tipped cane trembled in his fingers.

"Do be quiet, clever boy. Kim, come here," Anton requested, his smile widening in his face.

"No!" Shane held her behind him protectively.

"If you don't come, by the time I count to five Marcus here will put a bullet through Shane's heart."

"You bastard! She's staying right where she is," Shane cried, holding her in his viselike grip.

Two thoughts hit Kim in the same instant. The first was that Leonard knew they had come here and if they could stay alive long enough, help might arrive. The second was that she wouldn't allow anyone to harm Shane any further. They'd already killed his aunt, the one person in all the world he'd allowed himself to care about.

Her icy anger made it easy to pretend she was completely unafraid.

"Kim, do as I say!" Anton threatened. When she didn't move he sighed. "So be it, Kimberly...one... Marcus, on the count of five shoot Mr. Alexander...two..."

Grinning through yellow teeth, Marcus took a silencer out of his pocket and screwed it into place.

Claude looked as if he was going to be sick. Kim felt the same, but Shane laughed. "Melodrama is my milieu, not yours, Anton. Let's handle this like gentlemen."

Anton's eyes widened in mock surprise. "But, dear boy, Marcus isn't a gentleman...three...."

Fear for Shane overrode every option; she tore away from his side. In seconds she stood beside the judge.

"Anton, for God's sake!" Shane shouted, lunging after her. "Don't...."

Marcus savagely struck Shane with the gun and he dropped to the floor unconscious. Kim fell to her knees, cradling Shane's bruised head in her lap. Fortunately no blood came away with the hand when she checked the damage. Flinging back her head, she glared at their three captors. "Have you all gone crazy?"

Claude was leaning against the door, a pristine handkerchief pressed to his mouth. Anton shrugged, clasping the grinning Marcus on the shoulder. "Well done. It's better this way. I should have known Shane would try something."

Frozen in a protective posture over Shane, Kim asked the question uppermost in her mind. "Why?" Then in a blinding flash of insight she gasped. "This has nothing to do with voodoo, does it? You all are involved in extortion and blackmail and even murder just for personal gain."

Claude did not answer, he merely closed his eyes, crumpling in on himself where he stood. He looked old and weak.

Anton glanced at him with disdain and then met Kim's furious stare. "For Marcus here, it *is* a religious experience. But for Claude and I, voodoo provides us with services... goods which are not, you might say, readily available, and money."

"But you're both already wealthy men," she protested, gently stroking her fingers through Shane's hair, her arms still cradling him fiercely close.

Anton laughed harshly. "There's not enough money on this earth to recreate The Pointe. You see, some of the leading citizens in this fair city may have come from money. But none of us have been as successful as our illustrious ancestors. This is an industrial society, my dear, prone to favor businessmen, not landed gentry. And some of us need . . . funds."

"Anton, please, I beg of . . ." Claude whined.

"Oh, do be quiet, Claude, and be useful for a change! Check the hall. The car's already in the alley. Marcus can carry Shane down the back stairs." Anton took the gun from Marcus and aimed it at Shane's chest. "I can see you have become quite attached to our Shane. So you wouldn't do anything so foolish as to scream or attract attention, would you, Kimberly? Because I do assure you, I won't hesitate to use this."

"What can you gain by this, Anton?" Kim shook her head in disbelief. "Is this all to keep Marlena supplied with drugs?"

His smile burned through her like acid.

"How perceptive of you, Kimberly," he purred gently. "All these years no one else has ever discovered our little secret."

THE NIGHTMARISH JOURNEY must end here, Kim assumed bleakly. They'd been travelling for hours—far out into the bayou—when they stopped at an isolated cabin.

Marcus dumped Shane unceremoniously onto the bed before locking them in.

Kim rushed to him, calling his name, kneeling to press his cool hand to her cheek. He was still unconscious, not from the blow to the head, but from the ether used to keep him immobile during the trip.

She couldn't believe they'd been taken against their will through a major city, carried onto a boat, and delivered to the bayou without anyone noticing. The stairwell had been empty, the limo windows darkened, the out-of-the-way boat dock deserted. And now here they were at the mercy of three lunatics, in the middle of nowhere in a run-down shack. The frightened young girl who had let them in might be their only hope.

Kim listened at the door, then quickly checked to see if she could force open a window.

"They're all nailed shut." The judge spoke from the doorway.

She whirled in panic to face him.

Anton still appeared guileless. Behind him, Claude shriveled into helplessness before her eyes. Anton was clearly in charge and had been all along. The night they'd been attacked on the old bayou road . . . his rescue had just been a clever ruse.

"What do you plan to do with us?" she asked.

Smiling sardonically, Anton walked to her, cupping her cheek in his hand. It took every ounce of her self-control not to flinch from his touch, but she wouldn't give him the satisfaction.

"Such spirit. No wonder Shane has kept you with him. As to your question, dear Kimberly, your fate has not yet been decided. But I promise it will be unique and worthy of your spirit."

She stepped back angrily.

"Don't try anything, Kim!" he warned. "Marcus and his lovely wife, Angelina, have orders to shoot if you try to escape." He said, shrugging, "And where would you go in these aimless bayous, anyway?" At the door he looked back, smiling in mock sadness. "Farewell, dear Kim. Claude, let's go!"

Claude suddenly straightened. His face took on its customary aristocratic air, but his eyes showed some compassion. He took two steps toward her. "Kimberly, I'll see you're brought some food. I deeply regret this unfortunate turn of events. If only . . ."

"Please spare me your pitiful attempts at chivalry, Claude!" She attacked him with the only weapon left to her—scorn. "You once told me the past was a part of you, part of those whose heir you are. What would your honorable ancestors think of you?"

She had hit the mark; he looked so devastated that she turned away disgusted. It was a hollow victory anyway for she heard the bolt slide into place, locking them in.

Shane was still unconscious; he stirred slightly when Marcus opened the door and Angelina brought in a tray of food. Kim wouldn't touch any or try to give it to Shane; heaven only knew what they might have put in it.

She curled up on the bed beside Shane for comfort. He looked so young and vulnerable in sleep, color flushing his high cheekbones. She ran her fingers through his soft thick hair.

"We're going to get out of this," she whispered into his curls. "Just please wake up so we can plan. I need you...."

SHANE FOUGHT HIS WAY OUT of groggy lethargy and opened his eyes. For an instant he felt pleasure, finding himself pressed next to Kim, who soothed his aching head with her fingers. But in the next breath he remembered.

"Where are we?" he asked, pulling himself upright, focusing on her concerned face. "Are you all right? They didn't hurt you, did they?"

Smiling faintly, she shook her head. "I'm fine. But you've been out for hours so take it easy. We're in the bayou. They drugged you. Claude and Anton are gone. They left Marcus and a young girl, his wife I think, to guard us. This is probably their house." He watched her examine his eyes before she smiled. "I've been trying to figure out how we can escape."

Admiration. That was the only word to describe what he was feeling. She'd been kidnapped, had death threats made against her, witnessed a murder. Through it all she remained calm and optimistic; she gave him hope. He couldn't resist kissing her soft chin. "That's my girl. Always planning. Let's see what we've got."

Sliding off the bed gingerly, he was relieved to find his legs were steady. Once he stood his mind cleared. "Who brought the food?"

"The girl. I've been afraid to try it. She'll probably be back soon to get the tray."

"Good, that's when we'll make our move."

Kim moved beside him, raising wide curious eyes to his face. "How?"

Instead of answering, he pulled over a chair and stood on it. Then he reached up to remove the bleached white alligator skull from high upon the wall near the ceiling. It must be Marcus's juju, painted with a blue cross, surrounded by four red *X*s. It was intended to protect this house from evil spirits.

"Ugh! What is that thing?" Kim gasped, but came closer to examine it.

"It's their protective juju, Kim. And we're going to break it."

Her eyes widened, remembering. "Like your aunt's. But I'm not sure that will be enough to frighten Marcus."

"Look around, Kim. There's a little altar in the corner. See the candles and the skull. These people are believers. When we hear them coming I'll break it. I know a curse that'll bedevil them."

"I don't know whether I believe in this stuff, Shane," she muttered. Flushing, she looked down at her palm, absently rubbing it.

"It doesn't matter if we believe in it. They do! Quick! I think someone's coming. Get behind the door and stay out of the way."

With a defiant glance she did as he commanded.

Raising the skull high over his head he flung it down and broke it into three pieces. When the door opened he began to chant what he had learned in Africa.

The strange chant confused the girl. When she saw the broken juju she screamed, falling to her knees and covering her face with trembling hands. Directly behind her, Marcus was taken off guard. In that instant Shane flew at him, tackling him so they both fell heavily to the floor. Knocked breathless for an instant, he rolled sideways, then sprang up to launch a punch into Marcus's stomach. Marcus doubled over, but with a grunt rammed his head into Shane's chest.

Shane fell against the wall, then pushed himself away to land an upward clip to Marcus's jaw. The heavier man staggered back and . . . collapsed to the floor.

Kim stood triumphantly above him, the wooden dinner tray she'd bashed him with broken in two pieces. She grinned, jumping down off the chair. "We're quite a team, aren't we?"

Resisting the urge to hug her, he laughed ruefully before pulling Marcus out of the way.

Fear of the broken juju kept the young girl on her knees, mumbling and sobbing. But since Marcus wouldn't be unconscious for long, they bolted out of the room.

Kim looked up at him. "Now what?"

He held her hand in a fiercely protective grip. "Now we're getting out of here."

OUT OF THAT HOUSE and away. It had seemed the logical thing to do. But now they were lost, in a landscape of nothing but tall grass, gaunt gray trees which resembled stooped elderly men, and swampland. They were up to their knees in the green scummy water.

Shane climbed the nearest tree, trying to catch sight of a landmark. There was nothing to guide him but the slow flowing water and the endless bayou.

"Stay right behind me," he urged, taking her hand again. "There's quicksand and sinkholes. You could disappear quicker than I could turn and grab you."

"Shane, do you have any idea where we are? They brought us blindfolded by boat. I couldn't even tell you which way to go."

He gripped her shoulders, his eyes bright with determination. "I'll get us out of this, don't you worry," he promised.

As always, she believed him, just like from the beginning.

She wasn't certain how long she'd be able to keep up with him. He had heavy shoes and pants to protect his legs. Each step she took was hampered by vines and thorns that had scratched her stockings to tatters.

Grimly keeping pace, Kim clung to Shane's hand through tall grass, wild marsh flowers with white and purple buds, over cypress trees whose roots were turned up reaching for the sun from soil too shallow to hold them.

The worst part was wading through brown water covered with green algae. What were her feet sinking into? What horrors might lie beneath the murky depths?

Kim's eyes continuously searched from side to side. She knew there were alligators everywhere. If she'd seen one her hard-held control would have slipped.

Then she saw a shape move. "What's that?" she gasped, pointing.

He stepped back toward her, following the direction of her shaken gaze. "It's a snake, Kim," he said matter-of-factly.

Primal fear overtook her. In a moment her finely held control slipped. "Snakes, too?" she muttered, unable to go forward. His fingers were crushed by her grip.

"C'mon, we're almost to that island of bog grass." Urgently he pulled her rigid body away. He let go of her momentarily to climb over a particularly high formation of cypress roots, and then reached out both arms to help her. "You can do it, Kim," he encouraged her.

At the same time she reached for the safety of his grasp something slithered from beneath the dark roots, striking Shane's exposed forearm.

"Damn!" he bit out, clutching his arm, holding it tightly to his body. The next instant he grabbed the snake and flung it far away from them. "It's all right...I'll help you."

His hand was trembling.

She didn't need help now; she scrambled over the roots, crawling to where he sat. Already his face was drained of all color and dripped with perspiration. Yet when she touched him he was icy cold.

"Don't be afraid," he said softly through clenched teeth. "It was a yellow diamond water snake. Not deadly, but I'm going to be very sick with a headache and high fever." Blinking sweat from his long lashes, he smiled into her stricken face. "I'm not going to die, I promise."

"No?" Every cell of her body was filled with fear for him. Logically she knew there were events in her life she had no control over, but emotionally she couldn't accept them. Not now, not with Shane.

"I should say you're not going to die! You promised to get me out of this godforsaken place!" The words came tartly and were answered by his shaky laughter.

"That's my girl." Struggling to his feet with Kim's help, he stood to gaze around.

"We've got to find a safe place to stop. It'll be dark soon," Kim said. This was the first time she'd thought of the oncoming night. The sun was going down; when it was dark she'd be in the swamp, lost, with a man in the throes of delirium. How would she be able to cope?

One step at a time, she reassured herself. Just find a safe resting place—a place where Shane will be protected—until morning.

He closed his eyes, wincing. She knew his headache was beginning already. Now it was her, urging him on in the fading light. His weight rested ever more heavily on the arm she kept around him.

Suddenly she spotted oil storage tanks in the distance. She remembered the oil wells Leonard had showed her in the bayou and how the pipeline could lead her to civilization. There was no one around. But a boat was tied to a rickety wooden dock. It was equally old, in equally bad shape. She didn't have a choice. There was only a little water beneath the tarpaulin covering its bottom.

Shane had fallen silent, conserving his dwindling strength. "Take it, Kim. We'll be safer in it," he finally murmured.

It held her weight and she was reassured. With a deep sigh, Shane laid back as she threw off the frayed rope

and pulled them off from the dock. There was one paddle, and using it, she aimed them out into the bayou.
They passed under huge oaks bent over the water with
moss hanging so low she had to push through it.

"I hate this ugly moss," she muttered to herself.

Shane's eyes opened wide, the brown dissolving into
amber. "I've always liked Spanish moss," he replied in
a dreamy tone. "Look, Kim, when the sun shines
through, it becomes sea green and luminous like your
eyes."

He murmured more lyrical words, then stopped
abruptly.

She pressed her hand against his forehead. She'd been
afraid of this. The cold had been consumed by fire;
Shane had a raging fever.

If he hadn't already reassured her, his temperature
would have scared her to death. As it was he moaned and
thrashed about in the bottom of the boat. Letting the
boat drift, she tried to make him more comfortable.
Tugging at the tarp, she shifted it over him. Twilight had
fallen, and in the silence she could hear cicada locust
trilling. She tried to remember what Leonard had told
her that day they went to the honey tree. She focused on
the memory, but what she remembered wasn't encouraging: It was easy to get lost because there were hundreds
of small bayous and only the largest ones had markers.

Ahead in the water was a darker shadow. Quickly, she
padded toward it. It was rescue! A warning pole that an
oil pipeline crossed here. It was a good place to tie up for
the night and in the morning she'd be able to follow the
pipeline. She looped the rope around the pole several
times.

She didn't have time to be afraid. Shane needed her.
She ripped one corner of her blouse and dared to dip her

hand over the side. She sponged his forehead, trying to relieve some of his discomfort.

"Kim," he sighed in appreciation.

"It's all right. We're safe. I tied us up to a pipeline. Nothing can get at us by land." She kept rewetting the cloth to keep it cool. That seemed to help him.

"How do you do it?" he mumbled deliriously.

She was so tired she barely listened. She just kept dipping the rag and cooling him down. Tossing his head restlessly back and forth he began to ramble, the words flowing hot and urgently from his parched lips.

Several times she tried to quiet him, but found it useless.

He started, his eyes opened and he clutched frantically at her. "Kim . . . Kim. . . ."

"It's all right. I'm here."

"Have we found the doll yet?"

"It's all right," she soothed again. "The doll's not important."

It took all her strength to hold him down.

"Important," he rambled. "Find the doll . . . find the doll."

"Shane, the doll doesn't mean anything."

"Hurt you . . . they'll hurt you through the doll. I've seen it happen."

His body shook. Frantically, she opened his shirt and ran the cooling cloth over his chest until he calmed slightly.

"OK," he sighed deeply. "It's OK . . . I reversed the spell. . . ."

The words began to flow; bits and pieces about his parents and life in primitive cultures—how he'd seen the brutality and learned the power of evil.

Her imagination filled in the gaps. No wonder his plays were cynical and dark. Since he was a boy, he'd never given anyone a chance to break through his bitterness, to get close enough to him to show him how sweet love and caring could be.

She'd learned from her lonely childhood that the only way to survive was to press on—discarding the defeats as meaningless—cherishing the little victories and gaining strength from them for the next task. Unless you felt pain, pleasure held little meaning. Unless you knew sorrow, joy was unimportant. These were all things she could teach him.

A soft mist developed, and she noticed that Shane slept more quietly now. The mist turned to fat drips and she pulled the tarp completely over their heads, cocooning them in each other's warmth.

Exhaustion drove her lids shut and she gave in to the temptation to sleep, safe here with Shane. Her fear of the dark was at the moment held at bay.

Chapter Fifteen

Sometime during the night one of them must have pushed the tarp back because the sun was blinding her when Kim opened her eyes. Shane slept peacefully beside her. She pressed her cheek to his face, sighing in relief. His fever had broken.

The bayou was strangely beautiful in the sun's light. The water broke gently against the bow as they drifted.

Adrenaline pumped wildly through her system. Drifting! Scrambling to her knees, she gazed around in panic. Somehow the rope had untangled itself from its pole mooring. They had left the pipeline and were lost again. Squinting her eyes, she peered ahead. Then with fumbling fingers, she grabbed the paddle.

It wasn't just her imagination. The Three Sisters, home of the legendary honeycomb, was just off to their left.

A GNAWING ACHE BURNED behind his eyes, throbbed dully through his head, but at least Shane could stand up. Vaguely he remembered Kim soothing him through the worst of the fever. Now, she had found the Three Sisters. He knew the way home from here. The quickest way was cross-country.

She kept her arm supportively around him as they walked even though he really didn't need it. But he didn't discourage her, either. The weight of her body against his, the caress of her damp, tangled hair brushing his cheek was comforting.

This wasn't over yet. They had to make sure Claude and Anton didn't get away. He couldn't begin to guess who else was involved or who he could trust. Except Kim. Kim, who was like no one he had ever known before.

Kim needed to rest more than anything, he guessed, because she had been uncharacteristically silent on their trek home. He pulled her through the French doors of the library and stopped dead in his tracks.

DeSable turned from the fireplace.

Shane caught Kim fast in his arms, bracing himself for whatever was to come. "What in the hell are you doing here?" He panted. He knew he was being illogical, the police were the first people he should call, but he still couldn't shake the feeling that DeSable wasn't to be trusted.

"You're alive!" DeSable stared at them, his jowls hanging in astonishment.

"You're alive!" Leonard repeated from the doorway. With tears glistening in his watery blue eyes, Leonard rushed to embrace them.

Kim stared blankly up at him, and Shane kept his arm tightly around her shoulder. "What's going on here, Leonard?"

"Laddie, when you didn't come back from Judge Rudolph's I called the lieutenant here."

"Called my foot! He busted into my office demanding I take action to find you."

"That's when we found Judge Rudolph and his wife apackin'...."

"Wait a minute! Start at the beginning," Shane ordered, helping Kim to the couch before she fell over from fatigue.

"You both look like hell," DeSable stated brusquely, smoothing his palm over his balding head. "Where've you been?"

"You first, Lieutenant," Shane ordered as he collapsed onto the chair behind his desk.

"OK. Let's cut right to the bottom line. Leonard convinced me to call on Judge Rudolph and question him about your whereabouts. He said he hadn't seen you since you left his office yesterday. But a few hours later the man I left on stakeout reports he and his wife are on the way to the airport." DeSable shrugged. "He's still not talking, but he's not going anywhere. I booked them both on suspicion of kidnapping."

"What about Claude?" Kim asked coldly.

Shane shot her a startled glance. Her silence had lulled him into thinking she was too exhausted to deal with anything else, but now her green eyes flashed with angry energy.

"Claude LaCroix is just as involved in this as Anton Rudolph." Her voice was like ice.

"Leonard tried to tell me. That's why I'm out here," DeSable said, almost apologetically. "It took this long to get a search warrant. I'm heading over there now."

"I'm going with you," Shane stated grimly. Now that he knew Kim was her old self, he could leave her safely with Leonard.

"If you don't mind me saying so, you don't look well enough to go across the room, let alone all the way to

The Pointe," DeSable replied bluntly. "Don't worry, the police will take care of him."

"You don't understand! Claude was involved in my aunt's death and he's put Kim and me through hell. I'm going over there with or without you." Shane pushed himself to his feet.

"Me, too!" Quickly Kim crossed the room to stand beside him, twining her fingers through his. Once the contact would have shocked him, but now it felt right. Looking down into her face, the smudges of fatigue under her eyes, he saw again that spirit which had first drawn him. He didn't even try to change her mind. She'd been there at the beginning, she deserved to be in on the end. And he wanted her there, he suddenly recognized.

"You two are a real pair." DeSable lifted a brow, looking to Leonard for aid. "Talk some sense into them."

Shaking his head, Leonard clasped Shane's shoulder. "The lad's right. It would be better to take them with you than let them go on their own."

"Look, DeSable, we're damn tired, but neither one of us is going to rest until we see Claude behind bars."

Both anger and exhaustion filtered into Shane's voice. He had another good reason to settle this mess as soon as possible. He wouldn't feel secure until he knew Claude was in custody and the doll was found; then all the threats would be over.

THE LATE AFTERNOON SUN HID behind a large gray cloud as they drove up the statue-lined drive to The Pointe. Somehow it all seemed symbolic to Kim. She was totally spent. Physically, she'd passed her limit stumbling through the bayou. Emotionally, she'd been up and down with Shane's ramblings. Psychologically, she'd been conserving all her energy, all her thoughts, directing them toward Shane. It was totally illogical, she knew, but somehow she sensed he needed her strength.

She would have fought him tooth and nail if he'd tried to make her stay behind at Belle Rêve. She just couldn't let him face this final disaster alone—to accuse a lifelong friend of murder. Anton's perfidy had been bad enough, but with that well-defined instinct where Shane was concerned, she knew Claude's betrayal cut even deeper.

A servant let them into The Pointe and ushered them with great ceremony into the downriver parlor.

Claude stood all in white, a startling contrast to the black marble fireplace. He was perfectly groomed as always but leaned heavily upon his silver-tipped cane. Something flickered through his eyes as the three of them entered the room. Kim could almost believe it was relief.

"I've been expecting you, Lieutenant DeSable," he drawled. "But I'm especially pleased to see Kimberly and Shane."

"You hypocrite! If you'd had your way, we'd be dead right now!" Shane roared, stepping forward. Kim reached out to stop him, but DeSable was ahead of her, barring the way with an outstretched arm.

Kim knew Shane could have pushed it aside if he'd wanted, but he stopped, all rage suddenly draining from him. Perhaps he saw Claude as she did—an old man, reduced now to a hollow shell.

"Why, Claude?" Shane demanded, finally shoving past DeSable. From where she stood, Kim could see how deeply Shane breathed, holding himself in check. "I remember the three of you at Belle Rêve. Louise, Jerome and you. The laughter. The chess games. All the wonderful stories." Shane took one more step, anguish twisting his features. "She found out you were using the voodoo cult for your own gains, didn't she, Claude? She discovered your ugly little secrets so you had her killed!"

Claude's thin, blue-veined lids closed for an instant. "Anton and I didn't know what was planned for Louise." He trembled where he stood, staring at them. "They all said it was necessary for the queen to deal with her."

"Jeanne Carter you mean," Kim urged. She saw DeSable's face redden to scarlet at Claude's nod.

"Yes, Jeanne was our queen. But I didn't realize they planned to . . . to . . . murder Louise. I thought they just meant to frighten her into minding her own business. Don't you understand, Shane? I only became involved to help preserve our heritage. The Pointe belongs to all of us. It represents our past." He suddenly straightened, rubbing his fingertips over his mustache. "It is my duty to preserve the honor of my ancestors."

"Louise was murdered because she realized the truth about you all." Kim kept her voice steady, confirming everything they had already suspected. "Louise uncovered the extortion, the sudden death of your partner, and that led her to the two people she knew were desperate for money. You to restore The Pointe and Anton to support Marlena's habit. She confronted you and you killed her. The queen was really your pawn. She stirred up the superstitious, revived the voodoo cult. Followers no doubt came from everywhere . . . they threatened shopkeepers for money which was supposed to go to the queen, but was partly siphoned off to you."

"No! No!" Claude's hand trembled as he held it out in protest. "Louise never came to us. But the queen knew she was on to us. The queen had incredible power. The spirits guided her.''

Kim looked away, tears of compassion misting her eyes, but she couldn't hide from what was being destroyed here.

DeSable elbowed past Shane and pulled a small book from his pocket. In a matter of moments he read Claude his rights.

Claude didn't move a muscle from his stately pose. At the end he nodded, almost regally. ''I understand. If I might make one small request? A few moments to pen notes to my housekeeper and my estate manager. Things must continue on in my absence.''

''Mr. LaCroix, that is out of the...''

''Give it to him!'' Shane bit out. ''What possible harm can it do now?'' he added wearily.

Kim's heart ached for him. The hunt was finally over. He had found his aunt's killers, but the price had been high.

Just as they had done on the first day in Madame Loulou's room, Shane and DeSable locked gazes. This time the policeman looked away first. He nodded. ''We'll be right outside, LaCroix. You have five minutes!'' DeSable said gruffly and stalked from the room.

Shane stood staring into the face of his old friend. Finally Kim touched his arm and he peered at her, dazed. She sensed he had withdrawn again, back into the darkness that only acknowledged ugliness and defeat in life. But his eyes lightened slightly as he took a deep breath, and allowed her to urge him away.

Claude's voice reached them in the hall before the door closed. They both turned.

He threw back his shoulder and faced them. "You may not believe me, Shane, but I am so sorry. So terribly sorry."

On one level, compassion for Claude surged through her; he was a weak man who had allowed his obsession to destroy him. But there was no softening in Shane. He simply turned his back and shut the door.

Kim wanted to offer comfort. Tentatively she placed her fingers on Shane's arm. It was rock hard, every muscle tensed with the ultimate effort he was making.

"This is hard to swallow," DeSable shook his head in disbelief. "Jeanne Carter was my partner for five years!" He squinted his eyes into Shane's face. "I owe you an apology, Shane. I should have listened to you before." He thrust out his hand.

Grimly, Shane took it. "We've all been fools, DeSable. I . . ."

A shot rang out, echoing in the great hallway. Cursing, DeSable jerked open the door. Shane's face was stark white as he shoved past her. But she saw knowledge in his amber eyes as if he had guessed what Claude would do and had been in agreement.

Horror churned in her stomach as Kim leaned against the wall. She didn't need to follow the men into that room. She didn't want to see. She knew Claude had done the only thing possible for him.

SLOWLY THE SHOCK which had held her in its impersonal grip faded. It was over. Totally. Finally. Together, she and Shane had found the killers. Kim found it difficult to believe that Shane had known exactly what he was doing when he demanded DeSable give Claude time alone. Claude could never have endured a public trial; she recognized that now. Perhaps Shane had felt compassion after all. But he accepted these things so easily—this dark side of human nature. Whereas she had fought against it her entire life. Was there a way for two people who viewed life and its meaning in such different ways to share any kind of relationship?

There was a tenuous bond with Shane Kim didn't understand. She was positive she couldn't sever it easily.

She stared at the calendar on Shane's desk. Tomorrow at exactly three forty-two her plane left New Orleans. There was no excuse to stay now that Louise LeCarpentiers's murderers had been found. Her old life waited for her in Illinois.

Shane walked into the library with Leonard following. The last policeman and most persistent reporters had just left Belle Rêve. He had spared her that ordeal, insisting that he would handle all the curiosity. His face showed the ravages of fatigue and sorrow; the lingering effects of the snakebite.

He collapsed into the wing chair. His penetrating gaze swung quickly to her, but she kept her face deliberately relaxed as his eyes searched hers. "Are you all right?" he asked quietly.

"I just can't believe it's all over." Standing, she paced slowly back and forth between the fireplace and the desk. She could feel Shane's gaze touching her. "It was all on the genealogical chart. Anton. Claude. DeSable says he's going to question everyone he can find that was on it. But one thing bothers me . . . That one line wasn't completed."

"Lass, that's not odd. Often happens. The line dies out or is somehow lost. Come across it often." Sighing, Leonard patted her shoulder. "It's been quite a time for the both of you. Why don't I fix us a light supper and then you two can make an early night of it?"

"Thank you, Leonard, but I think I'll skip dinner. I leave tomorrow and I haven't even begun to pack," she said overbrightly. Her pulse quickened at the startled look on Shane's face.

The tension in the room was suddenly palpable. Leonard coughed self-consciously. "Well, I think I'll have an early night myself. I was up all last night worryin' about you two."

"I didn't realize you would be leaving so soon." Shane's voice, quiet and impersonal, reverberated in the surrounding silence.

Suddenly, she wanted nothing more than to go into his arms. For the first time in a life of hard-fought control and clear-thinking good judgment, Kim was ready to toss all her hard-earned security away. Only pride kept her from pleading with him to let her stay and explore these feelings.

"Yes, remember at the cemetery," she stammered, the heavy weight in her chest nearly unbearable. "It seems so long ago. I told you two weeks and . . . and now that we know what happened to your aunt . . . and everyone's under arrest . . . or . . . gone . . . we're safe. My time here is up."

His gaze passed over her questioningly and she saw him take a hard breath. "I understand, Kim. I just . . ." He caught himself and nodded. "I know you're exhausted so we'll talk in the morning. I hope you'll let me take you to the airport," he said with the well-remembered mild sarcasm.

A rueful smile tugged at his lips. He was being charming and gallant. She must acknowledge his efforts.

The tears could not be kept at bay as she climbed the stairs to her room. Her palm throbbed and she pressed it against her trembling lips as she shut the door, collapsing back against it.

There was no love spell. He was letting her go.

Chapter Sixteen

He couldn't let her go. Pacing back and forth in the library, Shane rammed his fingers through his hair in pure frustration.

Admit it, you fool! He chided himself; everything about Kim had become necessary to him. But old fears still lurked in the dark corners of his mind. He had spent his entire lifetime focusing on the dark side of man...of existence itself. It was hard to allow himself to believe in what Kim meant to him.

Fighting to conquer the habits of a lifetime, he forced down the barriers. His pacing ended at the desk still littered with manuscript pages. His characters were demanding a happy ending.

So was he.

He took the stairs two at a time, reaching her door to pound on it as if his life depended on it.

She opened it and stared in bewilderment. She was wearing a lacy cotton robe. Her eyes looked blotchy, as if she'd been crying. She had never looked more beautiful and he had never wanted anyone so much. Suddenly, for the first time in his life, he couldn't find the right words.

"Shane! What is it?" she asked, clasping her collar tightly about her throat.

His eyes dissolved into amber as they searched hers. "Kim, we need to talk."

His urgency shocked her so much she could do nothing but stare back at him. Her heartbeat accelerated in her chest, making her hands tremble as she moved the door wider so he might enter.

He lowered himself into the only chair in the room and she perched on the side of the bed, tucking her robe around her thighs.

She stared at him. Having him near, having him here in the room, increased her need tenfold. She had never felt this burning in her blood before she met Shane. She only knew she wanted to be in his arms again. To be close, wrapped together, as they had been in the bayou. To be close and talk about the feelings she didn't want to lose.

"I can't . . . I can't seem to find the right words." He laughed ruefully. His eyes bored into her and she was caught, as if every secret had been spread out before him. "The only thing I seem capable of doing is wanting to make love with you."

He didn't speak of love, he spoke of need. She was beginning to believe in love. And she understood need. Admitting that, she rose slowly from the bed and went to stand in front of him.

"Shane, you're supposed to be good with words, you're a writer." She lifted his hands, ever so softly, a caress, and he stood to meet her. "You're supposed to ask, you know."

He looked at her wonderingly, bemused, confused, as she had never seen him. Rising on tiptoe, she brushed his chin with a kiss.

"Lean down a little. Then you'll get your answer."

His face lowered. One slow longing kiss, a promise of all to come. Suddenly shy, she backed up a step. But his arms imprisoned her.

"Kim, I can't promise..."

She placed a finger over his lips, silencing him. Tonight wasn't about promises—or the past—or the future. It was about these feelings between them which had grown stronger and stronger until they could no longer be denied.

"I feel the need, the want, pulling at me too, Shane. Right now, that's all that's necessary...."

Slowly his hands opened the collar of her robe. Without words he drew her to him, raining kisses along her neck, sending shivers down her spine.

Her fingers combed through his hair, testing its silkiness, just as she had always longed to do. She breathed in the faint scent of sandalwood soap. Forever after it would remind her of Shane, of this night.

His hands refused to be still. They drifted down the front of her robe, testing, teasing, until he untied her sash, dropping it to the floor. Her opened robe revealed a very practical cotton gown. He'd bought it for her after the fire. How could he have known the lace would end at the very tip of her breasts? He stood mesmerized, reaching out one finger to touch her sensitive skin.

Their eyes locked, and desire, long denied, moved her to shrug out of her robe and into his arms.

"Kim?" he breathed.

"Yes." Could she make it any plainer than that? She would take responsibility for this decision and never regret it. Actions always spoke louder...she reached her arms wide to him. "Come to me, Shane."

They walked to the bed, where she found that his touch drove her to the edge, even though he never hurried. They pulsed together, a primitive force beyond their control.

When had she ever felt this way? Never before. The climb had been so high, the descent was so slow. Languor overtook her before she could come back to reality. She slept, curled in his arms. Trusting and trusted.

HE MUST HAVE SLEPT, TOO. At once he was awake, confused by the warm press of body against his. He should leave her now. He could make no promises.

He stayed. His hands rediscovered all the delight he'd found in her. She was unlike anyone he'd ever known. She gave everything, held nothing back in their lovemaking, and asked for nothing. But her giving had inspired him to depths of feeling, to heights of ecstasy he'd never felt before. It couldn't happen again that way, could it?

She was stirring to life under his eager exploration. He found he couldn't wait to begin again. His lovemaking was more demanding this time. He knew what she was capable of. This time he wanted to test their limits.

She wouldn't let him. Instead, she pushed him onto his back.

"Stay there," she ordered, "my turn."

He forgot to analyze under her tender touch; he could only feel. He forgot to hold back, to remain emotionless. He writhed in pleasure and found warmth he never thought existed.

Chapter Seventeen

As content, as loved, as completed as Shane felt on fall-ing asleep, he felt confusion, death and destruction on his sudden awakening. Kim curled beside him, peace-fully unaware of his distress. He waited for the after-effects of the forgotten dream to subside, but they did not. Instead the feeling of dread increased, as if a power outside his being was at work. For the first time in his adult life he'd been able to let go of the past, he'd seen a future with Kim that offered meaning and happiness. What could have surfaced in his subconscious to bring about this feeling of impending disaster?

The old house was strangely silent around them, their cocoon of love had effectively shut out the rest of the world. Now, abruptly, it seemed too quiet. He rose and pulled on a pair of jeans. For his own peace of mind, he would take a look around just to make sure the house was secure.

The hall was dark. He prowled into and out of every room on the second floor. Then he started up the stairs to the ballroom. Louise smiled at him from her picture on the wall. He turned to go back down to the first floor when a faint flash from outside drew him to the French windows.

Far out on the lawn a figure stood silhouetted by the light of the waxing moon. That figure held a powerful beam of light and was directing it into each window of the house as if demanding attention. No burglar this!

The figure turned, dipped and swayed in some ancient dance. Shane threw open the window, striding out onto the veranda. Before he could yell, the light shined full in his face. Then the light focused on the ground. The sight of what was there froze Shane's blood.

The light showed Kim's voodoo doll plainly. Around its neck was a simple twine of rope. The figure, carefully staying outside the illuminated circle, picked up the doll and motioned Shane forward.

He pounded down the steps and threw open the door to his bedroom. Kim was still there, safe. His relief was short-lived when she stirred uneasily.

The light shone through his window in warning and he crossed the balcony to look out onto the lawn. The figure had come around to this side of the house. Again the doll was lifted up and the twine tightened symbolically. Again the figure beckoned.

Kim coughed in her sleep.

He didn't believe, couldn't believe, that any power could force Kim to battle for breath. But he couldn't take a chance, either. She was too precious to him to take any chances with. The doll had to be secured. Never again would anyone or anything threaten Kim's safety or happiness.

By the time he reached the door, the figure had disappeared. But through the trees, deep in the bayou, he saw a flickering light. He raced toward it, desperate to get the doll back. As he ran, a refrain poured through his mind, "It's not over . . . it's not over . . . it's not over."

A NOISE REGISTERED deep in her sleep and Kim stirred, stretching luxuriously and instinctively for Shane. He wasn't there.

She opened her eyes to the darkness. The old stirrings of panic tightened in her chest. Stop it! she told herself . . . all I have to do is turn on the light and see that I'm alone . . . just like I always do.

Reaching out, she pushed the light switch.

A scream died in her throat.

Evangeline Paris, orange hair a wild tangle about her pale face, her eyes overbright, and her brilliantly colored lips curled in the fortune teller smile, stood at the foot of the bed.

"Yes, Kim, it's me. You really didn't believe you had won, did you?"

Clutching the sheet with trembling fingers, Kim rose to her knees, swallowing nausea. "Where's Shane? What have you done to him!"

"Shane is following his destiny." Her insane chuckle froze Kim's blood. "He thinks he's chasing me to get this." Evangeline thrust the voodoo doll in Kim's face and she recoiled. "He thinks he will wrest it from me and you'll be free of me!"

Kim lunged for the doll, but Evangeline danced back, away.

"Give it to me, Evangeline!" Kim demanded, all fear of this woman retreating before her fear for Shane. Wrapping the sheet around her, she tugged it off the mattress and surged to her feet. "Where is Shane!" she screamed, hoping Leonard might hear her.

Evangeline's eyes widened. "You want Shane, Kimberly? You wish to save him from the darkness in his soul? Then come." She danced back another step. "Come with me into the night. And I shall show you the way." Whirling around, she fled from the room.

Just as quickly Kim dropped the sheet, scrambled in her open suitcase for shorts, threw on the shirt Shane had discarded on the floor, and pulled on gym shoes.

Passing the windows, she saw lights flickering through the trees, way out, almost to the bayou. Could Shane really be out there? Even before the question was fully formulated in her mind, she knew the truth. He had gone into the bayou after that voodoo doll. Evangeline had lured him there, just as she was luring Kim. The horrors weren't over yet.

Leonard had showed her all the camping equipment stowed in the butler's pantry. That was where she could find a light strong enough to guide her. She rushed into the kitchen and tripped over a body lying on the floor.

New fear rose hotter in her chest. She knelt, trembling, beside Leonard. Quickly she determined he was just knocked out. She put a cold cloth on his forehead after checking to make sure his pulse was strong. Then she found the flashlight.

She wouldn't let Shane face the dangers out in the bayou alone. An unknown inner strength, the determination to protect Shane at any cost, surfaced. She could, she would, face the danger, face the overwhelming fright of the night for Shane.

She set out in a determined jog across the back gardens. The trees closed in around her, but she pushed back her fear with thoughts of Shane. In moments she was through the trees and into the clearing before the bayou. The lights were just barely visible, but she knew in which direction to head: the heart of the bayou—the bayou with its waters of dissolving shadows and its shrouds of gray Spanish moss.

She hesitated, looking up to the sky where a cloud closed over the moon. It would be darker in the bayou. She could get lost forever in its depths. There were creatures, snakes and alligators, to think of. There were the leftover fears of her childhood to confront. Could she do it?

How could she not?

Shane was in there and he needed her help. She knew that with a certainty that would not be denied.

Vines tangled her legs, holding her back. Spanish moss seemed deliberately to block her view. She was moving slower than she wanted to, and making more noise. Darkness descended around her, the suffocating blackness prodding her worst fears awake. Onward she went, disregarding everything, refusing to let fear overcome her determination to help Shane. She was well beyond any recognizable landmark. Instinctively, she realized she was being led in a direction that would be completely unfamiliar to her and to Shane.

She kept running. Finally a stitch in her side slowed her down and she gasped for breath. To her right there was a faint light. She stumbled toward it. A lantern hung on a low cypress branch and a darker shadow stood in front of it.

"Shane!" she cried, stumbling heedlessly forward. She would recognize his silhouette anywhere.

Shane stepped forward to catch her, a gasp releasing between his lips as his strong arms caught her up and held her.

"Evangeline. She's the power, Shane. Come on, we've got to get out of here," she begged, pulling away and grasping his arm.

"My power is stronger!" Evangeline suddenly shrieked, holding another lantern high so she was silhouetted before them in the darkness.

"Evangeline! You were behind it all!" Shane's voice was raw with shock.

A cackle of laughter echoed around them. "Fool! I have always been the power, for I, too, am descended from Maria Laveau. Like your aunt, I was drawn to the art, but I possessed the knowledge to wield the power stronger. She chose the way to light. I studied the ways of my ancestress, and learned the powers of control. Of darkness. You know all about the power of darkness, don't you, Shane?"

"Evangeline, it's not too late. Let me help you." Pushing Kim behind him, he stepped forward slowly, inching his way toward the doll still held in her outstretched arm.

"Shane, leave it! It doesn't matter!" Kim insisted, tugging at his arm.

"Too late!" Evangeline's voice rose in a high-pitched whine. "Too late for you both." She looked at the doll, then smiling slyly at him, tugged the piece of twine tighter around its neck. "Kim, such an inconsequential meddler, but she shall suffer her fate first I believe. Right before your eyes, Shane."

Kim rushed forward. Though she felt a twinge in her neck, she refused to show weakness. Still a niggling question rose to mind: Did she believe this magic more than she thought? "No, Evangeline, you're wrong! You have no power over me!"

Shane caught her, pulling her to his side. "Kim, stay back!"

Cursing, Evangeline backed stealthily away, stepping deliberately as if she knew the exact places her feet should tread. Shane followed carefully, seemingly aware that this wily old woman had planned a trap for them both.

"It's over, Evangeline. Your voodoo empire has crumbled. My aunt discovered Jeanne was masquerading as Maria Laveau. So you got rid of her, too, didn't you?"

"She was a stupid girl! Always scheming to take over, thinking that she had more power and would be able to turn the faithful away from me. I let her believe that. Fools! All of you!"

Still backing away cautiously, Evangeline shifted her gaze away for an instant to look behind her, then deliberately stepped to the left. Water there. But Shane moved to his left also, testing each step before he put his full weight on it.

Why did he follow Evangeline? Was it the doll he was after? Did he still believe in its power? Did she?

"But how could you hurt Louise? She was your friend," Kim shouted, trying to divert Evangeline's attention, trying to help Shane.

"She was my rival! She was one step closer to Maria than I and as such had access to the power. I knew she had discovered the link between Maria's long lost child and my heritage. I had to eliminate her. But Jeanne botched the job, and then you refused to be scared off."

"We've caught them all, Evangeline," Kim taunted, following carefully in Shane's footsteps. "All your powerful tools. Jeanne . . . Claude . . . Anton . . . There's no one left."

A demonic scream cut through the bayou.

"Come then," she teased. "If you think you can best me, come. I have what you want, Shane. Right here." She dangled it over a pool of water and laughed.

"The doll is not important," he lied. "I followed only to find out who you were and why you were doing these terrible things."

"Come then," she chanted, "Follow me into the lair of Dumballah and I will tell you all you want to know. When I am Queen of the True Believers, I will control New Orleans, not just the Quarter, but all of the city. Then I will exact my tribute and I will reign. People will come from around the world to hear my judgments and worship me as their queen."

She was mad, Kim thought as she watched Evangeline wind her way through the undergrowth, luring them deeper and deeper into the bayou. Shane followed the light from her lantern, guessing where to step. Kim had to stop him. Evangeline was insane, that was clear enough. Perhaps Anton and Claude had been in on this scheme for the money, but Evangeline believed in all that she was saying.

"You destroyed my dream, my empire. It will take time to rebuild. But have no fear, I will succeed and be stronger than before. Then you and your kind will have no power over me. For now, my revenge is that you will die, both of you, and you will die alone. You believe I can do that, don't you, Shane. Don't you!" she cackled.

Her insane words did not slow Shane. In fact, he was steadily gaining on her. In her madness, or delusion of invincibility, she was unaware of her peril.

Shane lowered his voice seductively, "Evangeline, let me help you." He stretched out a hand to grab for the doll.

In her realization that it was well within his grasp, Evangeline jumped away.

"My power is greater," she yelled.

"Shane, be careful!" Kim warned, following him.

"Shane, help me!" Evangeline suddenly cried. Her unwary jump away from him had put her into one of the well-concealed bogs, and the quicksand was sucking at her legs.

Instinctively, he reached to help her. Her clawing hand fastened like a vise around his wrist, drawing him toward her.

"That's it," she croaked triumphantly. "I've got you now. You must save me and the doll. You must save your Kim!"

"No!" Kim screamed. She felt the evil emanating forth like a living thing ready to grasp him in its jaws and devour him. The doll was held just beyond his reach. He would have to move toward Evangeline to get it. As she sank she was losing her mobility and wouldn't be able to pull away. He stepped forward.

"That's right, come to me. I have what you want."

"No. Shane, the doll doesn't matter!" Kim gestured pleadingly.

"My power over you has grown with every passing moment, you can't turn away from me," Evangeline taunted, the quicksand sucking to her waist.

Instinctively, Shane fell to his knees trying to pull her free, but instead Kim could see him being drawn in.

"Yes, Shane, help me!" Evangeline held the doll before her like a talisman. "Help me! Help me and save Kim!"

"Shane, no, don't listen to her!" Kim's entreaty echoed in the night air. She also fell to her knees and grabbed Shane's arm, joining her strength in the fight against the insidious mud.

Evangeline's frantic struggles to hold the doll away from Shane and fight the mud were causing her to sink more rapidly. "Don't let me go!" she wailed.

Kim knew what she had to do. She began to crawl toward Evangeline. "Let go of the doll," Kim demanded. "Let go and take my hand."

"No, Kim, stay back!" Shane bellowed.

Staring into Evangeline's wild eyes, Kim saw the instant all reason fled before her madness. Instead of taking Kim's outstretched hand, Evangeline's fingers tightened on the doll.

"I shall defeat Louise. I shall take Shane into the darkness forever," she cried out.

Recoiling in horror, Kim knew if Shane could not pull Evangeline free, she would try to take him with her to his death. Swallowing back a rush of tears, fear tore through her.

Throwing herself backward, she twined herself around his body. "Let go of her, Shane. You can't save her! It's too late!"

"No, Shane," Evangeline pleaded, the sand covering their outstretched arms now. "You must save the doll. Save Kim! It is your destiny. You've always known that. Always."

For a moment he knelt poised between the two, the quicksand covering his arm. Kim could feel its pull, the weight of Evangeline's body, Shane's tension as he vainly tried to keep her from sinking and dragging him with her.

"Shane, the doll means nothing! She's trying to kill you! It's not your fault! Let go!" Kim cried, tears streaming down her face. "No one can help her! No one!"

Their gazes locked, his dark and anguished, hers imploring.

There was only one choice and Shane took it. Twisting his body, he broke free of Evangeline's grasp and fell back, grabbing Kim as he rolled away. She cradled him in her arms, her damp face pressed to his throat as, with a sudden choked off scream, Evangeline and the doll were gone.

"Kim...Kim... You're all right," he murmured, pressing kisses over her wet face.

Kim couldn't stop shaking, but finally the reality of Shane's nearness soothed her senses.

They clung together, making their way back to Belle Rêve. In the distance she could just see Leonard standing at the back veranda, watching them approach.

Her head fell back upon Shane's shoulder and their eyes met. "I truly don't think I believe in the powers of darkness," she said, not feeling a twinge of pain since the doll had disappeared.

He squeezed her shoulder. "If so, there's always a spell...."

She smiled softly at him, and he held her fiercely tighter, pressing a kiss into her hair.

"There will be happiness here at Belle Rêve now, Kim, I promise you. As long as you stay."

Sighing, she rested her cheek close to his heart. "I know Louise would be pleased."

"I've finally found all she wished for me in the diary entries. Remember, Kim? I've been able to let go of the darkness because of you."

She stopped to peer up at him. "Oh, Shane, I love you so much."

He smiled and light filled his eyes. "I love you." He laughed wonderingly. "It's so easy to say, after all."

Then he leaned over and she felt the warmth of his lips, full of promise for the future, on hers.

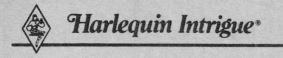

Harlequin Intrigue®

COMING NEXT MONTH

#131 BLACK MESA by Aimée Thurlo
To the Tewa tribe, Black Mesa was sacred land.
Navajo FBI Agent Justin Nakai had traveled a long
way to reach it—to see his old friend John Romero—
only to find the man missing and John's beautiful
friend Kelly Ferguson under attack and suspicion.
Neither Justin nor Kelly was willing to abandon
John without a fight. They could only hope their
separate talents and their newfound love would be
enough to protect them on the dangerous path they
followed together.

#132 PAST TENSE by Tina Vasilos
For months, Samantha Smith had successfully
eluded two men who knew she'd witnessed a murder.
Now, the murder victim had turned up safe and
sound in Tony Theopoulos's hotel—and Samantha
faced a dilemma. Could she trust Tony? Could their
sharp minds and keen instincts unite to piece
together what really happened that fateful night in
Montreal? Or would her gamble on the perceptive
hotelier lose Samantha the deadly game of cat and
mouse, and spell checkmate?

HARLEQUIN

Temptation

The Pirate

JAYNE ANN KRENTZ

At the heart of every powerful romance story lies a
legend. There are many romantic legends and
countless modern variations on them, but they all
have one thing in common: They are tales of brave,
resourceful women who must gentle and tame the
powerful, passionate men who are their true mates.

The enormous appeal of Jayne Ann Krentz lies in
her ability to create modern-day versions of these
classic romantic myths, and her LADIES AND
LEGENDS trilogy showcases this talent. Believing
that a storyteller who can bring legends to life
deserves special attention, Harlequin has chosen
the first book of the trilogy—THE PIRATE—to
receive our Award of Excellence. Look for it in
February.

AE-PIR-1

Harlequin Superromance®

LET THE GOOD TIMES ROLL...

Add some Cajun spice to liven up your New Year's celebrations and join Superromance for a romantic tour of the rich Acadian marshlands and the legendary Louisiana bayous.

Starting in January 1990, we're launching CAJUN MELODIES, a three-book tribute to the fun-loving people who've enriched America by introducing us to crawfish étouffé and gumbo, zydeco music and the Saturday night party, the *fais-dodo*. And learn about loving, Cajun-style, as you meet the tall, dark, handsome men who win their ladies' hearts with a beautiful, haunting melody....

Book One: *Julianne's Song*, January 1990
Book Two: *Catherine's Song*, February 1990
Book Three: *Jessica's Song*, March 1990

A compelling novel of deadly revenge and passion
from Harlequin's bestselling international
romance author Penny Jordan

Eleven years had passed but the
terror of that night was something
Pepper Minesse would never
forget. Fueled by revenge against
the four men who had brutally
shattered her past, she set in
motion a deadly plan to destroy
their futures.

Available in February!

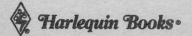
HPP-1A